D0556344

A NOVEL BASED ON THE LIFE OF
GIUSEPPE VERDI

THE
FAITHFUL

Collin Mitchell

Barbera Foundation, Inc.
P.O. Box 1019
Temple City, CA 91780

More information at www.mentorisproject.org

ISBN: 978-1-947431-11-9

Library of Congress Control Number: 2018939802

The Mentoris Project is a series of novels and biographies about the lives of great Italians and Italian-Americans: men and women who have changed history through their contributions as scientists, inventors, explorers, thinkers, and creators. The Barbera Foundation sponsors this series in the hope that, like a mentor, each book will inspire the reader to discover how she or he can make a positive contribution to society.

Contents

Foreword

First and foremost, Mentor was a person. We tend to think of the word *mentor* as a noun (a mentor) or a verb (to mentor), but there is a very human dimension embedded in the term. Mentor appears in Homer's *Odyssey* as the old friend entrusted to care for Odysseus's household and his son Telemachus during the Trojan War. When years pass and Telemachus sets out to search for his missing father, the goddess Athena assumes the form of Mentor to accompany him. The human being welcomes a human form for counsel. From its very origins, becoming a mentor is a transcendent act; it carries with it something of the holy.

The Barbera Foundation's Mentoris Project sets out on an Athena-like mission: We hope the books that form this series will be an inspiration to all those who are seekers, to those of the twenty-first century who are on their own odysseys, trying to find enduring principles that will guide them to a spiritual home. The stories that comprise the series are all deeply human. These books dramatize the lives of great Italians and Italian-Americans whose stories bridge the ancient and the modern, taking many forms, just as Athena did, but always holding up a light for those living today.

Whether in novel form or traditional biography, these books plumb the individual characters of our heroes' journeys. The power of storytelling has always been to envelop the reader in a vivid and continuous dream, and to forge a link with the subject. Our goal is for that link to guide the reader home with a new inspiration.

What is a mentor? A guide, a moral compass, an inspiration. A friend who points you toward true north. We hope that the Mentoris Project will become that friend, and it will help us all transcend our daily lives with something that can only be called holy.

—Robert J. Barbera, President, Barbera Foundation
—Ken LaZebnik, Editor, The Mentoris Project

Prelude

1814

Luigia gripped the top rung of the ladder and pushed her shoulder against the trapdoor that connected to the belfry above. Her bare feet trembled under the weight of the door as she leaned down to soothe the baby clutching the billows of her blouse. The rumble of soldiers marching on the road below shook the church's walls like a distant thunderstorm rolling in. The air hummed with a whisper of warning that hiding was a mistake. If she hid, it would only make it harder for Carlo to find her. But staying in the house, their tavern, with its food and wine would only lead more soldiers to her and the baby. Run and hide. In a storm, instinct is a sound harbor.

Not yet two years old, little Giuseppe looked up from his mother's arms and studied the room. His serene expression produced in Luigia a trust that ignored the striking fear that she, Carlo, and the boy would be split forever. Death would be preferable to being without the family—or worse, a spoil of the Russian Cossack soldiers. History repeats itself, and this was not the first time their tiny village of Le Roncole had been invaded by foreigners.

Carlo and Luigia had been credulous when Napoleon brought the democratic values of the French Republic to Northern Italy nearly a decade before. Being young, the couple was idealistic about their future. The singular message from France was "liberty" and Le Roncole prospered as a result. But now, not long after the French defeated the Austrians in Italy, the Austrians were fighting back to reclaim what they had lost. And the citizenry continued to be pawns in an endless game of political chess.

Luigia slid her head along the jagged wood of the trapdoor, the rough splinters catching in her hair as she wiggled her body into the belfry. The church bells glimmered through the dank haze of gunsmoke, their curves catching the light of the soldiers' torches below. Despite fear and fatigue, Luigia's senses were sharp. She thought about her friend Caterina, whom she often teased for jumping with nerves at the sound of her husband's cleaver chopping through the day at their butcher shop. Embarrassed, Caterina would laugh, sharing in the absurdity of her delicate nature.

Luigia snapped out of the daydream. "She would only be a burden," Luigia whispered to herself, though she longed to be in the familiar company of her friend. She unwrapped Giuseppe from his blankets and he pawed expectantly at her chest. She leaned back and pulled a knife from the folds of her dress, placing it gently on the floor next to her. Finally, she opened her bloodstained shirt and gave the boy her breast.

Just that morning Carlo had happily suggested they expand their modest tavern. And why not? Under Napoleon's rule Le Roncole was transformed into something more than a trivial bump in the road. "The Kingdom of Italy!" Carlo exclaimed buoyantly when France pushed Austria out of the northern Italian states, making room for the self-proclaimed king,

Napoleon Bonaparte, to govern. He enunciated the word "Kingdom" as though it carried two disparate concepts to be blended and savored like wine.

Napoleon's Grande Armée was swift in ejecting Austria. Or at least that's how it was sung by French soldiers who passed through Le Roncole in the weeks after their victory. Carlo recalled the incredulity of the men and the irrational fact that they had survived battle—a tribute to Napoleon's power, he reasoned. But Le Roncole had been spared the corporeal violence of battle and Carlo took for granted the human cost to install France's dominance.

Luigia's father made the point that their new leaders would rule miles away from France. Considering his modest farm, he lamented the fact that France would likely make no considerations to the region's farmers. But Carlo believed in the Revolution. Most farmers, and certainly not the sons of farmers, hadn't the time or mind to consider the value of democracy. But Carlo possessed an unassuming pride in the belief that he could pursue his own happiness.

Several years into their marriage, Carlo secured a promising agreement with the local wine and food wholesaler, Antonio Barezzi. He returned home after signing the contract, tossing several freshly minted *lire* into the air. Carlo laughed as they dropped on the table with a bright, sharp clang. It was with these coins and many others that Carlo and Luigia eventually opened their tavern, taking several societal steps away from their parents' humble farms. The coins' smooth metal, embossed audaciously with *Regno d'Italia*—Kingdom of Italy—connected them for the first time to their neighbors in the surrounding countryside. It was like they were opening their front door to the world.

Luigia forced herself back to reality again. Gunshots ripped through the night air. She gripped her knife as the snapping blasts ricocheted around the belfry. Giuseppe continued to sleep, satiated in his mother's arms.

Despite warnings that the Austrians were traveling north through Le Roncole, Carlo made the journey that morning for Busseto in order to settle his accounts with Barezzi. Through the afternoon, Luigia, Caterina, and their neighbor Maria stood vigil as Austrian and Russian troops ambled wearily through the town toward Milan. Maria, whose husband, Pasquale, owned a general store in the village, gripped Luigia's hand so tightly that her rings left irritated marks on Luigia's fingers.

More troops streamed endlessly into Le Roncole like figurines rotating in a music box. By late afternoon, the soldiers appeared increasingly tired and despondent, their uniforms tattered and stained from days of marching. Grizzled Russian Cossacks perilously allied with the Austrians barely cast an eye to the women as they made their way north. When night fell, Luigia dashed home, tales of the Cossacks' reputation for brutality lingering in her mind. Through the evening, Luigia sat by the kitchen fire, soothing Giuseppe the way she wished Carlo could if he were there.

The front door opened with a familiar creak and moan. Carlo was home. Luigia put Giuseppe in his cradle and smoothed out her dress.

"Hello," she called, lighting another candle. "We're back here."

A silhouette silently appeared in the doorway. Its arms hung slack by its sides and its head swung back and forth like a clock pendulum. Although she couldn't see the figure's eyes, Luigia knew they were looking at her. Two more shadows appeared from behind, peering into the kitchen. By sheer mass, the first shadow pushed through the threshold, revealing his ravaged body.

The man was large and lopsided, hunched like a sack of grain. He waited for the others to fan out from behind him before walking into the kitchen. In the dim light his hair gleamed with grease and blood. His uniform, more suitable for burning than wearing, was covered in a thick layer of soot. The other two soldiers, equally haggard by war, split across the room, entrapping Luigia like a pack of wolves. Expressionless, the man sat at the table, placing his muddy boots on the chair beside him. He put his soiled hands to his mouth and squinted.

"We're hungry," he said in Russian.

The other men watched their comrade with nervous apprehension. The man grinned and peered down on the boy.

"A widow," he quipped, leering at Luigia.

The others laughed. A cold throb pushed through Luigia's stomach.

"I can give you wine," she said, habitually pouring each man a glass. *Surely, these men will be missed by the others and will be on their way*, she thought.

The biggest one downed his wine and then, with the whole of his arm, swept the glasses off the table, sending them shattering to the floor. The clatter startled Giuseppe and he wailed as though sounding an alarm. The smallest man grabbed Luigia around the chest and pushed her into the table. The jagged edge of the wood pressed into her back as the third man pulled her wrists from behind, dragging her body across the table until her feet dangled above the floor. The largest of the three unsheathed a knife from his belt and brushed the pitted blade along the soft of her neck. The edge slid along her collarbone, slicing her like the skin of a ripe peach, and a thick line of blood ran down the front of her blouse.

Luigia stared up at her captor. His face was gaunt and pale, revealing the contours of his skull and the wiry veins around his eyes. She could hear the other men laughing as they rummaged through the kitchen looking for food and alcohol.

The man gripped Luigia by the neck, pushing her body so her head dangled off the end of the table. The blood rushed to her face and she began to feel faint as the weight of his crooked frame forced the air out of her lungs. She tried to listen for the baby's cries, but all she could hear was the thrum of her heart pounding in her chest.

The men's laughter was suddenly replaced by shouting and the crackle of broken glass. The man was abruptly tossed off her, his fingernails tearing at her neck. Luigia felt light and lucid as the piercing weight of his body lifted itself from her torso.

A pair of rough hands reached underneath her arms and dragged her to her feet. The blood rushed back to her head and she staggered, trying to catch her breath. When she finally focused her eyes, she gazed upon several Austrian soldiers standing in the kitchen, their rifles hanging from their shoulders, their uniforms reasonably clean. The leader, dressed smartly in a blue wool jacket and a plumed shako calmly gave orders to his men. They swiftly detained the Russian soldiers and pushed them out of the kitchen.

The Austrian soldier made a cursory effort to pick up the broken glass by Luigia's feet, kicking the shards aside with his boot. He sniffed, taking appraisal of the room, and then turned to Luigia, taking a deep breath.

"I'm sorry, madam," he said in broken French, his leather belt creaking as he bowed.

He straightened himself and, eying the carafe of wine, took a deep pull and stuffed the bottle in his jacket pocket. He glided out the door, joining the stream of Austrian and Russian soldiers still marching through Le Roncole.

"Wake up."

Luigia startled awake, her hands frantically feeling for the knife. Carlo stood over her, his eyes reflections of concern and guilt. He had hardly suffered a scratch from his journey back from Busseto. Behind him, the village priest peered over Carlo's shoulders mumbling prayers. Carlo helped Luigia to her feet and cautiously looked down the front of Luigia's bloodstained blouse.

"You're hurt."

Weary, Luigia revealed the Cossack's knife wound across her neck.

The priest placed a soft hand on her shoulder. "Do you need to confess for your sins?"

Luigia shook her head and bounced the baby, cooing in his ears.

In the morning light, Le Roncole looked the same as it always had. Each shingle, rock, and tree was in place. Only the animals were gone. The sun rose over the low eastern hills as the priest rang the church bells, sending the nesting blackbirds back into the world. Giuseppe lurched toward the clanging sound, his hands stretched out as if to catch the peal.

When the clangor faded and the bells hung silently in their tower, the town slid back into its patterns, impervious to the changes about to come.

Part I

Chapter One

1821

It was a light spring day, the clouds dashing the sky in spotted, chalky lines. The poppies were in full bloom and embraced the Verdi tavern in droplets of white and purple.

Kneeling at the tavern's entrance, Giuseppe took a deep breath and tugged at the front door hanging sternly on its hinges. Every muscle from his feet down to his hands strained under the inertia. Carlo laughed to himself—finally, something as stubborn as Giuseppe.

Giuseppe shared his father's compact, broad frame and his mother's dense black hair, always stiff at attention. At seven years old he already carried a solemn, contemplative gaze well beyond his years. And it was for this reason that Giuseppe was popular among the adults of Le Roncole, who referred to him affectionately as "Carlo's Old Man." It was all in good humor, of course, especially after dinner and a few bottles of wine at the family's tavern. Giuseppe would smile politely as not to embarrass his mother, who took reserved humor in the nickname. In an attempt to entertain his often-dour son, Carlo mimicked Giuseppe's pensive stare, pretending to be so absorbed in a book or the flicker of candlelight that his eyes would cross. Luigia would laugh encouragingly, but Giuseppe rarely acknowledged his father's humor, sitting tight-lipped and red-faced.

Giuseppe hardly complained when Carlo asked for his help repairing the door. The prospect of learning something new enthralled him, and his father was pleased to see Giuseppe so eager to help. They spent the day hiking in the surrounding woods, eventually finding a squat oak clinging to the side of a creek bed. They chopped down the tree and dragged it back to the tavern.

Their neighbor Pasquale, pleased to take on an odd job, cut and planed the wood into boards under Giuseppe's watchful gaze. Carlo was impressed but slightly weary of his son's diligence in finding perfection in the minutiae. Though he was inclined to indulge Giuseppe in something so tedious, Carlo couldn't ignore that Giuseppe was nothing short of a purist. The new door would open and close and keep the wind out, Carlo reasoned. Yet Giuseppe insisted that nearly every wood grain be true for it to function.

"I don't think it's finished," said Giuseppe to Carlo after he hung the unwieldy door in its frame.

Carlo handed him the mallet and wedge and lay down to rest his back. "The first step in fixing the door is taking off the door." He stretched out in the wet grass and was soon fast asleep.

"Papa, I can't pull these pins out!" hollered Giuseppe minutes later, tugging at the door.

Carlo's mind had just touched upon a dream. He sat up slowly.

Giuseppe shook his hands. "It hurts."

Carlo walked over and grabbed the bottom edge of the door and lifted up, easing the pressure off the hinges. "Now try."

Giuseppe knelt and placed the wedge between the pin and the hinge. After knocking several times with the mallet, the pin crept out of its cradle.

"The weight of the door was keeping the pin in," Carlo explained. He nodded toward the middle hinge. "Try that one."

Giuseppe ran his hands along the hinge, visualizing the simple solution. Straining under the weight, Carlo whistled at Giuseppe to hurry up.

In the years since France's defeat, Carlo feared the worst for Le Roncole. The family prospered under the strength of the *lira* and French democracy made room for the budding idea of being an Italian. It was regression to return to the regime of their former rulers and Carlo braced himself for firm retribution from the Austrians. But Carlo and Parma were fortunate.

The Duchy of Parma where Le Roncole was settled was ceded to Napoleon's wife, Marie Louise, herself an Austrian. And for the years following her placement, Carlo and Luigia's way of life was relatively undisturbed. He knew they were lucky to have been able to keep the tavern and their daily routines. The verity that travelers came through Le Roncole proved that the world had not turned upside down without the benevolent French to protect it.

But the return of the Austrians still left much to be desired. Most destructive was the state's consumption of livestock, surpassing that of the French Army. Felice and Caterina struggled to make ends meet from their modest butcher shop, and with little trade available after the war, Maria and Pasquale closed their small store and farmed with wanting success on a small plot of land leased to them by a Milanese landowner. Carlo and Luigia were an exception to their neighbors. Carlo was expedient if not wholly lucky in business thanks to his wholesaler, Antonio

Barezzi. An artful pragmatist, Barezzi kept political ties with the Austrians, helping his position amid contrived tax and trade laws. Bolstered by good business and good timing, Carlo became a leader and confidant among his peers.

Carlo took Giuseppe's hands and helped him move the wood plane down the length of the door. After several tries, Giuseppe slid the tool evenly until the shavings fell like a light snow.

"Signor Verdi!"

A young girl stood smiling at the tavern fence, her linen dress hovering loosely over her slight frame. Precocious, Margherita Barezzi presented herself as an adult—expectant and formal.

"Mademoiselle Barezzi, to what do we owe the pleasure?" asked Carlo in exaggerated French.

"My father is in town looking at land," she said, handing Carlo a small leather coin purse. "You overpaid last month's invoice."

"Your father is a kind man, but not half as kind as you," said Carlo, bowing. He pushed the purse back into her hands. "Please tell him to apply it to next month."

Margherita returned Carlo's mock formality, bowing back as if to a noble. "It would be an honor," she said, playacting in stride.

She watched Giuseppe plane the door. Undisturbed by her presence, he didn't bother to look up. Ignoring his churlish behavior, Margherita playfully blew a handful of wood shavings into his face. Giuseppe brushed the flakes out of his hair and went back to his work.

"Giuseppe is helping get this door back into shape," said Carlo. "He's very particular."

Giuseppe ran his hand over the smooth surface of the door as a shipwright to the hull of his boat.

Margherita looked on, amused. "I can see."

Down the road, a reedy voice wavered up the hill shouting, "*Ehi, ehi!*" Margherita and Giuseppe walked to the fence to see what the commotion was about.

A bearded man dressed in a worn overcoat and tattered hat wildly swung his arms across a fiddle as if working a runaway loom. The whirly sound pulled the neighboring kids out of their houses and into the road. With a broad smile, the musician stopped in front of the tavern, bowing the strings of his fiddle. Children and adults encircled him in a makeshift auditorium and the fiddler addressed his small audience, tipping his hat.

"Greetings, good people of Le Roncole! I come as a friend, musician, and messenger of accord." He paused as more of the townspeople gathered around. Margherita grabbed Giuseppe's hand and pulled him to the edge of the small crowd.

"I come to entertain," said the fiddler, bowing the strings in a playful waltz. "And I bring news of our fair land as well. The people of Sicily and Naples have brought up a revolution against King Ferdinand I of the Two Sicilies."

Unfazed, the children looked on as the adults murmured among themselves.

"May God and these songs bring peace to all of us," said the fiddler, placing the instrument under his chin. "In these troubled times, every heart can join and beat in unison. All mankind should dance in the fraternal embrace of their friends and neighbors!"

Giuseppe watched, transfixed, as the fiddler moved his hand slowly over the instrument, his eyes closed in a trance. The notes meshed into an agreeable pitch and Giuseppe felt a wave of melody wash over him.

> *I am only a plain old man,*
> *The fiddler of the hamlet here,*
> *Yet some consider me a sage;*
> *I take my wine both strong and clear.*
> *Around me, 'neath this spreading shade,*
> *Rest from your tasks, my comrades dear.*
> *And while I play, ye village folk,*
> *Can dance beneath my ancient oak.*

Giuseppe associated music with the chore of group activities and organized religion. For him, church had been nothing more than a family obligation. This attitude he took largely from Luigia, who largely discouraged prayer in the house and did not keep a Bible by her bedside. French rule had made this schism socially acceptable, but Carlo, always the social opportunist, persuaded Luigia to make occasional appearances at church. It was under this somber duty of decorum that Giuseppe followed his mother's lead of silent opposition. Listless, Giuseppe would count down the minutes, hardly taking notice of the sweeping organ pieces and choral arrangements at the weekly Mass.

In church, arms didn't swing, feet didn't tap, and rugged men in overcoats didn't captivate a town by banging on a fiddle. This traveling minstrel was a revelation and Giuseppe took in the music like water in a desert.

> *Have pity for your feudal lord,*
> *The master of yon castle great;*
> *For he your quiet country life*

Must envy, with its happy fate;
How sad he looks within his coach,
When driving by in lonely state,
While tea la la, ye village folk,
Are dancing 'neath my ancient oak.

When gentle peace shall shed its balm
O'er evils wrought by war's array,
Oh! drive not from his early home
The blinded one who went astray;
The storm is over; welcome back
Those whom the blast had swept away,
And tra la la, ye village folk,
Come, dance beneath my ancient oak.

The fiddler quickly brought his bow to a stop and bowed to his audience. The crowd clapped appreciatively and Giuseppe unwittingly joined in, his ears reeling.

"Lord or peasant, I do not judge you," said the fiddler, flipping his cap, "in the capacity of your generosity."

Carlo dropped a coin in Giuseppe's hand, breaking him out of his trance. He handed Margherita a coin as well and pushed them toward the fiddler, where they placed the silver into his droopy cap.

"What is this news from the Two Sicilies?" asked Carlo, adding to the man's coffers.

"There have been revolts against King Ferdinand. In the south they are calling for a constitution."

"How have you come into this account?"

The fiddler smirked. "It is my occupation, good sir, to travel and to tell stories."

"So they are just stories."

"It's the privilege of the musician to say what I mean without actually saying it. But I assure you, it's true. I have come from the south and have seen Austrian soldiers myself. I have heard too, that some are on to the Kingdom of Sardinia." Smiling toward Giuseppe, the fiddler plucked the fiddle with a dirty fingernail as if to emphasize his point.

"I have heard the Carbonari are here in the north," said Carlo.

"Perhaps. But if I knew any more about the whereabouts of the secret group, then I would say their efforts have failed."

Carlo looked aloofly toward the horizon. "I don't approve of their ways."

Directing his attention to Giuseppe, the fiddler struck a few chords. "As it's getting late, I could use a place to sleep this evening."

"My wife and I run this tavern. We can make up a room for you."

"An idea by half. But I would be remiss to return the coins you have just given me." The fiddler stood and handed Giuseppe his instrument. "Your boy seems to have taken quite an interest in this fiddle. Perhaps I can regale him and teach the boy a few things in exchange for your hospitality."

Carlo took the fiddle out of Giuseppe's hands and examined it as if it were for sale. He looked to Margherita. "Do you play an instrument?"

"I play the piano."

"And do you like it?"

"I actually find it quite boring."

Carlo smiled broadly at the minstrel. "You'll find our son an apt pupil. I wish you luck in getting any sleep tonight."

Chapter Two

Low late-summer sunlight filtered through the hallway windows that gazed onto the garden below. Carlo knocked hesitantly at Giuseppe's door. For months now it had been regularly closed to the narrow hallway that connected their bedrooms.

Carlo called down to Luigia, picking spinach from raised flowerbeds. "I'm taking Giuseppe with me to Signor Barezzi's."

Luigia squinted into the window's reflection. "It's Sunday, can't you go tomorrow?"

"I'll be busy with repairs."

Carlo could hear her resignation echo off the courtyard walls.

"You'll both need something to eat before you leave," she said.

"We'll take it with us. And some cheeses for Signor Barezzi."

"I'll let you do that yourself."

In his room, Giuseppe transcribed sheet music given to him by Don Pietro Baistrocci, Le Roncole's music director. Meticulously tracing staff lines onto fresh paper, he hummed along to the music eddying in his head, taking pleasure in the faithful reproduction of each line, note, and lyric. As Baistrocci explained, these sheets would be his to memorize and practice. Note by note, hour by cloistered hour, the music mysteriously plotted its course in Giuseppe's head.

Giuseppe relished the countless solitary hours needed to bring the written pieces to their evocative ends. Hunched over a narrow wooden table, he took inspiration from the foreboding process of writing. The miracle of the living sound, given birth through his pen, drifted through his mind's ear and he could sit accompanied by his new companion for hours.

Not long after starting lessons with Baistrocci, Giuseppe began to treasure the concerts that made up his weekly visits to church. Much to the annoyance of those in front of him, he would lean over the pew, stretching to behold his teacher play the organ. With its hypnotic melodies, the organ helped Giuseppe turn a deaf ear to the rote castigations of the sermon.

Carlo eased open the bedroom door. Giuseppe sat over his desk, his head hardly visible.

"Come, Giuseppe. We need to leave soon."

Giuseppe hardly lifted his head. "Where?"

"To Busseto, to see Signor Barezzi. I'll need your help loading the wagon."

Giuseppe stopped writing and turned toward his father. "What are we getting?"

Carlo never understood why Luigia disliked Antonio Barezzi. The merchant was guilty of being successful, if that was something to be critical about. If nothing else, Barezzi was the sole reason Carlo and Luigia's tavern kept its stock during the transition to Austrian rule. He was generous in his attention to their account— and for that, Carlo was grateful and considered himself lucky to be on such agreeable terms with a man of Barezzi's position. He was also the only person Carlo knew who could help procure an instrument for Giuseppe. The boy could make do with his weekly music lessons, but Carlo's pride took precedence over the expense of owning an instrument. If maintaining the tavern was the soil to raising his son, then indulging his musical interests was the germination of his being.

Their horse and wagon ambled along the cobblestone streets and through Busseto's gates. By comparison, the town of Busseto was considerably larger than Le Roncole. But to any urban Milanese or Roman it was a speck of buildings surrounded on all sides by farms and the poor farmers who farmed them.

Giuseppe marveled at the Rocca Pallavicino towering over them. It was the first time he had seen any building taller than Le Roncole's bell tower. Despite its seeming impenetrability, the fortress's walls crumbled into a stagnant moat, a testament to the battles of time.

The carriage wound down the main boulevard and through several narrow streets before arriving at the home of Antonio Barezzi.

Settled between two residences, Casa Barezzi was visibly modest despite its conspicuous wealth. Three stories with four chimneys flecking its pitched roof, the home sat adjacent to an unassuming town square sprinkled with lush, manicured trees. The oversized wooden shutters hanging from the townhouse's windows helped provide respite from the unseasonable heat.

Carlo and Giuseppe pulled in front of the corralled arches enclosing the main door. A valet rushed to meet them and, with hardly a glance, took their horse and cart to the stables. A maid whose hair sat coiffed under a lacy bonnet escorted them into the tiled entryway. As they waited, Giuseppe could hear the soft plunking of a piano and the airy singing of a girl. The maid returned with Barezzi following ardently behind.

"Signor Verdi, welcome!"

Barezzi carried the uncompromising gaze of a man self-righteous in his wealth—a face molded for large oil portraits or paper money. He spoke with a humored gait that made one feel as though they were the exact relief he was looking for. Barezzi's neatly trimmed mustache rose and fell in tandem with his thick eyebrows.

Carlo bowed slightly. "Thank you for having us."

"It would be illogical not to, given the circumstances," said Barezzi, putting his arm loosely around Giuseppe's shoulders. "This must be the other Signor Verdi."

Giuseppe reddened and looked down at the floor. "A pleasure, sir."

Their host led them into a cavernous room with parquet floors and thick furnishings. Before anything else, Barezzi aspired to be a man of letters and education and this parlor was the substantive manifestation of that projected success. To Giuseppe, the wood molding lining the ceiling looked like thick vines installed to keep the walls and roof intact.

Sunlight filtered through the broad windows under which Margherita graced a grand piano. She stood and bowed.

"Good afternoon, Signor Verdi," she said in the exaggerated French that Carlo had teased her with before. She turned to Giuseppe and smiled, clutching her music book to her chest. "Giuseppe."

Barezzi coughed. "I wish I could spend as much time in this room as my daughter," he said, lurching to other side of the room, swiftly pulling a white sheet off a spinet. The instrument's glossy book-matched grain took on an illusion of depth that made its existence appear endless. "Besides youth, you both share the agility to cultivate the mind." He looked directly at Giuseppe. "I understand from Signor Baistrocci and your father that you are a considerable student of music."

Giuseppe tightened, uncomfortable with the attention.

Barezzi continued. "I am keen to support artistic talent and I want to help further your musical education."

Margherita slid the bench from the grand piano and pushed Giuseppe on the shoulders, imploring him to sit.

Giuseppe hovered his hands over the keys, plotting their course. He looked up to his father, who gave him a slight smile.

"Signor Barezzi has been generous enough to suggest that you give Margherita weekly lessons," Carlo said. "Of course, after some progress with Signor Baistrocci."

Giuseppe walked his fingers up and down the keys, carefully placed his hands, and pushed down. The thrum of the chord took him to his room in Le Roncole—a place in the mind where, like the fiddler, he could be completely present and completely alone.

"I would like that," Giuseppe replied.

"Of course you would," said Barezzi, smiling.

Margherita placed her music book on the spinet's music stand, and without pause, Giuseppe picked up on the open page, seizing the earnest admiration of his small audience.

Outside, Carlo and Giuseppe stood by Barezzi as he instructed two servants strapping the spinet to their cart. Carlo handed him a small purse. "Thank you. I hope to pay the other half soon."

Barezzi handed back the purse. "Signor Verdi, it is a pleasure. We cannot let talent be minimized." He grinned. "Or bought, for such a paltry sum."

Carlo reached to give the purse back, but Barezzi laughed it off. "You are a good friend, if I may be so bold."

"You may."

For the length of the trip back to Le Roncole, Giuseppe kept his eyes fixed on the horizon, the cart creaking and whining to the beat of the horse's hooves, the spinet secure and silent.

Chapter Three

Giuseppe stood outside the church clutching the leather sleeve enclosing his papers. The children of Le Roncole meandered back from school, teasing, taunting, and running to nowhere in particular. Bespectacled and burdened with folders, Baistrocci walked fervently to the church steps where Giuseppe was waiting.

Giuseppe was a favorite among his teachers, especially Signor Amici, who taught Latin. Among other things, Giuseppe excelled in rote memorization, repeating back verb conjugations on command. This caused ridicule among his peers, who were eager to find his weakness. But it was obvious that Giuseppe was trying to win the favor of no one and his natural reticence gave him reprieve. The other kids didn't want to be anything more than acquaintances and this suited Giuseppe just fine.

Baistrocci had lived in Le Roncole for the majority of his adult life. The youngest in a wealthy merchant family, he came to the small town by way of Rome, where he studied to become a priest. He excelled in music and quickly gave up the priesthood, taking a position in Le Roncole. As the town's music director he pursued a quiet and productive life in a manner that reflected his affinity for the town. He didn't have the stomach for the politics of a priest and he appreciated the tranquility of country life.

Baistrocci stood huffing for air at the bottom of the steps. "Always early."

"And you're always late," said Giuseppe.

The teacher removed his gloves and opened the door for his young pupil. "And in music the goal is to always be on time. I suppose we both could practice more," he said, sweeping Giuseppe inside.

The worship hall was encased by portico windows that gently lit the pews from their curved alcoves. Adjacent to the small upright piano on which Giuseppe practiced was the pipe organ. Standing nearly twenty feet tall, it held pipes encased in dark wood and capped with a golden crown. Several angels peered down from the top of its massive cabinet, watching everything that passed below their feet.

Giuseppe untied his leather sleeve and carefully laid out his compositions. His work was so painstakingly accurate and thorough that Baistrocci found himself overlooking Giuseppe's habitual irreverence. The boy's rude manner was not something he would have tolerated from any other student—especially one so young. Perhaps it was his old age that allowed the boy to humor him.

"Excellent work, Giuseppe," said Baistrocci, leafing through his compositions.

"Shall I transcribe more?" asked Giuseppe hopefully.

Baistrocci looked out the window into the courtyard, where students splashed each other in a small fountain. "I'd like you to perform the organ for tomorrow's Mass. It will be a good opportunity to show your talents to Father Felli."

Giuseppe looked down at his manuscripts as if to apologize to them that they were no longer the topic of conversation. "I don't think I want to do that."

Baistrocci pulled his chair next to Giuseppe and sat down. "Well, what do you expect from our work together?"

"To write. Practice more. Teach when I have to."

Baistrocci paused, searching for the right words. "You will naturally improve. You practice as much as one can." He looked out the window at the playful chaos of the children outside. "Let me ask you—why? Why do you want to continue to pursue music?"

Giuseppe shifted. Despite his maturity, matters beyond basic exchanges were obscure, like watching fish frantically swim in cloudy water—their behavior and reasons unclear.

Baistrocci prodded him. "I am asking *you*, Giuseppe. Don't make it hard."

"I suppose it's a matter of working."

"Working?"

"Yes, just working."

"You're an intelligent boy. I owe much of your progress to this. But to what point will working hard continue to bear fruit?"

"Practicing will make me better," said Giuseppe, defiant.

"I am not going to discourage that thought. But as an old man, I can assure you that we are not on God's earth to simply become better. For the further purpose of our lessons together, we need to focus on *why* you are doing it."

Giuseppe squinted. "To become a better musician?"

"I do not take for granted that you have no interest in impressing others. But you might consider what being a better musician means to people other than yourself."

"That doesn't concern me."

"Then you are not the person I thought you were. Frankly, Giuseppe, your intolerance is disdainful."

Giuseppe leaned back in his seat, chastened.

Baistrocci took him by the arm and led him to the organ. "More important than your compositions is your regard for others." He lifted Giuseppe's hands and moved them in a flowing movement over the organ's keys. "It will serve the music in ways that practice never will."

Giuseppe took Baistrocci's lead and began playing, filling the sanctuary with the low hum of the organ.

"When someone asks you to do something," said Baistrocci, "you say 'yes.'"

Chapter Four

Margherita held up her hand and looked Giuseppe in the eye. "Yes, I promise I will practice every day."

"Excellent. Your father has asked that I accompany you once a week." Giuseppe lowered his voice, mindful of the hushed conversation next to him. "So it would be a good idea if—"

Giuseppe interrupted himself and leaned forward as a servant began making his way down the table with the evening's main course, *cotoletta alla milanese*. Giuseppe's stiff suit coat strained at the shoulders as he waited for the servant to find a spot for his dish. Attempting to make room, Giuseppe tilted to the side, bumping the woman next to him

"*Excuse!*" she exclaimed.

Margherita giggled.

"Sorry," said Giuseppe, looking apologetically to the woman and then to the servant who continued his task undaunted, serving Parma's dignitaries, businessmen, and their wives. Guests of Antonio Barezzi, these denizens of high society sat along his prodigious dining table topped with a dozen flickering candelabras and waited on by as many staff serving the evening's meal from silver platters.

Mocking Giuseppe, Margherita poised her hands with exaggeration and walked her fingers down the tablecloth as if playing a keyboard. She stuck her tongue out.

"Anyway, I am practicing now," she said, her brow furrowed, mocking playfully. "So, I'll be ready for his majesty when you honor us with your presence."

The fact that Margherita never took anything seriously confused Giuseppe. So he contemplated his dinner plate, its edges painted with romantic depictions of leafy vines and soaring blue jays commingled in a dramatic depiction of their daily lives.

Resigned to the banality of the evening, Margherita sighed and looked up at the glittering chandelier hanging like a glass constellation. The massive orb swayed under the currents of warm air that puffed from the candles lining the dining room.

"I hate Sunday dinners," she said, poking at her food with a fork. "So boring."

Giuseppe looked around the table and back at his food, unable, as usual, to find a response to one of Margherita's rhetorical comments.

Barezzi watched the counts and legislators, money brokers and minor royalty politely find conversation. Since Napoleon's defeat by the Austrians in 1815, Barezzi found himself increasingly in the position of host and socialite rather than businessman wholesaler. It wasn't a difficult adjustment, but entertaining for the sake of business left a simplicity of life to be desired. He longed for the early days working for his father, cheerfully haggling prices over cheap wine and grains.

Although the Austrians ruled much of the Italian peninsula once again, the liberal temperament of the French lingered. This evening was designed to maintain that sentiment. Good business was keeping relationships on friendly, gracious terms, and this was judiciously—if not dispassionately—accomplished through the stomachs of his peers and betters.

A small bell tinkled from the end of the room and a servant ushered in a stolid, severe man dressed in a crisp navy uniform, a dozen gleaming medallions festooned along his breast. He gazed across the room with his single eye, the right covered by a black silk eyepatch crudely knotted in the back. Several men in lesser livery took his side.

"*Signore e signori*: Count Adam Albert von Neipperg!" bellowed the servant.

Everyone in the room stood and then quickly sat, resuming their conversations, the formality a stale occurrence.

The count greeted Barezzi with the confidence of a man who did not take his title and duty lightly.

"A pleasure, as always," said Barezzi.

"Please sit," assured Neipperg as a servant pulled out his chair. "My apologies for confirming your invitation so late this afternoon."

"It has been too long since we've had the pleasure of your company. I'm sorry the Duchess Marie Louise could not attend."

"As is she," said Neipperg contentedly. "We recently received word that Napoleon has taken ill in exile in Elba. The duchess has taken to mourning, but she gives her sincere regards."

Well traveled and educated, Neipperg earned his societal stripes accordingly. His military exploits were well known and within his social circles he was rightfully considered a brave soldier and a competent officer. But as such, his pride was easily won and lost.

The count was well aware of the rumors circulating about his affair with Duchess Marie Louise, and without the security of royal blood flowing through his veins, his acceptance by the public depended as much on the fickle opinions of others as it did on his own volition. He admitted to himself as well as to his close friends that his sudden relationship with the duchess had been nothing less than planned. Assigned to accompany her on holiday by her father, Emperor Francis I of Austria, he and his associates successfully diverted the duchess from visiting Napoleon in exile. Neipperg's subsequent seduction of the wife of his enemy was a category of success of its own. Having joined the Austrian army at fifteen, the entire extent of his military career had been in the service of defeating the French under Napoleon's rule. With his smooth manner and easy wit, Neipperg swiftly won the heart of the duchess, fourteen years his junior, and tactfully took the title of "advisor" in order to justify their regular companionship. It was, to say the least, his defining victory and the appropriate restitution for losing his right eye at the tip of a French bayonet.

At the other end of the table, Margherita leaned into Giuseppe. His ill-fitting coat pinned his arms back so that his hands protruded like an extension of his stomach and he struggled with his silverware.

"I've heard the count is in love with the duchess," said Margherita, helpfully cutting Giuseppe's food while placing some on her own plate. She looked conspiratorially across the room. "And she's in love with him," she whispered.

Giuseppe graciously took a bite. "So what?"

"So..." Margherita adjusted her hair. "Duchess Marie Louise is still married to Napoleon, that's what."

"Oh," said Giuseppe, unsure of what to do with this new knowledge. "How do you know that?"

"One of our maids heard it from another maid who works for the duchess." Margherita took a satisfied bite. "The count apparently dissuaded the duchess from visiting her husband in exile." She glanced at Neipperg, who nodded gravely in conversation with her father. "It's quite obvious, I think," she smirked.

"Why would the maid tell you this?"

"Because I'm fun to talk to."

Giuseppe's fork skidded off the plate and onto the floor as he choked on his food.

Giuseppe wondered how he would retrieve the fork when his suit made any kind of movement a challenge. He felt extremely annoyed with his father, who, upon receiving the invitation for Giuseppe to attend dinner at the Barezzi house, had been anxious to ensure Giuseppe was outfitted properly. Barezzi had instilled himself as the benefactor of Giuseppe's musical education and Carlo did not want his son to look anything less than worthy of the patron's generosity. Short of time, Carlo took Giuseppe's measurements and with his crude approximations went to the tailor for a new suit. When he returned the following week with the ill-fitting garment, Luigia fretted over the cost and Carlo's obsequiousness. Meanwhile, Giuseppe struggled to walk or even sit in a coat and pants that felt less like a piece of clothing than a harness designed specifically to keep him from doing anything at all.

Concerned about calling attention to himself, Giuseppe discreetly leaned off his chair and reached for his fork, which had landed between Margherita's feet. The tips of his fingers just touched the floor when the sound of tearing emanated from his backside. Stretching further, his jacket suddenly burst across the back with the unmistakable bawl of ripping material.

Margherita turned beet red as she took in the absurdity of Giuseppe's torn coat. "You, sir, have ripped your entire backside," she laughed.

"At least I can eat now," said Giuseppe, finally taking a bite of his untouched food.

Back at the far end of the table, Barezzi was measuring Neipperg's words carefully. The man's reputation as a deft general preceded him, but with the rumors circulating of his relationship with the duchess, his authority over the Duchy of Parma carried an air of ill-gotten gains. Yet the count was born into wealth and he had the aplomb to reassure.

"How is the duchess coping with Napoleon's exile?"

"Well. All things considered," said Neipperg diplomatically. "As duchess she understands and takes quite seriously her role in governing the duchy."

Barezzi nodded. "I have been impressed with her support of the arts."

"An advantage of Napoleon being away. It has given the duchess an opportunity to govern with more autonomy." Neipperg paused to take a bite. "The arts are something she has the authority to contrive. It is a simple gesture to build confidence within the coalition."

"It is commendable," said Barezzi, twisting his wine glass between his fingers. "I am curious, however, about her reaction to the uprisings in the south. I have heard many things about the Carbonari making inroads here in the north." Barezzi signaled for his glass to filled. "As a businessman, I am concerned."

"Signor Barezzi, I am well aware of this small band of pseudo-intellectual terrorists in Naples. As you are aware, Austria quickly restored order."

Barezzi nodded. "The rebels were persuasive enough to get King Ferdinand to sign a new constitution," he said indifferently.

"Naples is back under the leadership of Ferdinand and that farce of a constitution has been destroyed."

"With military force," said Barezzi, sipping his wine. "Frankly, the Austrians seem to be spending more of their resources padding the tax code than governing."

"Please do not tell me you are allergic to taxation."

"The Austrians are making things very difficult for me. I can't go to church without my carriage being taxed. Surely you can take my complaint to the duchess."

Neipperg narrowed his eyes. "What are you saying?"

"It's no secret that tax evasion runs rampant. The deficit is evidently being made up in Parma. I do not wish to take political sides, but as a businessman I need a reason to assure my colleagues that we should support the Austrian government."

Neipperg smiled and gazed on the distinguished guests dining and talking among themselves. "A lovely group of people here."

Barezzi softened. "I am concerned with Austria's business interests in Italy. What happened in Naples makes clear that it's the lower classes with whom Austria should focus its attention. Surely the Austrians are taking notes from what happened in France."

"Signor Barezzi, I appreciate your concerns and I will certainly take them up with the duchess," said Neipperg wearily. "But before anything else, we—and that includes *you*—are beholden to Austria."

Flushed, Barezzi pushed back from the table and clinked the side of his wine glass. "*Signore e signori.* Citizens of Busseto and the Duchy of Parma, I want to thank you all for coming to my home tonight."

As a young man, Antonio Barezzi, considered the profession of law, an expected position that his father, also a wholesaler, had planned for his only son. Whether it was a lack of imagination or the ease of simple inheritance that kept him on the same course as his father, Antonio continued in the family business. He loathed the minutiae of accounting (preferring the security of thrift) and the uncertainty of politics. But like a sea captain, he assembled those who could help him guide his enterprise safely from one port to the next. And those at the table, to varying degrees, were a crew waiting eagerly to set sail.

Barezzi raised his glass and put his hand on Neipperg's shoulder. "And I am especially grateful to Count Adam Albert von Neipperg for attending on behalf of the Duchess Marie Louise." Neipperg bristled at the social slight, nodding appreciatively in polite deference as Barezzi continued. "But this evening's dinner is not just about financial nourishment. I want to take this opportunity to introduce you to a young man, an Italian, a musician: Giuseppe Verdi."

Piqued with curiosity, the high society of Parma turned to-ward Giuseppe. Blankly, Giuseppe looked up, his fork halfway to his mouth. Margherita took his hand.

"Papa is having you play," she whispered excitedly. "Thank God *I* don't have to do it."

"In a short amount of time Giuseppe is already showing tremendous progress," said Barezzi, maintaining an affectionate smile. "So much so, I have entrusted him to teach my daughter in her compositions and technique."

Margherita grinned, clutching Giuseppe's hand even tighter.

Giuseppe assumed he would be asked to play that evening, perhaps after dinner, discreetly plunking away in the corner of the room. But as the servants pushed the grand piano to the threshold of the room, it quickly became apparent that his small debut would come unrehearsed, hungry, and in a torn suit.

"As you know," Barezzi said, "our patrons, the Austrians, are strong supporters of the arts and I want to share our local talent with them here tonight."

The room turned once again toward Giuseppe, expectant.

Barezzi looked at him proudly. "Giuseppe, please gratify us with a short performance."

Giuseppe rose sheepishly from his chair and ambled to the piano, his mind and confidence in a muddled fog. He sat at the piano, his torn coat revealed to everyone, and put out what grace and confidence he could muster. Baistrocci's advice to be agreeable and amenable was already finding its faults.

His mind raced for a piece, any piece he could play from memory, but performing unexpectedly blocked his mind from any clear thought. The hours of practice coalesced into a brief, forgotten snap of time. His mind failed to deliver what it contained in its sticky folds to the tips of his fingers. Each key was indistinguishable from the next and the piano wobbled like a set of ivory blocks assembled at random.

He took a deep breath and closed his eyes and thought of home—the church bells and his morning routine on the spinet. Slowly the music box of memory hummed in the back of his head and the image of the traveling musician grew louder and more distinct.

As the ocean recedes from the shore, the melody revealed itself like shells on the sand and Giuseppe's hands stirred into action. The song that had first captivated him with its honesty and zeal flowed through his fingers and he began to sing.

I am only a plain old man
The fiddler of the hamlet here
Yet some consider me a sage—
I take my wine both strong and clear.

Neipperg turned swiftly to Barezzi. "Who is this boy?" he whispered heavily.

"A local. The son of a merchant."

"This piece is wholly inappropriate and, frankly, insulting."

Aroused, Barezzi considered the count's sentiment. Perhaps inappropriate for dinner, but there was something amusing about the choice. It was provincial.

Giuseppe played on, his young voice singing confidently.

The good old times saw hatred die,
And friendship reigning here serene.
Our grandsires, meeting happily,
Its verdant branches oft have seen!

"This is absurd," hissed Neipperg.

Before Barezzi could protest, the count stormed out the door, with one of his men draping his cape over his shoulders as he moved.

Barezzi discreetly removed himself from the table and followed Neipperg into the hall.

"Signor Neipperg, I am sorry if something has offended you," huffed Barezzi, trailing behind.

"I am an Austrian by blood and by rank, *Herr* Barezzi," said Neipperg placing his hat on his head and looking out the front door, impatient for the footman to fetch his coach. "And based on our conversation this evening, I cannot help but believe you intentionally had that song performed to undermine myself, the duchess, and your Austrian superiors in front of your peers."

"I assure you, Herr Neipperg, I meant nothing by his performance. By all accounts I cannot fathom what you have found offensive about the piece."

"Well, I should expect a provincial man such as yourself wouldn't. That song—written by a *Frenchman*, no less—asks the conquering Bourbons to give forgiveness to the partisans of Napoleon. The parallels to our current political situation are more than just a coincidence."

"I am confident that—"

Barezzi was interrupted by the arrival of the count's coach. It rumbled to a stop on the cobblestone street, waiting for its lone occupant.

"It's combative," said Neipperg, placing his booted foot on the carriage's side rail. He climbed inside the coach, adding, "And irrespective of your slight, for you to think that a country boy in rags would be appropriate entertainment for the duchess and me is nothing short of impudent."

He forcefully shut the door. The count's men loaded themselves onto the carriage as it lurched forward, quickly making its way back into the narrow streets of Busseto.

Barezzi ambled back into the entry hall and took a healthy swig from an errant wine glass sitting on a sideboard. When he returned to the dining room, he addressed his guests in a strained geniality.

"Thank you all. If you could please take your drinks into the parlor, we shall continue our evening together."

A servant opened a tall partition door and the guests flowed into the parlor, its walls painted with a muted pastoral scene that surrounded the guests from all sides.

Margherita took Giuseppe's arm. "You were wonderful and absurd," she said, tugging playfully at Giuseppe's torn coat.

Giuseppe suppressed a smile, pushing her hand away as Barezzi approached.

"You made quite an impression on the count," said Barezzi.

Giuseppe's smile faded and he steeled himself. "I'm sorry, Signor Barezzi, I—"

Barezzi handed Giuseppe his half-drunk glass of wine and watched the guests file into the ornate parlor, admiring his art and antiques.

"I would like to say I foresaw this, Giuseppe, but I didn't."

"If I had known…I was going to play tonight, I…" Giuseppe stammered.

Margherita took her father's hand. "Everyone thought he was wonderful, Papa."

Barezzi firmly put his hand on Giuseppe's shoulder. "We have certainly tempted fate this evening—"

"Next time I'll—" said Giuseppe, repentant.

"—and in the process you have stumbled upon the subtle politics of music."

"Papa, are you mad at Giuseppe?" Margherita asked.

Barezzi took the wine glass out of Giuseppe's hand and finished what was left. He turned to his daughter.

"*No, mio amore*. But the count is. Your little song made him see how weak his position is." Barezzi beamed. "Let's enjoy the rest of the night," he said, leading the children into the parlor.

Giuseppe took his seat at the piano and played for his countrymen through the rest of the evening.

Chapter Five

Baistrocci took Giuseppe's hands off the keyboard and turned the page in the frayed notebook. "This is not a time to impress the congregation with your musical prowess, Giuseppe."

Giuseppe and Baistrocci sat at the piano where they now practiced daily. Its chipped edges and worn finish had disappointed many ambitious students over the years, but Giuseppe was unencumbered by pretensions of appearance.

It didn't take much persuasion to convince Carlo that his son required more musical instruction. Lessons consumed the majority of Giuseppe's day and the boy spent increasingly more time away from home. Luigia had been hesitant to the change, but Baistrocci appealed to her motherly instincts with the reassurance that composition and practice would make Giuseppe happy. A part of Luigia tugged at the notion that Giuseppe would benefit from more time with her and Carlo, helping in the tavern or even playing with the neighborhood children. Assuaging her anxieties, Carlo suggested that Giuseppe's musical education would "bring out more of who he is than who he isn't"—a reality Luigia found difficult to disagree with.

Giuseppe came to the church each morning before his school lessons and again in the afternoon. Baistrocci, despite the toll on his own health, taught Giuseppe well into the evening, appealing to the boy's inclination to refine what had already been mastered. He hoped Giuseppe would soon be prepared to lead the music programming at the church—a reasonable position for a boy of Giuseppe's age and talent. Under Baistrocci's supervision, Giuseppe had played a few organ pieces at the occasional Mass, but Father Felli, conservative in his approach, was reluctant to let a child take over such an important aspect of his church. Baistrocci was eager to allow Giuseppe the space and confidence to grow, but became increasingly frustrated with the politics of power between himself and the priest.

Baistrocci's slender fingers glided over the keyboard and he played in a slow, deliberate rhythm—a farmer diligently tilling a familiar field. He eyed Giuseppe to follow his lead. Once a competitive student himself, Baistrocci patiently tampered Giuseppe's need to impress in an attempt to create a sense of artistic propriety.

"Sometimes the music is less a mirror of the performer than a body in and of itself," he said.

Giuseppe watched, bored, noting the lack of flourish in Baistrocci's playing, like a chef discovering he has only flour and water to cook with.

"As musicians of the church we are in service to the Lord," said Baistrocci. "These are His words and His music."

"Then why doesn't He play them?" asked Giuseppe derisively.

Baistrocci smiled, mindful of his charge's impetuous manner in conversation. "You miss the point, Giuseppe. It is His inspiration that allows us to write, sing, and play. God gives us the ability to create the things that help us understand life." Baistrocci played a scale as an interlude to his improvised pulpit. "The music we play in church helps us come closer to understanding our experiences on earth."

Lacking a retort, Giuseppe blew a shot of air out of his nose and walked to the window overlooking the church courtyard. Outside, several of his classmates shouted playful insults at one another and banged long sticks in a mock sword fight. The clouds overhead broke, spilling crisp afternoon light across the stone floor of the chapel.

"Perhaps you are too young to understand, but I know it is in your heart," Baistrocci continued.

Giuseppe shrugged. "I just want to play music. No more, no less.

"I think you'll find that very difficult."

The front door creaked open, echoing through the sanctuary as if a tomb were unsealed from centuries of solitude. Cloaked in a black winter cape, Le Roncole's priest, Father Felli, floated across the room.

Baistrocci stood and bowed. "I am pleased to see you, Father."

Like Baistrocci, Felli had come by Rome, but not by choice. He had served Le Roncole since French rule and itched to leave, aspiring for a higher position in Rome. But lacking the political connections and will, he languished in what he considered a backwater assignment. His relationship with the village and his musical director was distant at best and adversarial at worst. Once hopeful for a transfer, he was resigned to the fact that he was in Le Roncole for good.

Felli took Baistrocci's hand, smiling wanly. "It is always a pleasure to watch the growth of youth." He placed his hand on Giuseppe's shoulder. "Your father is a good friend of the church, Giuseppe." As if searching for his next thought, Felli leafed through the sheet music scattered on the table. "I can only hope that we can see more of you and your mother."

Baistrocci closed the lid of the piano. "Giuseppe is making great progress, Father. His understanding of the material is unprecedented in my experience."

"I look forward to hearing more," said Felli absently. "In time, of course."

Then as quickly as he came in, the priest turned and left the chapel on resounding footsteps.

Lit by the late-afternoon sun, Giuseppe and Baistrocci walked into the small graveyard at the back of the church. The gravestones cast slender shadows on the grass like sundials. Giuseppe's peers had long gone home and the yard hummed in the sound of silence. Baistrocci wobbled on his cane, trying to find his footing.

Giuseppe took him by the arm. "You're getting old."

"A master musician *and* a keen observer," said Baistrocci drily.

They walked to the edge of the grass where the road met the churchyard. Two farmhands lurched by, each pulling a cart filled to the brim with vegetables. Beyond them stretched patches of farmland sewn together in stitches of intersecting paths. Baistrocci dug a bag of pine nuts from his pocket and offered them to Giuseppe.

"Over the years, I've found the expectation to serve to be overwhelming," he said, chewing on the nuts. "But we continue to do it, so often with unwavering conviction."

Baistrocci considered the lives of the men passing by, their carts filled with the bounty of someone else. Born with little means, these men were taught to be grateful for what little they had. Be humble. Give thanks. And how could a person in their position not do so? Life was filled with rules. Service to the Lord, service to a ruler, service to family. But where and when do they apply what individuality they have upon the world?

Baistrocci saw a lot of himself in Giuseppe and could recall once having the same bounding ambition. But now in old age, Baistrocci's desires simmered in muted memories, like an object fixed in place, just beyond reach. He rarely made decisions without the guidance of God or in adherence of a simple life. And though he longed to do more, his ambitions percolated from a sense of duty rather than passion.

He watched Giuseppe contemplate the horizon beyond and considered the shifting world in front of him. As man progressed from wanderer to statesman, perhaps service to a king or God was no longer required to keep civilization intact.

Socially, it was certain that the political influence of those outside of the church and the royal palaces had grown. These men of commerce grew with the land and hired the beleaguered farmhands in front of them to push wheelbarrows filled with vegetables to sell at market. The rich would use these profits to pay to be entertained. Baistrocci had missed that boat, but Giuseppe was there, at the dock, on time. Perhaps serving God was less about seeking to please Him than it was to answer the passion within oneself—selfish or otherwise.

The sun was beginning to set and the remaining rays of sunlight bounced off the walls of the church in an amber hue.

"Giuseppe, I want you to lead the services this Sunday. You'll play everything."

Giuseppe knelt down on the cold ground and rummaged for a rock. Standing, he tossed it a few times in his hand and threw it across the road where it landed with a thud. "I thought I wasn't ready yet."

"You are," said Baistrocci. "You have been for some time." He repositioned his cane. "I suppose I was waiting for time to pass. I wanted to gain the confidence of the church. Of Father Felli."

"I'll begin this Sunday?"

Baistrocci nodded. He looked up at the bell tower, a foggy halo hovering over its roof. "I can't think of any reason not to. Keeping you from playing would only sanctify what it is that I do. There's enough aggrandizement in the world already." Baistrocci turned and shuffled back toward the church. "I know you are not one for bragging, but please tell your parents."

Giuseppe watched his teacher make his way up the uneven path, his cane sticking in the mud with every step. "They just want you to be happy."

Giuseppe kicked his boots against the back wall of the tavern, knocking the mud off the soles.

Luigia swung the door open and pulled him inside. "I've asked you a hundred times not to do that," she said, putting his notebooks on the side table by the front door.

The kitchen was warm with the smell of roasting meats and vegetables. A stew simmered in an iron pot hanging over the stone hearth. Stealing a moment, Luigia kissed Giuseppe on the cheek and pulled his jacket off before going back to the fire to stir the stew.

"We have guests this evening, so I'm going to need your help."

Giuseppe pushed a stool up to the counter and took a few pieces of chopped carrot.

His mother turned to him. "That's not for you. That needs to go in the stew."

"Then why isn't it?"

"Because it will turn to mush if it stays in there too long." Luigia pushed him off the stool. "Stop being a know-it-all and go wash up. Your father brought hot water to your room." Her knife went through an onion with a snap. "And tell him I need him down here."

Giuseppe walked up the stairs that connected the bedrooms to the dining room on the first floor. He glanced at the four men sitting at the large communal table—their lodgers for the evening.

When they had overnight guests, the family spent the evening accommodating their needs and prepared bedding and the following day's breakfast. Giuseppe often helped his mother with these chores and he knew this evening would be spent taking care of these tasks. The men picked at a roasted pheasant sitting on a pewter platter in the center of the table. They all slouched, exhausted from riding, their tunics spotted with dirt from the road. Giuseppe sighed as he made his way to his room. He'd be helping with the laundry as well.

Upstairs, Giuseppe unrolled his compositions and placed them on the spinet's music stand. Arranging the organ pieces in the order he was to play them, he noted their similarities to one another. Either hushed or bombastic, the pieces lacked nuance. But playing in church was a clear milestone in his progress as a musician and he was pleased to have earned Baistrocci's trust. Giuseppe held great respect for his teacher and was flattered that he thought him competent enough to play. He considered his forthcoming performance as a student would approach the recitation of a poem—something conjured from memory, its meaning neglected. Just because he played the music of God didn't mean he had to believe in Him. Rather, Giuseppe would play to honor Baistrocci.

Carlo knocked outside the bedroom. "Giuseppe, time for dinner," he said, opening the door.

Giuseppe reluctantly shifted off his chair and washed his hands in the ceramic basin.

Carlo studied him. "How was your lesson with Signor Baistrocci?"

"Good."

"Ah, 'good.' That certainly tells me a lot."

Giuseppe wiped his hands on his pants and sat down at his spinet.

Carlo tossed Giuseppe a towel. "Wash your face as well," he said, pushing his son out of his seat and sitting on the edge of the bed. "Signor Barezzi sent me a letter regarding lessons with Margherita."

Giuseppe rubbed his wet hands over his face. The water warmed his nose and mouth in the winter air. He patted his face dry and draped the towel across the back of his chair.

"Things have changed, Papa. I won't have time to do that anymore."

Carlo stood, crossing his arms. "And why is that?"

"My time is going to be short now with school and my commitments with Signor Baistrocci at the church," said Giuseppe staring down at his spinet.

Carlo laughed with a short cough. "I don't believe it's up for conversation, Giuseppe."

"But things have changed. I—"

"If this is because you feel uncomfortable around Margherita, I am sure we can talk to Signor Barezzi."

"No, it's nothing like that." Giuseppe looked up at his father. "Signor Baistrocci has made me the organist. I'll be leading the services."

Carlo leapt off the bed, taking his son in his arms, nearly knocking him over. "That's extraordinary news!" He pushed back from Giuseppe, beaming. "Why didn't you say something?"

Giuseppe shrugged, nonchalant. "I just did."

Carlo pushed him off to the kitchen, bounding through the door with Giuseppe under his arm. Luigia stood over the kitchen counter, removing the innards of a small fowl.

"Luigia, you are in the presence of our son, the church music director."

"No, Papa, I am not the director," corrected Giuseppe.

"I'm sorry, the what?" asked Luigia, distracted with the carcass in her hands.

Carlo spun around the kitchen. "We should celebrate. Where's the wine?"

"I gave the rest to our guests," said Luigia. She put the bird down on a stone platter and placed it near the hearth. "Now what is this about?"

"There's more wine in the shed," said Carlo to himself. He dashed out the back door. Giuseppe sat next to his mother.

"I'll be playing the organ for the full service on Sunday."

Luigia knelt down and wiped her hands on her apron, leaving translucent grease spots.

"I'm very proud of you, Giuseppe," she said, running her hand on the top of his head. "I hope you're proud, too."

He smiled. "Thanks, Mama. I am."

In the dining room they could hear Carlo laughing and the sound of clinking glasses.

"Sounds like your father found the wine," Luigia said. She handed Giuseppe a platter of roasted vegetables and they went into the dining room to serve dinner to their guests.

"My son, the church organist!" Carlo boasted as Luigia and Giuseppe entered. Carlo raised his glass and the rest of the men followed suit.

"You must be quite good for someone your age," said one of the men to Giuseppe.

"He is," said Luigia, pouring herself a glass of wine and raising it. "To my son, the musician."

Giuseppe blushed. Carlo poured him a glass of wine and he joined in the toast.

When the guests retired, Giuseppe dutifully began to clear the table. Carlo whipped him up and playfully spanked his rear. "The church organist does not do the dishes," he said.

"At least for tonight," said Luigia.

Giuseppe rose with the sun as it made its way over the eastern hills. Just beyond the tavern, the vineyards twinkled from the crushed quartz the vintners threw beneath the vines, the reflected warmth smoothing out the grapes' sweet, earthy flavor. Refreshed from a good night's sleep, Giuseppe dressed and walked to the church.

Giuseppe opened the heavy door and strolled into the main sanctuary of the church. Surrounding oak trees filtered the morning light, keeping the church interior gray and cool. Giuseppe called out for Baistrocci. No answer. He called out again, his voice echoing endlessly.

He was answered by the tiny sound of footsteps followed by the presence of Father Felli, his robe flowing assuredly around his body. He had a rosary wound tightly around his fist and the attached cross swung quickly back and forth, keeping time. He stopped, surprised.

"Good morning, Master Verdi."

"Good morning," answered Giuseppe.

"Was Signor Baistrocci expecting you so early?"

"No, I came to prepare for this morning's services."

Felli walked toward Giuseppe. "Of course, of course," he said, folding his hands over his stomach, his body in limbo. Then, as if assuming the role of a magistrate delivering news from far afield, he said, "I'm sorry, but I have very sad news." He laid his soft hand on Giuseppe's head. "Signor Baistrocci passed away in his sleep last night."

Baistrocci lay on a small bed, barely room for one. The attending nun had laid his body prone and straight with his feet together at the heels and his hands resting at his sides. Baistrocci was still in his black suit from the day before, as if prepared to mourn his own death. His cane rested against the desk, mud still caked on the tip in a hard shell.

The nun stepped back so Giuseppe could approach the bed. From the warmth of the room, Baistrocci's face still appeared flush with life. Giuseppe had never encountered death before. On occasion, he helped his father slaughter the chickens. They would thrash about the yard, headless, more alive in the throes of death than in life.

Giuseppe was not prepared for the unexpected feeling of grief that came over him. Baistrocci's lifeless body belied the fervent memories Giuseppe had for the man who had stoked his passion for music. He knelt down and silently thought a small prayer, overcome with the sanctity of the moment.

Felli took Giuseppe by the shoulders and sat him down on a chair beside the bed. "Signor Baistrocci was a dear friend to me and to the church. I know he was very special to you as well, Giuseppe." The priest placed his hand on the corpse's forehead. "We can be happy that he is with God now."

The swelling in Giuseppe's throat worked its way up his neck, to his cheeks, and finally to his eyes, where small tears began to drip. He wiped his sleeve across his face, sniffling.

"He lived a good, pious life. One of service. There is nothing to be sad about. He is in a better place now."

Giuseppe tightened. *If this were true, then why would we not kill ourselves at the earliest opportunity?* he thought. He looked at Baistrocci for an answer. The church forbade such an act. Rules. Always rules.

The nun sat at the foot of the bed, her head bowed in repose.

Giuseppe looked up to Father Felli, his cheeks red with sadness. "I am supposed to play today."

Felli paused, considering the situation. "I see." *Is there no one else capable in this town other than this dour little boy?* he thought. "Is this something you discussed with Signor Baistrocci?"

"It is."

"Well," said Felli, considering his options, "I suppose if you are prepared for today, then we mustn't let your training go to waste." He nodded to the nun, who stood and helped Giuseppe out of his chair, leading him to the door.

"Giuseppe," Felli called out, "I will need your help with communion today. We can have someone else play the organ as you serve."

The service began like any other with a barrage of hymns as people found their seats. Giuseppe played from the page as Baistrocci had required of him, creating the familiar milieu the congregation expected. Carlo waved to Giuseppe, who nodded back with a mix of pride and grief. After taking her seat next to Carlo, Luigia turned and smiled at her son. Father Felli took the pulpit, addressing the church with abrupt solemnity.

"It is with great sadness that I announce to you that our music director and organist, Signor Baistrocci, died this morning."

The congregation murmured, shaken by the news.

"As this occurred in the early morning, I have not yet been able to prepare the appropriate service or remarks for our esteemed friend." Felli put on his glasses and flipped his Bible open. "We will find an appropriate replacement for music director as soon as time will allow it." He looked about the congregation for a reaction. "Now a reading from John 11:25–26."

During the Lord's Prayer, a nun relieved Giuseppe of his duties at the organ. Father Felli walked down the altar, blessing the sacrament, while Giuseppe lost himself trying to place the hymn. As he hummed quietly to himself, an acolyte nudged Giuseppe and nodded toward Felli, who stood staring, impatient for Giuseppe to follow. Another hymn unfamiliar to Giuseppe began to play, and again he closed his eyes and murmured the tune, trying to predict its pattern. The notes skipped unpredictably and Giuseppe considered the nun's select playing. What would Baistrocci have thought?

As he considered the hymn's peculiar charms he suddenly became aware of the fact that Father Felli was yelling, his voice full-throated, specifically at Giuseppe. The horrified look on the congregation's collective face confirmed that a priest was yelling at a boy in front of the entire church.

Suddenly, Giuseppe felt a sharp kick in the middle of his back. He tumbled down the altar stairs in a violent gush of limbs. He scrambled to stand.

"You impudent boy, pay attention!" seethed Felli from high atop the altar. His piercing voice reverberated about the church. The effect, however, was less menacing than pathetic.

Finding his bearings and his pride, Giuseppe adjusted his suit and cleared his throat in the awkward silence. "May God strike you with lightning!" he bellowed, and stormed out of the church.

Felli's robe seemingly drooped with shame. "It seems that I am overcome with grief for our beloved Baistrocci," he stammered, trying to save face.

The congregation was silent in its rebuke.

The following day, Giuseppe prepared the music for Baistrocci's funeral, practicing throughout the day on his spinet. His selections and performance received much praise from the members of the church and they quickly embraced their young prodigy—a formidable evolution of the esteemed and beloved Baistrocci.

Chastened, Felli blessed Giuseppe as a new addition to his church, unable to push back against the passion of public opinion.

Chapter Six

1828

His attaché in hand, Giuseppe crossed the public square in front of the Barezzi house. Tea lights hung from lush trees, guiding Giuseppe's path to the front door. After a year of weekly piano lessons with Margherita, Giuseppe's discomfort with the elegance of the home had subsided and he knocked on the door with pluck.

The boy was still as stiff as a steel rod, but Antonio Barezzi's patronage took on a paternal grace that tempered Giuseppe's disposition to something more agreeable. Every day, Giuseppe walked three miles along the rutted road between Le Roncole and Busseto to fulfill his commitment teaching lessons, attending school and producing pieces for the Busseto Philharmonic. His success gave him pride, though he kept this sentiment close to the chest. To most, he still exuded an air of constant irritability and dissatisfaction.

Giuseppe rang the bell. A servant promptly opened the door and took his coat.

"Mistress Margherita is upstairs in the music room."

"Thank you," said Giuseppe, already ascending the curved stairs.

On the second-floor landing Giuseppe could hear the tinkling sound of the piano wafting from the music room. The hesitation between chords was unmistakably from Margherita's hands. Though it pained Giuseppe's ear, he was comforted by its predictability. Between his Sunday organ duties in Le Roncole, vigorous studies, and prolific compositions, the music lessons had become a familiar, safe ritual.

Giuseppe placed his attaché on a circular table and lit a candle. He placed it on top of the piano. "An original composition?"

"It is," said Margherita concentrating on the keyboard, her head swaying to the rhythm. "I have lyrics as well. But I won't share them unless you promise to cancel today's lesson."

"A composer and a librettist," said Giuseppe. He sat on a buttoned love seat to the side of the piano and crossed his legs. "I should say you no longer require a lesson ever again."

"You would hate that. Admit it."

Giuseppe traced his fingers along the couch's trim. "Hm."

"Well, you should know that the song I wrote is about a boy who forces a girl through a very peculiar routine of piano playing."

"Are you making fun of me?"

"Hardly," she said, rolling her eyes. "If I were making fun of you, that would mean I like you." Margherita stood and smoothed out her dress. She outstretched her arms and wiggled her fingers. "Walk with me."

Nonplussed, Giuseppe remained on the couch as if forbidden by law to do otherwise. Margherita pulled him from his perch, and wrapping her arm in his, they shuffled across the room to the window.

"What are you thinking about?" she asked.

"That we should get to your lesson."

"No, you're not."

"I am, actually."

"You're thinking about…" Margherita paused, watching a carriage on the road below. "Something very boring."

"Exactly."

Margherita smiled, hitting Giuseppe on the shoulder. "Unfair." She turned toward him. "But I do like you, you know. I was only joking."

"Of course."

Margherita lowered her eyebrows and jutted out her chin. "Of course," she said, mimicking Giuseppe.

He laughed, losing his composure for a moment.

"Ah," said Margherita, smiling. "You can laugh. That makes me feel good."

"Come on, we have work to do."

Giuseppe was all business. His music career had taken off quickly since Baistrocci's sudden death. Giuseppe's reputation had spread thanks to his relationship with Barezzi, enabling him to begin lessons with Ferdinando Provesi—music teacher, school director, and renowned composer in his own right. Under Provesi's guidance, Giuseppe's skill as musician and composer grew. One late evening, looking over an eight-movement cantata that Giuseppe had composed, Provesi declared he had no more to teach his pupil. Giuseppe's skill of arrangement and composition was exemplary. But it was his apt comprehension of the human condition that made a man of Provesi's stature weep. His student was fifteen years old.

Barezzi, Giuseppe, and Margherita sat at the table as a servant poured a ladle of pumpkin soup into their bowls. The windows were open to the night air, letting in the smell of chimney smoke from across the plaza.

"Signor Provesi and I had a conversation last night," said Barezzi, closing the window. "He thinks you have an opportunity to study in Milan at the conservatory."

"Oh."

"It would be an excellent opportunity for you."

"Would that mean I no longer have music lessons?" asked Margherita expectantly.

Barezzi laughed. "I suppose you would benefit as well." He took a sip of soup and then a mouthful of wine. "I do bring this up prematurely. But it's something to consider."

"What did my father say?" asked Giuseppe.

"I haven't spoken to him about it yet. But I suppose he would be supportive. Don't you?"

Giuseppe nodded.

"The trick is that we will have to apply for a sponsorship," said Barezzi, "a petition to allow you to audition."

"My compositions and role at the philharmonic aren't enough?"

Barezzi smiled. "Giuseppe, you're talented, to be sure. However—" he took a swig of wine, "the Royal Conservatory is in Lombardy, another state. I will need some letter from a statesman, supporting you. That said, I do believe my relationship with the duchess is in good standing and I'll start making the necessary arrangements."

"She's never heard me play. How would she know what to write about me?"

"Politics is without substance, Giuseppe. You could play the hurdy-gurdy for all they care."

Chapter Seven

B arezzi sat in a small armchair, uncomfortably crossing and uncrossing his legs in the late-morning heat. Sunlight filled the narrow hallway, floating down from oblong windows lining the vaulted ceiling. Heavy tapestries depicting fierce battles, noble hunting parties, and the gentility of court life hung from the pine support beams. Barezzi noted that happy, obedient dogs were a consistent theme in these fabric worlds.

He left Busseto early that morning, riding twenty-five miles on horseback to the Ducal Palace of Colorno, the palace of the duchess. He hoped to make his appeal regarding Giuseppe's sponsorship to the duchess directly. But upon arrival he was informed that he was to meet with Count Neipperg, who fulfilled his role in the palace by delicate obfuscation.

A servant led Barezzi to a small outdoor courtyard, its stone walls topped with metal lattice resembling trailing ivy. Groomed hedges planted along the granite and marble walkways created small rooms and segues, like a maze built for a child or small animal.

From the far side of the courtyard, the unmistakable clang of metal on metal could be heard in brief gusts of fury. Two middle-aged men, each dressed in stiff riding pants—one red, the other camel—flung their rapiers at each other, equally emboldened and cautious of the danger into which they had put themselves. A group of Austrian military officers made a ring around the men, sipping wine and giving silent encouragement. The man in red swung wildly at his opponent, his shirt torn and flapping like an errant appendage.

Neipperg was seated on a stone bench, watching the duel in rapt attention. His elegant silk and linen coat contrasted sharply with his simple black eye patch. The man in camel lurched, stabbing his opponent in his right side. Blood drew immediately and the soldiers rushed to his aid.

"Ah. Aha!" shouted Neipperg, both humored and relieved. He turned his palms upward, imploring Barezzi to sit. "It's always about money."

"Who owes whom?" asked Barezzi, getting his bearings.

"Hardly," said Neipperg.

As soon as Barezzi had made himself comfortable, Neipperg stood and adjusted his coat. He looked down on Barezzi.

"Both men are beyond rich." He motioned to the man in red pants. "The duke demanded satisfaction that *he* be recognized as the richer of the two," he said, laughing. "And I should say, by rights of both courage and stupidity, he should be." Neipperg tightened the strap on his eye patch. "Animals, all of us," he continued, pouring a glass of peppered brandy from a crystal decanter. "As gentlemen, they are solving this disagreement in the most civilized of terms. Don't you agree?"

"Of course," replied Barezzi.

"I tried to talk them out of it, but neither would back down." Neipperg downed his glass of brandy and bellowed to the loser,

"Have you have not found satisfaction, Duke?" as the bleeding man was carried away by a doctor.

It was simply by chance that Neipperg had intercepted Barezzi's request to speak with the duchess. He was wary of granting Barezzi an audience. It was a particularly inopportune time and Neipperg was concerned about giving him the chance to express a genuine grievance.

Recent reports of nationalist uprisings in Rome and Milan were funneling south and it was particularly troubling for Neipperg as it suggested strong organization among the dissenters. And who was responsible? The heads of the mobs were difficult to find without starting at the tails. And any inquiries in the slums and public houses, no matter how discreet, would suggest a lack of confidence on the part of the Austrian government. Word travels fast. Eventually, the Austrian military had to be deployed—guns spoke louder than words.

If Barezzi came to complain of violence, Count Neipperg hardly wanted to give the matter to the duchess. Marie Louise could be liberal to a fault and would certainly entertain Barezzi's dissent. *Hell, she might concede the whole duchy to the Italians*, he thought.

"Anyway," said Neipperg, directing his attention back to Barezzi, "I wanted to personally meet as soon as I received your letter."

"I appreciate that. I know your time is short."

"Mm," said Neipperg, putting on an air of impatience.

Barezzi cleared his throat. "My visit here does not concern tariffs or taxes or anything of that nature. It's actually a matter of personal interest. I would like to request of the duchess a letter of support for a young musician."

"He is in need of employment?"

"I have high hopes for him to attend the music conservatory in Milan."

Neipperg looked on, silent, nodding vacantly.

"I would like a letter of recommendation," continued Barezzi.

Neipperg poured a fresh glass of brandy and sniffed the glass. "Surely if his musical gifts are so great, he would be granted admission based on his talent alone."

"It's not so much a matter of talent as it is the duchess's particular influence." Barezzi lowered his voice. "As you can appreciate, Count Neipperg, the conservatory is in Lombardy. As a citizen of Parma, the boy is precluded from enrolling without some political intervention."

Neipperg flicked a speck of lint off his coat. "Why would the duchess be inclined to do this?"

Throughout their territories, the Austrians were enthusiastic about supporting the arts, and Duchess Marie Louise was an enthusiastic manager of these enterprises, producing dozens of plays and musicals as well as overseeing the construction of several museums and opera houses.

Barezzi softened, appealing to this impressionable side of her diplomacy. "Frankly, the boy is a prodigy. I would suggest to you and the duchess that his current success is in large part due to the support the Austrian government has given to the arts."

"I see the appeal. But it's no small matter to send a letter of support for something so…" Neipperg looked around the garden, toward the palace, "…so representative of this duchy. I wouldn't want to export someone we aren't proud of."

"What do you suggest?"

"We would have to have him audition for the duchess."

Barezzi hesitated, balking at the specificity of the request. "Of course," he conceded. "When would be most convenient for you and the duchess?"

Neipperg tipped back the dregs of his brandy. "Tonight."

"So soon?"

Neipperg shrugged. "The surprise should be the perfect challenge for your young man." He walked back toward the palace. "If you'll excuse me, I need to check on the duke. I fear his money has really cost him something this time."

Luigia opened the front door of the tavern to find Barezzi nearly nose-to-nose with her. She moved a step back, taking a deep breath.

"Signora Verdi, please excuse my unannounced visit," said Barezzi, removing his hat.

Luigia wiped her hands on her apron and opened the door. "Signor Barezzi, please come in. I'll let Carlo know you're here."

She trotted off. Barezzi stood in the kitchen as a cast iron pot warmed over the open fire.

"Signor Barezzi!" said Carlo, bounding through the kitchen with Giuseppe in his wake.

"Please excuse the intrusion, but something urgent has come up," said Barezzi in his most conciliatory tone. "Giuseppe and I need to ride to Parma immediately."

"He has school lessons tomorrow," said Luigia.

"It's inconvenient, to be sure, but it's a matter of his application to the conservatory."

"The conservatory?" said Carlo, looking to Luigia and Giuseppe.

"Yes, Giuseppe needs to audition for the duchess," said Barezzi matter-of-factly.

"The duchess," said Carlo wistfully, caught in the mystique of such an encounter.

Luigia untied her apron and placed it on the counter. "This is the first we're hearing of anything about the conservatory," she said, breaking the spell. She stole a hard glance at Giuseppe.

Barezzi composed himself, maintaining the course. "I admit, this is short notice. However, Giuseppe's music instructor and I believe that he would be a prime candidate for the music conservatory in Milan. At this juncture, it's a matter of getting a sponsorship from the duchess."

Carlo and Luigia stood still, stunned with the revelation.

"Politics as usual," said Barezzi with a nervous laugh.

"Signor Barezzi, this is a matter that we need to discuss as a family," said Luigia.

"I think," Carlo broke in, directing his thoughts toward Luigia, "that it's certainly something we would want Giuseppe to do."

"They're leaving tonight," she interjected.

Barezzi coughed. "This afternoon, actually."

Giuseppe tugged at his mother's dress. "Mama, please."

Luigia kneeled down and ran her hand firmly over Giuseppe's hair. "Is this what you want?"

Giuseppe nodded, his eyes adrift, flustered with the position in which he placed his mother. She lifted his chin, meeting his gaze.

He looked at her intently. "Yes, it is what I want."

Luigia stood and took the pot off the fire, dropping it on the table with a thud. "Signor Barezzi, this soup will not travel well, so please join us for an early lunch. I hope you will find cheese and bread suitable for you ride."

As she ladled the soup, Giuseppe gathered his things from his room.

Giuseppe and Barezzi mounted their horses and rode hard to Parma without stopping. Stiff and nearly immobile from their saddles, they were quickly received at Ducal Palace. Neipperg came down the main steps to greet them.

"Signor Barezzi, you made it back."

"As instructed," said Barezzi, pushing Giuseppe forward. "Count Neipperg, please meet Giuseppe Verdi, perhaps the finest young composer in all of Italy."

Neipperg's convivial tone demurred, as he recognized Giuseppe from the ill-fated dinner several years before. "Ah, yes. I believe I am acquainted with this boy," he said derisively. "The farmer's son?"

Giuseppe nodded matter-of-factly.

"Well, come on then," said Neipperg, his demeanor now less familiar. He pushed them into a small parlor, several hallways and vestibules from the main entry hall.

Ensconced in a plush velvet chair, Duchess Marie Louise sat adjacent to a grand piano. The curtains were drawn, casting light over the gilded furniture and glassware that filled the room. A sunbeam caught the diamond pendants laced in the duchess's hair, casting beads of quivering light across the walls. She held her hand out to Barezzi to take in his. He bowed.

"We are honored to be here," he said, rising.

The duchess smiled and held her hand toward Giuseppe. He stiffly took it to his forehead, imperfectly mimicking Barezzi.

Barezzi puffed up his chest. "Your Grace, please meet Giuseppe Verdi of Le Roncole. I have the distinct joy and honor to be his patron."

The duchess returned to her seat and smoothed out the lace on her dress. "The honor is mine. It's a pleasure to have a gifted young musician in our palace. I adore the arts." She looked to Neipperg, who stepped obediently to her side. "The count has told me that I am to approve of his playing in some capacity."

"That's right," said Barezzi, nudging Giuseppe to take his position at the piano.

"And what will you be playing for us?" asked the duchess.

"A piece by Haydn, your Grace," said Giuseppe.

"Nothing original?" snorted Neipperg.

"An Austrian composer, not original?" chided the duchess. "Please, Giuseppe, ignore the count. Play for us."

Giuseppe ran his fingers up and down the keyboard and then began the playful strokes of *Piano Sonata no. 59*. He soon lost himself in the music, easily moving his fingers to the logical place of the notes. Enchanted, he hardly noticed the duchess's appreciative gaze, Barezzi's pride, or Neipperg's agitation. The duchess was charmed.

"You play with a natural tranquility. Truly exceptional for someone your age."

"Thank you, your Grace."

The duchess stood and her gown unfolded into a perfect cone, as if she were seated on a pedestal. "It would be my pleasure to send my recommendation to the conservatory," she said with admiration.

"Your Grace," said Neipperg firmly, "I would be remiss if I did not inform you that this boy performed a base and ill-timed protest song at a dinner party I once attended. I do not believe he represents the Duchy of Parma in a manner that we see fit. Or the Austrian Empire, frankly."

The duchess burst out laughing. "Please excuse the count. He can be overzealous with propriety. He rose at four this morning to oversee a silly *and* illegal duel," she said, throwing an accusatory gaze at Neipperg. "Ghastly business, if you ask me. Grown men stabbing one another." She scribbled in a notebook and handed it to the count. "Please have my secretary draw up the recommendation immediately."

The duchess bowed to Giuseppe. "Truly an honor," she said as she walked out, her dress trailing obediently behind her.

Rattled, Neipperg vainly gathered his temper and led Giuseppe and Barezzi out of the parlor. "I hope you have found satisfaction."

"We all have," said Barezzi diplomatically.

Chapter Eight

It was several months after the audition, but still no word had come from the offices of the duchess about the status of the letter to the music conservatory.

"I don't understand," said Giuseppe. "I played quite well that day."

Barezzi stared out the window at the town square. "Mm," he conceded. "It's politics, Giuseppe. We'll have to go back."

Giuseppe packed his sheet music into his attaché. "Politics? Of what? It's a waste of time, if you ask me. I can't focus on my music. If I can't play in the foolish school by their foolish rules, then they can go stuff themselves."

"Don't say that."

"Don't say what?" asked Margherita, setting down a silver tea set on a coaching table. She poured a cup and handed it to her father.

"Giuseppe, you cannot play in a vacuum," Barezzi said. "For better or for worse, you have to fight for recognition. Merit is only half the battle. You need others in your life to get by."

"Hmph," smirked Margherita. "He certainly needs me," she said, handing Giuseppe a steaming cup of tea.

"Hardly," said Giuseppe, handing the cup back to Margherita and pouring his own cup of tea. "Case in point."

"Oh, really? If it weren't for these lessons you'd never leave your room."

Giuseppe rolled his eyes and took a sip of tea. "I must be going home."

"Of course," said Barezzi, patting Giuseppe on the back. "Tell your parents we need to go to Parma again and make an appeal."

Giuseppe grimaced.

"Oh, he doesn't like that," observed Margherita.

Barezzi took Giuseppe by the shoulder. "Let me worry about the injustices of the world, Giuseppe. They're for you to use in your music."

Giuseppe and Barezzi started for Parma before dawn, stopping only so their horses could drink. A palace footman recognized Giuseppe from his previous visit and led them in without question. They waited for the count on a landing overlooking an English-style garden with dozens of palm trees and spiraled topiaries radiating from a gushing fountain.

"I'm sorry, Signor, but I cannot find the count's assistant," said the footman, returning to the landing.

"Ah, thank you, my good man, but we are here to see the duchess."

"Yes, I see," said the footman, growing impatient, "but the count typically receives unexpected guests."

"And what about the count himself? Or is he indisposed?"

"I wouldn't know, Signor, I'm sorry."

Giuseppe tugged on Barezzi's coat sleeve and cocked his head toward the far end of the garden. Several men shuttled back and forth, the glint of their swords giving them away. Barezzi practically pushed Giuseppe down the stairs as they ran across the gravel walkway.

"Signor! You can't go down there," yelled the footman, chasing after them and trying in vain to keep up.

They found Neipperg much as he was on their previous visit, sitting comfortably, legs crossed and sipping brandy, his rapier hanging from his belt. He nearly dropped the decanter when he saw Barezzi marching toward him.

"Ah, Signor Barezzi. To what do we owe the pleasure?" he said, maintaining his composure.

Barezzi casually extended his hand to Neipperg, who reluctantly shook it. "We happened by the palace and thought we would give our regards to you and the duchess."

"How nice," said Neipperg, excusing himself from the ongoing duel. "And now, I am sorry, but I must ask you to leave as I have other matters to attend to," he huffed under his breath.

"Count Neipperg, we have failed to receive any letter from the conservatory about Giuseppe's appointment to audition. Not only did we want to give our respects, but we wanted to make sure this had been done."

Neipperg blanched and took a step toward Barezzi. "If it isn't immediately apparent to you, I do not believe you acknowledge the natural order of decorum between us."

"And what might that be?"

"As your superior, I—"

"My superior?"

"*Herr* Barezzi. By birth and by nationality I am an Austrian. You are not. And if you or your young friend here has not noticed, an Austrian flag flies over this palace. I owe you no favors." Neipperg examined the handle of his saber. "Now if we were to duel...."

Emboldened by the indignation apparent in Giuseppe's face, Barezzi collected himself and took a deep breath. "Count Neipperg, despite your rather popular rule, that flag represents opposition. The Austrians have been good rulers, but there is no disguising the fact that a revolution of independence has moved into Italy."

"That's simply a point of view."

"It's not a point of view that Austrian troops have been deployed within your holdings, fighting against the very people you occupy."

"I would consider that a gross exaggeration and simply ignorant."

"The Carbonari rebel group is growing, and you know as well as I that the leaders in that organization carry much influence." Barezzi crossed his arms. "I have the means to—"

Neipperg stepped to Barezzi, his hand on the hilt of his saber. "Are you threatening me?"

"I am simply telling you that you have a situation. A person in my position can help quell dissent."

Neipperg's face turned scarlet and he put himself nose-to-nose with Barezzi. "I could have you arrested for threats against the state," he said, gritting his teeth.

Barezzi shrugged and handed Neipperg several of Giuseppe's compositions. "Please see that the duchess's secretary receives this," he said, tapping the folder. "I hope she can take credit for young Verdi's success."

Giuseppe and Barezzi's feet crunched on the gravel as they passed the ongoing duel, whose members had stopped to witness the heated exchange. Neipperg adjusted his tunic and barked at the footman incoherently.

"My boy," said Barezzi, adjusting the saddle on his horse. "I am sure we'll receive a letter quite soon."

"You're not concerned about threatening the duke?"

"Hardly. He has an opportunity to distance himself from the resistance." Barezzi cinched his saddlepack. "We did him a favor."

Chapter Nine

1832

As it happened, the letter from the conservatory arrived unexpectedly, almost a forgotten relic from a forgotten time. With little fanfare, Margherita casually tore it open, much to the dismay of Barezzi, who hoped to have the honor himself. Unsentimental as always, Giuseppe was unconcerned with the lack of ceremony and continued to begrudge the pandering it required. It was good news, but it was an opportunity to audition, not an admission, he argued.

What Giuseppe was most concerned about when the letter arrived—and what he kept to himself—was the growing admiration and feelings he had for Margherita. Their scheduled music lessons had evolved into casual social engagements, a friendship, and then to Giuseppe's own surprise, a passionate expression of his tenderness for her. He had always been indifferent to friendships, let alone love, but was now willing to admit that he had a fondness for something more than music. It was a precarious place, to be sure.

"As soon as we get to Milan, I'll send the address of where I'll be staying," he told Margherita.

She folded a linen handkerchief, putting it Giuseppe's breast pocket. "Why would I need that?" she asked coolly.

"Well," said Giuseppe, anxious, "I suppose it would be for the occasion that we would write to one another."

"You want to write while you're away?"

"Don't you?" asked Giuseppe, thumbing nervously at the handkerchief.

Margherita ran her finger over the rough edge of the envelope. "Our lessons have taken up so much of my time. I think I'll be quite busy catching up on the things I would have been doing if we weren't together so much."

"Oh, I see," said Giuseppe, his heart struggling, a butterfly caught in a headwind.

Margherita barked a laugh, covering her mouth. "Of course I'll write, you dolt." She shoved the letter into his chest. "You'd better, too."

Giuseppe smiled and his heart regained its ascent.

"You're going to miss me," she said with accusation or joy. Giuseppe could never tell which.

In his bedroom, Giuseppe closed the brass latch of his travel trunk, everything for his trip laid neatly inside. He made a silent good-bye to his spinet, laying his hand across its keys.

In the days leading to his departure, Giuseppe continued to practice in preparation for his audition. The conservatory requested a fugue composition based on the theme of the seasons. Working tirelessly on balancing originality and the expected—a maddening exercise to solve the mystery of pleasing others—he conjured recent memories of Margherita as inspiration. Being away from a book of music was a new approach for Giuseppe.

In anticipation of his long absence from home, he let Luigia sit in his room as he practiced, an indulgence he rarely granted. Giuseppe would miss her silent solace the most.

He stood outside the tavern with his parents, eagerly waiting for Barezzi's arrival. As the coach crested the hill, Luigia impulsively grabbed Giuseppe in a hug. He dropped the composition books clutched across his chest, the papers scattering across the walkway.

"Mama, I won't be gone forever," he said, quickly picking the papers up off the ground.

"If you're successful, you will."

Carlo stuffed a small leather purse into Giuseppe's vest pocket. "Just to help you get settled. Or maybe a new suit. I've heard they're quite fashionable in Milan." He smiled, tugging at Giuseppe's ill-fitting pants. "Not so much in Le Roncole."

The coachman opened the door to the carriage, and with the fast click of the latch, Giuseppe and Barezzi made off on the three-day journey to Milan.

They traveled the broad, open valleys and flatlands of Northern Italy over dirt roads clogged with ruts and ditches. They jostled and bounced endlessly. Dozens of turnpikes monitored by the Austrian authorities lay scattered between the small towns and villages along the trip. Barezzi grumbled about the expense and inconsistent stamps the soldiers placed in their passports, and more often than not, he paid the same fee several times over. Giuseppe grew weary of the soldiers' scrutiny of his passport:

Age: eighteen. Height: tall. Color of hair: chestnut-brown. Color of eyes: gray. Forehead: high. Eyebrows: black. Nose: aquiline. Mouth: small. Beard: dark. Chin: oval. Face: thin. Complexion: pale. Special peculiarities: pock-marked.

He was a foreigner paying a fee just to travel outside the town where he was born.

After lunch on the third day, they crossed into Milan, the capital of the Austrian-ruled state of Lombardy-Venice. The city's labyrinth of bridges, elongated canals, verdant parks, and cathedrals stood in sharp contrast to the more austere Busseto a hundred miles to the south. Even the wealthy Barezzi was silenced by the splendor and sheer opulence of the Duomo di Milano and the stoic Sforza Castle as they made their way to the boarding house near the conservatory.

Their rooms on the third floor of a modest townhouse faced west toward the city center. Amber twilight settled into the room as Giuseppe eagerly unpacked his clothes and laid his compositions out for study. As soon as he sat down, his head hit the desk and he closed his eyes, exhausted from the journey and the anxiety of missing someone for the first time. He longed to hear Margherita crack a joke at his expense.

The Milan Conservatory of Music stood in the middle of the city, a short walk from the gilded La Scala opera house. The school's simple buildings, which were shared with a neighboring church, appealed to Giuseppe, reminding him of something not far removed from Le Roncole.

Not long after they arrived, a small man in a black frock coat and tapered pants greeted them in the courtyard.

"Pleased to meet you," he said cheerfully. "I'm Alessandro Rolla, a professor here as well as a composer."

"Signor Rolla, a pleasure," bellowed Barezzi amicably. "I am familiar with your work. I've had the pleasure to hear some of your pieces by our orchestra in Busseto." He tugged at the lapels of his vest. "Of which I am a board member."

Giuseppe bowed slightly. "And I've had the pleasure of studying your work with my instructor, Piave," he said, removing his hat.

Rolla was well established in the Milan music scene as both a violinist and the orchestra director at La Scala.

"I'm honored that my work has perhaps brought you here," he said politely, leading them through the courtyard into a small room at the back of the campus. Several wooden chairs surrounded an upright piano.

"Did you bring the fugue?" Rolla asked rather suddenly.

Giuseppe promptly handed his composition to Rolla, who pulled a pair of glasses from his waistcoat and briskly scanned the page.

"Mm," he mumbled. "Promising." Rolla stuffed the composition into a folder overflowing with paperwork. "Allow me to find some of my colleagues who will need to listen to the audition."

Rolla returned with professor Vincenzo Lavigna, who brusquely introduced himself, acutely distracted from whatever it was Rolla had pulled him from.

With no introduction, Giuseppe performed his fugue. He looked up from his performance, eager and euphoric, to barely a nod of appreciation. Lavigna stood abruptly and whispered a perfunctory comment to Rolla.

"I agree," Rolla replied. "His hands are off." He made a notation in his notebook.

"Has he turned in the paperwork?" Lavigna asked.

"He has."

Lavigna took the application from Rolla, reading it with seeming contempt. "You're eighteen?" he asked Giuseppe.

Giuseppe nodded. "I am."

He looked Giuseppe up and down, smiled a cursory smile, and left the room, dead silence trailing after him.

Rolla smiled and stood, clapping playfully. "Very good, Giuseppe. Quite remarkable. Though we would need to work on your positioning."

Giuseppe cast a skeptical glance at his hands. "Shall I continue playing?"

"No, no—that won't be necessary." Rolla glanced at his pocket watch. "Thank you for taking the time to be here," he said, escorting them out of the building.

Out on the Via Conservatorio, Giuseppe spat on the ground. "A three-day journey just to turn in paperwork? We could have mailed it!"

The heat of the high summer sun reflected off the cobblestones. Barezzi leaned his cane against a wall and took off his coat.

"Well," he said, adjusting the tenor of his voice to something reassuring, "perhaps they already made their decision before they saw you, Giuseppe. This was just a formality."

"It was a waste of time," muttered Giuseppe, kicking the cane off the wall. Immediately ashamed, he rushed to pick it up and handed it back to Barezzi.

"You need to watch your temper, Giuseppe."

"But I am 'remarkable,' with 'off hands,'" said Giuseppe sarcastically, mimicking Rolla.

"Let's get some coffee and take a walk. I don't want you to think this day was a total waste."

Giuseppe took a deep breath and followed Barezzi down the narrow road, trying hard to be grateful.

Barezzi stayed in Milan for several days, anxiously awaiting a response from the conservatory. After a week of waiting and business to attend to, he made the arduous trip back to Busseto.

Giuseppe stayed behind in Milan. He took long walks around the city center to kill time or lingered in the boarding house to avoid the heat. When he grew tired of writing compositions—a masochistic struggle of deduction without his beloved spinet—he wrote fervent letters to Margherita.

Dearest Margherita,

As you well know, I am blunt almost to a fault. Admittedly, always to a fault. With this delicate fact notwithstanding, I hope you will not fault me for saying I miss you terribly. The sacrifice I would give to sit in your parlor, frustrated at your lack of practice, a teacup shaking in my hand, is immeasurable. I could only hope you feel half of what I feel for you. If you asked me to forgo my musical career to please you, I might entertain the idea.

In the late afternoon of Milan, the sun strikes harder than on the surface of Mercury. On my long, meandering walks, I rush for shade more than I ever did in our relative hamlet of Busseto. In short, it's oppressively, resentfully hot and on these stifling days I think of the cool, collected hours spent with you. The heat is only aggravating my sensibilities as I impatiently await confirmation to this blasted conservatory.

The journey to Milan and my audition make me feel like an outsider in my own country. My father sentimentalizes the French but I cannot see what use there is in that memory. It hasn't gotten us Italians anywhere or anything. In my brief escapade from home it's clear that the Austrians are nothing more than indifferent administrators. I can't help but ruminate on the fear that my audition was nothing less a reason to snub me. I am not a citizen of Lombardy-Venice but a citizen of Parma. Though it is unspoken, it is what defines me here, away from home and away from you.

Please give my best to your father and tell him I am holding the Milanese in contempt, though I am doing my best not to. Thinking of you helps in this valiant effort to be agreeable and hopeful.

Faithfully,
Giuseppe

Chapter Ten

Giuseppe awoke to a pounding on his door at the boarding house. A diminutive servant, not unlike himself when he was a boy, handed Giuseppe an envelope with "Milan Conservatory of Music" embossed in the left corner. Giuseppe's name was scrawled in red ink across the front.

Giuseppe took the letter back to the writing desk and held it to the light in the window, revealing the delicate crisscross of the paper fibers. He carefully peeled back the flap and pulled out the letter, unsure of what he wanted it to say. Would an acceptance confirm his skill as a musician? Or would it mean that they only approved of what he represented? Why should a letter dictate whether he belonged or didn't belong, or was too short, too competent, or too conspicuous with his hands? Couldn't he be accepted for his pursuit of truth and beauty?

Giuseppe unfolded the letter and read it quickly like swallowing an offensive medicine.

"No," said the letter.

Not in so few words, but "no" was the point written cautiously over several paragraphs. The school softened their decision with "thank you," "a pleasure," "competent," and "future success," but in short, they turned Giuseppe by the shoulders toward his hometown, the tavern, and his aging spinet, and closed the door. The rejection didn't come from an insecure priest or his peers uninterested in being a friend. These were professionals, Giuseppe's artistic brethren, concluding that he was not fit for their world.

The letter's concluding paragraph settled on the point that Giuseppe was too old for the student body. Entry-level students were fourteen, and by his age now, at eighteen, his bad habits were worn in like an old dog unable to adjust to a new home. Strange then that Giuseppe woke, ate, and slept to write. The daily habits and preoccupation with music that his maturity allowed belied the existence of time.

Silently fuming, Giuseppe headed to the conservatory to wait for Professor Rolla. He wanted an explanation beyond his age.

"Ah, Signor Verdi, good morning," came a voice from behind Giuseppe. "Vincenzo Lavigna," the man said affably. "You auditioned for me."

"Good morning, Signor."

Lavigna stared at Giuseppe, trying to gauge the boy's stoic expression. He smiled, putting a pipe to his mouth. "A formidable feat just to audition," he said, lighting the tobacco. "Is there a second audition?"

"Unfortunately I was turned down," said Giuseppe, holding the letter as proof.

"Mm." Lavigna tossed the matchstick on the ground. "Do you have time to talk?"

Lavigna's office was cluttered with piles of books lining the walls. Compositions were strewn across anything with a flat surface. An upright piano sat in the corner of the room with an assortment of ashtrays and dishes settled on top.

Lavigna drew the blinds, revealing the whole of Milan. From the second floor the view was both above and within the city, bearing the tight alleys and merchant tents below and the sprawling skyline above. The untold church steeples and apartments rambled toward the city center, melding into a seamless pile of red tile and stone.

"I am sure you are disappointed," opened Lavigna. He lit his pipe again, blowing the sweet smoke out of the open window. "You're a fine musician. I am certain you can make a living for yourself with or without the school."

"Apparently I'm too old."

Lavigna nodded. "Age is an important factor. The difference of three or four years can make a big difference."

Giuseppe shifted on his feet. "But I've being playing as long as many of the students here. I even have a letter of recommendation from the duchess. Surely that counts for something."

Lavigna casually exhaled a thick cloud of smoke. "If there were a school in Parma, you would be studying there. We never would have met. But here," he puffed on his pipe, "support only goes so far."

"But surely, the duchess's mandate—"

"I really wouldn't know about it," interrupted Lavigna. He paused, considering his words. "I was fortunate. I studied at a conservatory in Naples, and it was after my schooling that I came to Milan and took a position at La Scala."

"But there's nothing in Parma," said Giuseppe. "There's really no other place for me to study."

Lavigna shrugged. "You'll find your way."

"It's not fair."

Lavigna snorted. "Giuseppe, if life were fair, none of us would like what we have."

That evening Giuseppe prepared for bed early. He was ready to return to Parma, his parents, his spinet, and Margherita. At least his music would be appreciated by the congregation in Le Roncole.

But Lavigna was right. Nothing was fair. And paradoxically he benefitted from this inequity. If he was fortuitous enough to have parents who embraced his talents, the support of Barezzi and Provesi, and a girl who admired—perhaps loved—him, then what room was there for complaint? As much as Giuseppe despised the idea of fate, perhaps it was the very thing that led him away from home and was now scheming to send him back.

There was a knock at his door. Expecting Barezzi's return from Busseto, Giuseppe instead opened the door to Lavigna. The professor peered into the orderly room, a far cry from his cluttered office.

"May I come in?"

Giuseppe unlatched the chain lock and Lavigna took a seat on the travel trunk.

"I appreciated the opportunity to talk this morning," said the professor. "Thank you." He rapped his knuckles on the trunk's brass hinge. "I was hoping you might consider staying here in Milan."

"Is the school reconsidering my application?"

"No, it's nothing like that. But I have some time in my schedule." Lavigna fingered his coat pocket, extracting a pouch of pipe tobacco. "I would be your instructor."

"I already have an instructor in Busseto—Signor Provesi," said Giuseppe, crossing his arms.

"But Busseto is not Milan."

Giuseppe peered out at the lights below. "Once I return, I will play regularly with the philharmonic," he said defensively.

"I understand that." Lavigna leaned forward, putting his elbows on his knees, packing his pipe. "You're separated from your dream because of an arbitrary line between where you come from and where you want to be." He leaned back and smoothed out his pants with the palm of his hand. "If you stayed in Milan, with me, I could help you."

"That's what I thought the duchess was for."

"She's a person to know, but not the right one. She may be the duchess, but she has little influence in the Milanese music scene, I can tell you that much."

Giuseppe considered what Barezzi would think. He came all this way to study at the conservatory, not to change instructors. And since receiving the rejection letter, Giuseppe had his heart set on returning to Margherita. It was the salve to his bruised ego. Staying in Milan might just worsen the pain.

"You don't have to make a decision tonight," continued Lavigna, measuring Giuseppe's reticence. "I came to reassure you. I agree that it's unreasonable for you to not study at the conservatory. But the reality is that Milan and Busseto are virtually separate countries." Lavigna ran his fingers through the pile of Giuseppe's compositions on the desk. "I want to give you the opportunity that the conservatory can't."

Giuseppe was tired and depressed. "I need to go to bed. Thank you for coming."

"I see a lot of students, Giuseppe. Your talent is no different than theirs."

"Then why bother with me?"

Lavigna tapped the compositions with the bowl of his pipe. "Because I know you'll do the work."

Chapter Eleven

1833

Even after a year of strenuous study in Milan with Lavigna, Giuseppe still breathed in awe of the city's size and improbable mix of rich and poor. Milan's forty-odd cathedrals best exemplified the social dichotomy, and Giuseppe attained a new, albeit cynical, appreciation for the church and its conspicuous wealth, which snubbed the flock who walked through its pious doors.

Most weekends Lavigna took Giuseppe to performances at La Scala, introducing the young composer to the exaggerated characters and costumed pageantry of the opera. In the evenings they took to the salons of the music world's inflated personalities, where impresarios, producers, actors, and the Milanese beau monde mixed.

But rather than get lost in the glimmer, as Lavigna knew he wouldn't, Giuseppe put the sights and sounds, fears and joys on the page. Humored by Giuseppe's story about performing Haydn for the duchess, Lavigna secured a position for him to conduct Haydn's *Creation* for the Milan Philharmonic Society.

On the evening of the performance, Giuseppe made little conversation backstage with the musicians and singers as they waited for the audience to fill the house. When the stage candles were lit and the musicians took their place on stage, a hush went through the theatre as everyone waited for Giuseppe to make his appearance.

The tenor stood backstage next to the young conductor. "Signor Verdi, please, we'll follow," he said.

Startled, Giuseppe rushed out onto the stage, hardly acknowledging the applause. He stood facing the orchestra, forgetting to bow to the audience. The musicians eyed each other as Giuseppe kept his head down in repose. As soon as the last clap of applause echoed off the theatre's walls, Giuseppe raised his arms and the clamor of drum rolls and horns in the opening piece, "Chaos," began. He brought the house down, the concertgoers mesmerized by the impassioned performance. Impressed, Pietro Massini, an impresario and the director of the philharmonic, employed Verdi as the co-director of Rossini's *La Cenerentola*, Massini's directorial debut.

Returning to Lavigna's flat after the inaugural performance, Giuseppe flopped onto a chair, overwhelmed with adrenaline and bliss.

Lavigna poured him a snifter of brandy. "Aren't you glad I stopped you from going back to Busseto?"

Giuseppe could only smile and hold his glass up in gratitude.

Lavigna peeked into the music room where Giuseppe was studying. "I left your mail on the front table."

Bleary-eyed, Giuseppe tucked the composition into the desk drawer. He studied constantly, refining his piano technique and composing endless canons and fugues assigned by Lavigna.

But his original material he kept to himself, reluctant to watch Lavigna edit the orchestration in the mold of his teacher, Paisiello. It was too distressing. Keeping things close to the heart was not a challenge for Giuseppe, however, and Lavigna's editing was the only complaint he could muster against his teacher, whose support of his talents was obvious.

Giuseppe read copious amounts of Shakespeare when the translations were available, conceptualizing melodies for the Bard's wrought soliloquies that would be ripe for the opera. Inspired by Shakespeare's sense of tragedy and irony, Giuseppe kept a delicate ear, complementing the characters with melodies layered thick with nuance.

Despite the creative challenges and endless inspiration, Giuseppe missed home. The peace and quiet of Le Roncole, his parents' unquestionable support, and the gratifying frivolity of being in love were things he didn't know he missed until they were gone. He wrote nearly every day to Margherita—much to her surprise—painting a picture of what his life, the good and the bad, was like in Milan. The good was that he loved her. The bad was that he loved her and she wasn't there. He knew it was unfair to write this—what could she do?—but it was the only catharsis he could manage for his self-pity. Music, Shakespeare, and Milan were a volatile mixture for a young man's emotions.

Lavigna's apartment was no different from his office at the conservatory—stacks of books stood in for furniture and anything of importance was at risk of being swallowed forever in the folds of a chair or an overstuffed drawer. One day, Giuseppe found several letters addressed to him sticking out from under a pair of gloves. The thickest was from his parents. In order to save on postage, Carlo and Luigia sent letters infrequently, writing near essays on town gossip, recent tavern guests, and Carlo's latest hobby. Giuseppe placed it aside and tore open a letter from Margherita. More of a casual memo than a formal note, the script was written in long, loopy letters.

Giuseppe,

I hope this letter finds you the same as when I last saw you in Milan—distracted and madly in love with your music.

I'm sorry, but I write with sad news. Signor Provesi died this past Sunday. I don't mean to upset you and your work, but I would be remiss if you didn't know as soon as possible.

If you get this letter in time, perhaps you can make arrangements to return to Busseto and attend the funeral. And for selfish reasons, I hope you can make the trip. I miss you terribly.

Please read the other letters I've sent of late so that the last thing you read from me isn't so horrible.

Affectionately,
Margherita

Giuseppe tucked the letter into his coat pocket and walked back to his study in the rear of the flat, cursing Lavigna and his cluttered apartment. If he had received the letter sooner, perhaps he could have made it to the funeral, but Provesi had died nearly a month earlier.

It was a long time since Giuseppe had given thought to his former instructor and the memories reminded him of being a child in Le Roncole. Provesi's death was sad, to be sure, but his death marked the end of an earlier, more innocent time in Giuseppe's life—before the conservatory, before leaving his parents, and before a fondness for Margherita. Giuseppe's eyes welled up. People, alive or dead, moved on and that was endlessly tragic.

Giuseppe opened a letter from Barezzi, who wrote matter-of-factly of Provesi's passing, making an effort to note that there was nothing to indicate that the man was in poor health. But true to form, Barezzi conceded that Provesi's death offered a considerable opportunity for Giuseppe to take over his position as Busseto's music director. It would be a coup: The son of Busseto returns from studies in Milan to take his beloved professor's place. It would be good for Giuseppe and it would be good for the town. Of course, there was the rigmarole of submitting an application and glad-handing, but Barezzi, as always, would grease the wheels, confident his efforts would be vindicated.

The turn of events intrigued Giuseppe, but he resented the conflict thrust into his present course. He was a boat headed to multiple horizons, all as promising as they were unfamiliar. The music director position would be important and career-affirming, but his studies with Lavigna were just as assuring and had the added benefit of mixing with his musical peers in Milan. If he returned to Busseto he would be a big fish in a small pond, but in Milan he might discover dozens of ponds, perhaps a lake.

Giuseppe fingered one of Lavigna's cigars and chewed the end, savoring the dank tobacco juice. *The rote careerist or the passionate artist?* he thought. Barezzi's professional agenda, Lavigna's insistence on fugues, and Giuseppe's own animus toward the conservatory gnawed at his sense of free will. Even love, which he wanted, was out of his control.

Giuseppe pulled out a sheet of paper and wrote at the top: "What do I want?" His hand hovered over the page and he sat in the uncomfortable chair unable to write anything with conviction. He wanted everything equally. The truth, comfort and novelty, passion and success. Why was it so hard to choose and why did he feel like he had to exclude one for the other? A life well lived couldn't be this black and white.

He crossed out "What do I want?" and wrote "What is the only thing I want?" After a moment of resolve, he tossed the cigar into the waste can and with a steady hand wrote "Margherita," adding "Barezzi" for good measure, smiling to himself, like a boat captain spotting land. The equation was simple: with Margherita, everything else would fall into place.

Out of the emotional storm, Giuseppe felt his heart slow and his eyes relax. He opened a second letter from Barezzi postmarked from the previous week, which stated simply that he was on his way to Milan.

Barezzi arrived the following evening, exhausted, his hair matted to the top of his head and his suit stained with the scree of the open road. With nothing more than a suitcase and a hat in hand, he bounded through the threshold of Lavigna's flat.

"Where are we eating?" he asked.

They found the restaurant packed with diners sitting shoulder-to-shoulder along deep communal tables scattered under hanging candelabras. Giuseppe faced Lavigna and Barezzi as if in an interrogation. If he was looking for a trip back to his childhood, facing these two grown men was the ticket.

They arrived in time for the set serving hour, managing to get their own table. The waiter placed a hearty loaf of bread between them and served the only item on the menu: a tangy meat consommé with crystallized sugar and barley. Barezzi took a sip off his spoon and exhaled in satisfaction, a string of onion hanging from his chin. The noise was overwhelming and they had to shout to hear one another.

Lavigna lifted his glass. "A pleasure to have you with us, Signor Barezzi."

Barezzi raised his glass and took a long pull of wine followed by another spoonful of the consommé. He laughed and looked around the room. "This city is a marvel."

"How is Margherita?" asked Giuseppe.

Barezzi winked. "She's fine, Giuseppe, and she says hello. She misses you terribly."

Giuseppe blushed, taking a bite of bread. Lavigna chuckled at the immaturity of his pupil.

"Let's get down to it," said Barezzi, wiping his mouth. "I am sure you and Giuseppe have spoken about this opportunity that has come up in Busseto."

Lavigna cut a slice of bread. "He has my full support. In fact, I've been able to secure a commission for Giuseppe with Pietro Massini, director of the Teatro Filodrammatici." He took a small bite. "Giuseppe could work on those while performing his duties in Busseto."

"When would I start?" Giuseppe asked Barezzi.

Barezzi took a deep breath. "The position has been filled by another musician. I wanted to tell you both in person."

Giuseppe blanched. "What? Then why are you here?"

Barezzi shook his head. "The good news is that the Philharmonic Society will not fill the position permanently until you've finished your studies. But in the meantime, this man, Sormani, will be taking over at the church and some of the other musical duties in Busseto."

"Who is he?"

"Sormani?" Barezzi brushed the crumbs off his mustache. "I don't know, honestly. A friend of the priest or the provost."

Giuseppe huffed. *Why was the church always meddling?* "Damn it."

"Giuseppe!" said Lavigna, crossing himself.

Barezzi cleared his throat. "This has really divided the town, Giuseppe. You should be pleased to hear that the vast majority of people are up in arms that you weren't appointed."

This revelation didn't so much concern Giuseppe as it provoked a growing sense of unfairness in him. True, life was unfair, but why should it manifest itself under such blatant stupidity?

"Well, it's settled then. I'll stay here in Milan and never return to Busseto. They obviously don't want me," he said indignantly.

Barezzi chuckled at Giuseppe's dramatics. "It will be a matter of time," he said, unbuttoning his shirt collar. "You'll complete your studies with Signor Lavigna and we'll simply keep the music society up to date on your progress."

"Why? What's the point? I'll be working here in Milan by then."

Lavigna smiled reassuringly. "Giuseppe, I have no doubt of your talent, but I can tell you from experience that making a living as a composer is an unstable proposition and I have been both fortunate as I have unfortunate." He extended his arm toward Barezzi. "If I weren't being paid for lessons, I'd be a nervous wreck—financially speaking, that is."

"The point is, Giuseppe," said Barezzi, "this is going to take time."

"That's an understatement," Giuseppe replied.

"But it's really for the best," Barezzi added.

Giuseppe knew their advice made sense—and truly, he was a pragmatist at heart. It was distressing that so much was fated on the politics and prejudices of others.

"I suppose you're right," he said, composing himself. "I'm just disappointed."

"That's understandable," Barezzi replied.

"And if I could be so bold…" Giuseppe continued, "I miss Margherita."

Barezzi beamed. "Ah, the heart of the matter, as it were." He took a draw from his wine glass. "Which leads me to the next point of why I'm right," he laughed. "The life of a musician is not predictable. A position as music director would secure you and Margherita just fine."

Giuseppe reddened, a teenager again.

"And with these commissions that Signor Lavigna has arranged at La Scala, you could still further your personal career," said Barezzi.

Giuseppe felt his boat lurch, moored in the middle of the ocean. "We'd still be apart."

"Not forever, Giuseppe," Barezzi assuaged him.

Lavigna patted Giuseppe on the back. "Have faith that things will work out."

"Leave it to chance?"

"What Signor Lavigna means," said Barezzi, waving down the waiter for another bottle of wine, "is don't lose sight of the land."

Chapter Twelve

1836

Pietro Massini walked into the empty auditorium of the Teatro Filodrammatici. "Amateur theatre," he huffed, sipping his morning coffee. He leaned over the stage littered with props, hoping to find one of his actors silently rehearsing or at least waiting restlessly for his direction. "Not a soul," he said to himself, shaking his head. He slurped the last dregs of his brew.

The Teatro Filodrammatici was completed on Napoleon's arrival in Italy, erected in his vision to evict the cathedrals and religious institutions that peppered Milan. Thirty-five years later, the spirit of French liberalism continued to arouse the libertine habits of the Filodrammatici's actors and Massini struggled daily with his employees' capricious schedules. Nicknamed the "Patriot Theatre," the opera troupe seemed content to self-destruct on account of its individuality, like a child forgoing dessert to protest her bedtime.

The theatre stood four stories tall with a singular bay window overlooking the street. Patrons could gaze out onto the city, mingling over drinks before and long after a performance. Austere Corinthian columns and curved windows lined the arched doorways throughout the theatre. A dome roof, painted with a pastel floral relief, nestled over the main auditorium.

As money flowed into Milan, the finer theatres installed plush velvet seats to accommodate a more critical, expectant audience. But the Teatro Filodrammatici remained standing room only—opera for the people. Performances were a riotous affair with applause and heckling that could easily drown out the carefully rehearsed singing of any soprano.

"Sorry I'm late," said Giuseppe, arriving through the theatre's side door.

Massini looked at his pocket watch. Nine o'clock. On time.

"Ah, the young maestro. Good morning," said Massini, placing his coffee cup on the stage. "How are you?"

"Fine."

"And Signor Lavigna?"

"Fine...I think."

Massini smiled. Giuseppe's charisma was a rough stone wall compared to the colorful garden tents of the other theatre members.

Massini had plans to expand the theatre to include a school, but the Austrians, as much as they paid lip service to the arts, made it difficult with their cumbersome bureaucracy and censors. Hiring Giuseppe felt like one of the last threads of autonomy Massini could grasp. As much as Massini loved the disarray of the opera, he welcomed Giuseppe's work ethic and eagerness to get to the point.

Giuseppe laid his musical composition on the stage between the ornate candle reflectors that lined the perimeter. "I've been making a lot of mistakes on this, I think."

He was writing the score to a libretto about Oberto, Count of San Bonifacio, who, recently returned from battle, finds his estranged daughter abandoned by the man she was supposed to marry. He dies defending her honor.

Massini walked along the stage, pausing at each page, then placed his hands in his pockets and stooped to read. "The orchestration is original." He rocked back and forth. "It's interesting. I can't quite place your influences."

Giuseppe grabbed a pen. "Well, here I have paid homage to Haydn," he said, pointing at the page. "But I—"

"No, it's not that. It's a good thing," said Massini, peering down at the composition. "We pride ourselves on performing new works. But…" he reached for his empty coffee cup, "there is a certain expectation for the predictable."

Giuseppe squinted, his eyebrows forming a V. "That doesn't make sense."

"It's excellent work, Giuseppe. But it needs some fine-tuning." He pointed to one of the pages. "It could use some more melody here, and…don't be afraid to push the singers, really exploit their voices." He continued to look it over and chuckled. "I see you spend a long time on the dueling scenes."

"I'm sorry it isn't finished yet."

"Lavigna is working you hard."

"Fugues," said Giuseppe, rolling his eyes.

"Ugh. Well, there's no rush." Massini collected the pages, looking anxiously for any of his actors who might have arrived. "There's plenty of work already in development."

"I'd like to make a few changes to the libretto."

If keeping the seats filled wasn't the biggest challenge for Massini, it was dealing with the Austrian censors who worked extra hard in Milan to keep the opera free of any political offense. As it was, this libretto had already received the seal of approval. Even changing a name from Antonio to Angelo could cause a complete reexamination, perhaps revoking the work completely. For all of the Austrian support of the arts, the final products tended to be short of actual artistic expression.

"Let's focus on the musical themes," said Massini. "I wouldn't want to insult the librettist."

A low moan came from the rear of the stage. What looked like a papier-mâché rock suddenly lifted up from under a prop tree and opened itself like a butterfly expanding its wings. What emerged was a portly, bearded man dressed in the gray tunic and slacks of a soldier. A plumed cap sat askew on his sweaty head.

"Good morning!" he boomed, rattling the chandeliers. "I'm not late, am I?" He took a swig from a wine bottle tucked under his tunic.

Massini shook his head. "My bass singer," he said to Giuseppe, then turned back to the man. "No, Signor Salvi, you're not late…relatively speaking. I want you to meet Giuseppe Verdi. He's working with me and Signor Lavigna."

Salvi smiled broadly and brought the bottle to his lips. "Hallo Verdi!"

"Why don't you regale Giuseppe here with your vocal warm-up."

"Gladly," said Salvi, wiping the wine off his mouth with his sleeve. "But there's no need to warm up—I'm a professional!"

Massini patted Giuseppe on the back and went outside to find himself another cup of strong coffee.

Giuseppe returned exhausted to Lavigna's apartment. For most of the morning, Salvi made sure to impress his full range of voice and the particularities of gargling wine. "To loosen the instrument," he explained. Giuseppe was anxious to finally get some work done.

"How did it go at the theatre?" asked Lavigna, tinkering at the piano.

"Actors are mercurial," said Giuseppe, trying his hand at diplomacy.

"They are human, just like the rest of us."

"What do you mean?"

Lavigna shook his head, his sarcasm lost. "Nothing. Did you get any notes on *Oberto*?"

Giuseppe plunked down on a backless divan, upending a pile of books. "Yes, some." He closed his eyes and ran his hands along the fabric. "It could be years before this is produced."

Lavigna held up a letter and shook it. "Well, until it is, I have some good news right here."

"The Austrians have put a moratorium on practicing fugues?"

"Ha, no," said Lavigna, taking a seat next to Giuseppe. "The Busseto Philharmonic has accepted you in the music director position! In fact," he continued, "they are more than happy to accommodate your schedule here in Milan."

Giuseppe pressed his fingers on the thick wax seal at the bottom of the paper.

Lavigna waited for a reaction. "Signor Barezzi has been very busy on your behalf."

Giuseppe silently reeled. If this were to be believed and not just another step in an endless staircase, he would once again be ahead of the curve. He'd be able to finish his studies with Lavigna, have real commissioned work, and have access to Milanese society, all while starting his professional career in Busseto. *This would truly be the start of life as a composer*, thought Giuseppe.

"I'll miss you," said Lavigna, handing Giuseppe a pile of letters. "Though I'm sure you won't miss all your lost mail."

Giuseppe rifled through the letters looking for Margherita's languid handwriting. Of all this, she would be the best part of moving back to Busseto.

Chapter Thirteen

From his apartment window, Giuseppe looked out at the Rocca Pallavicino, the twelfth-century fortress that he and his father marveled at when they picked up his spinet in Busseto nearly twenty years before. Now Giuseppe was Busseto's music director and a happy husband—both arguably a result of the fateful day they brought home that modest instrument.

Giuseppe never assumed that he would be back in Busseto, entrusted with such responsibilities. Nor would he want to. But there was something affirming about sticking to a plan, even if other opportunities came his way. Life was becoming increasingly unpredictable for Giuseppe: demands from the philharmonic, coursework for the students he was now teaching, papers to sign…the list was endless. Best-laid plans often ran their own course, catching the tailwinds of uncertainty—and Giuseppe was learning to hold the rudder steady.

He sat at the baby grand piano in his study reviewing student compositions. The relative permanence of the Rocca Pallavicino was a daily reminder to do good work. If the fortress moat leaked, only the architect could be blamed. The same could be said for composers and their music.

Margherita kissed Giuseppe. "How are you?" she cooed, sleepy, rubbing her pregnant belly. Her hair hung in thick tendrils, bouncing as she nuzzled his neck.

He wrapped an arm around her waist. "I shouldn't have given you such a hard time during our lessons. My students' work isn't much better than yours."

"Hey," she said admonishingly, slapping Giuseppe's arm with the palm of her hand. "I was a small girl coerced into playing the piano." She pouted and put a hand on her hip. "I actually take the comparison to one of your students as a compliment."

Giuseppe took her hair in his hands, tugging gently. "I love you so much."

Margherita's eyes glistened from his simple honesty. "I love you, too."

"I have a lesson this afternoon," said Giuseppe, rubbing her belly. "And then your father and I are meeting with the President of the Interior of the Duchy of Parma."

"Stand up straight and say it again. Like an aristocrat."

"Come on." He stepped back and sorted his papers.

She placed her hands behind her back, sashaying in place. "Please?"

"The Pres…ident OF…the INterior of…the Duchy uv Paarmaa…" exhaled Giuseppe with a high nasal tone. "Satisfied?"

"I am so proud of you," said Margherita, hugging him. "Everyone adores you."

"I doubt that."

"Well, *I* adore you."

He placed a tall black cylinder hat on his head, tucking his hair behind his ears.

"How fashionable."

Giuseppe grimaced. He put the hat on the table and took his coat off the rack. Margherita lifted the coat over his shoulders and placed the hat back on his head. "How about…handsome? It's a very handsome hat."

He adjusted the brim and kissed her on cheek. "Be good."

From their bedroom window, Margherita watched Giuseppe cross the street below and she brushed the side of her cheek with the tips of her fingers and lingered, happy.

Giuseppe was loath to find comfort in anything, let alone his own skin, so the wafting nature of travel between Busseto and Milan he found perfectly suited to his well-being. It afforded him the time to muse on his surroundings and separate his mind from his professional duties at home and his aspirations in Milan. It had been a year and he was hardly tired of it.

The deluge of writing and teaching responsibilities in Busseto was welcome to a man who didn't think twice about shutting himself away for hours in his study while his wife tended patiently to their baby. Baby Virginia was now nearly a year old and the pride and joy of Margherita and Giuseppe alike. She shared her father's pensive eyes but was quick to smile and laugh, a trait she took from her mother.

Like a wheel needs its grease, Giuseppe depended on his work to keep himself useful to his family and he bore no grudges from Margherita for his long absences at home in his study or away in Milan. This kept life smooth and pleasantly idle. Giuseppe's schedule and deft circumvention of the domestic was no surprise to Margherita. If Giuseppe had suddenly taken to reading the evening paper while she knitted or nursed, she would know she had married an imposter. He made no demands for dinner, content with a roll and butter, nor was he fussy about his clothes, apathetic toward the threadbare pants and loose-fitting shirts that increasingly consumed his wardrobe. Unlike most wives, Margherita was indifferent to Giuseppe's detachment from the trivial matters of couture, and with her passion for reading novels and writing the occasional poem fulfilled, it made for a very happy home.

Since much of Giuseppe's income as music director was given to Barezzi—who had shouldered the majority of his expenses for travel and school—the Verdis weren't preoccupied with extra coins jangling in their pockets, a distraction that would likely take other young couples on weekend shopping trips for new curtains or bed sheets. Giuseppe preferred this arrangement of austere self-reliance that didn't carry the threat of missed meals or overdue rent. With gainful employment they could live simply and comfortably, furnishing a promising future.

Oberto was nearly complete and Giuseppe hoped this would be his last visit to Milan before the theatre began rehearsals. Working within the confines of an existing libretto had been a creative challenge and he was anxious to move on to the next project, where he hoped to better control the music *and* the lyrics.

A few weeks before his departure for Milan, when Giuseppe was ensconced in the final scenes of *Oberto*, Margherita innocently asked him about the theme for the upcoming spring concert.

"I'm sorry, a spring concert?" asked Giuseppe absently, struggling with his necktie before giving a music lesson.

As Margherita wistfully described childhood memories of the town's annual spring celebration, Giuseppe hurriedly began his obligated composition for the concert, all while scheming melodies for his opera in the far corner of his mind. For a less confident man, these unexpected expectations would have been maddening, but Giuseppe's pride, rather than projecting itself as conceit, simply humbled itself to the work.

Giuseppe faithfully fulfilled his duty and the new piece premiered, much to the delight of the town. Held in the central square, the philharmonic performed under a cloudless sky as children darted between chairs and twirled around the maypole. An older man threw a red cap over a lone boxwood and saluted the makeshift *arbor de la libretto*—"liberty tree"—a throwback to the glorified Napoleonic campaigns. Margherita sat next to her father with Virginia gurgling in her arms, and watched as her husband conducted one of the traditions she cherished the most. With each swoop of Giuseppe's arms, she was transported back to the joyful days of childhood and she bounced Virginia to the beat of her husband's creation.

Preparing for bed, suffused with nostalgia, Margherita kissed Giuseppe goodnight and left him alone to work through the night on *Oberto*. He finished the last scene the following day as his coach—and nightfall—crept steadily into Milan.

"You look exhausted," said Lavigna, opening the door and dragging Giuseppe's luggage into the entry.

Giuseppe's ride into Milan had been particularly tiring with long interruptions on the Austrian toll roads. The procedure was always the same: present citizenship papers and pay the tax. At each interruption Giuseppe felt no less a stranger in his own country as he watched his money go into the gloved hands of foreigners.

"Very...taxing." Giuseppe pushed past Lavigna and stumbled into the study, where the housekeeper made up a bed. The comforter billowed and then swallowed Giuseppe whole as he sank into the mattress. "*Oberto* is done," he murmured through the sheets.

"That is fantastic news!" Lavigna turned up the gas lamp, illuminating the room. He adjusted his bowtie in a tabletop mirror.

"What are you doing?" whined Giuseppe, covering his face with a pillow.

Lavigna, wearing a double-breasted waistcoat and a starched shirt, crossed the room and took his coat from the closest.

"Why are you dressed like that?"

"You and I are going out tonight."

"That's ridiculous. I'm not going anywhere."

Lavigna turned down the light and opened the window. A warm summer breeze blew into the room. "We've been invited to the Maffeis."

"Who are they?"

"They," said Lavigna, straightening his tie, "are an evening of stimulating conversation." He slammed the closet door shut. "I'll get you up in an hour."

Cavaliere Andrea Maffei and Countess Clarina Maffei were an odd couple. Andrea, sixteen years Clarina's senior, was an admired poet and man of letters, while Clarina was committed to outspoken politics and social climbing. Together, they comprised one of the most cosmopolitan salons of political and artistic conversation in Milan.

Clarina greeted Lavigna and Giuseppe in the foyer of her townhouse, placing their hats on an antique Chinese demilune table. A maid quickly whisked the accessories away.

The countess possessed a coquettish smile and her thick black ringlets of hair covered her eyes when she laughed. She grabbed Lavigna in a hug.

"Too, too long," Clarina said, kissing his cheek.

"You exaggerate." He paused while the maid took his coat. "I was last here in…uh…"

"Exactly."

Dozens of candles lit the oblong room in a bright haze, illuminating the contours of the textured blue wallpaper. It was an eclectic foyer with an array of African masks, Russian lacquer boxes, and neoclassical landscapes filling every conceivable space. A low murmur of conversation emanated from the back rooms.

Lavigna laughed. "I'll make sure to invite myself over more often."

"And who is this?" asked Clarina, watching Giuseppe struggle with his coat.

"Countess Clarina Maffei, please meet my student and the current music director of Busseto, Giuseppe Verdi."

"Busseto?"

"Yes, in Parma," said Giuseppe.

"Of course." Clarina sipped her wine. "I've heard there's been some recent activity with the Carbonari there."

"I…wouldn't know," stammered Giuseppe. "I've been traveling so much."

"Well, I suppose we can wait on discussing politics. Not a pleasant topic when you're tired."

"Giuseppe has been working on an opera at the Teatro Filodrammatici."

"Oh yes!" said Clarina, her eyes suddenly twinkling with familiarity. She gripped Giuseppe's hand. "Vincenzo has bragged about you for ages." She hit Lavigna on the shoulder. "See, you never come here—embarrass me like that." Clarina turned back to Giuseppe. "You're a composer?"

"I am." Giuseppe nervously tried to elaborate. "Um…for the opera."

"Oh, God, another composer."

As Giuseppe wondered how to respond, Andrea Maffei strolled into the room, chuckling.

"Maffei!" exclaimed Lavigna. "It's like seeing a ghost!"

Andrea gave his wife a kiss and shook Lavigna's hand. His slender frame gave him a strong, graceful presence and the natural glare in his eyes concealed the artist inside. He came across more a statesman than a poet. "None of you ever want to write with me."

"Andrea considers himself a librettist," teased Clarina.

Andrea smiled. "Well, I don't see why not. People seem to enjoy my poetry. But none of my more lyrical output, I suppose."

"Perhaps it's too sophisticated for the stage," Giuseppe said simply.

"Who is this? I like him already," said Andrea, swinging his glass in Giuseppe's direction.

"This is Giuseppe Verdi, a student of Vincenzo's." Clarina wrapped her arm around Giuseppe.

"Pleasure, truly." Andrea shook Giuseppe's hand with a forceful thrust. "So, two composers in our home. God help us."

Clarina suddenly twirled around to Lavigna. "Oh! You just missed Alessandro!"

"Who?"

"Alessandro Manzoni," clarified Andrea. "I'm helping him compile a complete version of *The Betrothed*."

Lavigna shook his head in surprise. "That's wonderful. I had no idea."

"The challenge has been standardizing the language," said Andrea. "I think his novel has far-reaching implications."

"Of course," Lavigna nodded.

"I am so proud of him," said Clarina, taking Andrea's hand. "He's so averse to politics, yet he's the one who gets to spend hours alone with Alessandro." She pouted. "I'm jealous. But if anyone can get this book read by more people, it's Andrea."

"It's not as exciting as all that," Andrea assured her.

"Aren't you concerned about the Austrians implicating you in some kind of conspiracy? It's not a flattering book," said Lavigna.

Andrea waved him off. "We have our protections."

"What Andrea is too polite to say is that we are simply too wealthy for the Austrians to force our hand in anything. Which is why it's our responsibility as elites—"

Andrea sighed. "Here we go…"

"No, I am not ashamed to say this, Andrea." Clarina put her hand on Giuseppe's shoulder, dragging him back into the conversation. "As elites, I believe our money gives us the moral responsibility to unify this country. Don't you agree?"

She looked back and forth to no one in particular. Giuseppe grinned nervously and shrugged.

"Well, I've said my piece." She turned to her husband. "Are you happy?"

"I'm always happy," said Andrea. "Let's join the rest of the party."

The Maffeis spent more of their time entertaining in the main salon than anything else. Servants placed food on the various sideboard tables for the guests who drifted in throughout the evening—some to exchange pleasantries, others looking for heady yet inconclusive conversation. Chairs and divans were scattered over an enormous Persian carpet lining the width of the room and portraits hung staggered from thick moulding along the walls.

Giuseppe sat in a small armchair next to the windows overlooking the city.

Andrea handed Giuseppe a glass of wine. "How long have you been working on this opera of yours?"

"Over a year now."

"That's not long at all."

"I thought I'd have it done sooner, but there have been so many other things to work on."

"That's the problem with the artistic life. We have to be involved in nearly everything just to have any influence." A door slammed and laughter emanated from the entryway. "Speaking of which, there's someone you must meet."

By any standard, Giuseppina Strepponi was an alluring woman with a voice to match. She maintained an approachable beauty that made her as amiable as she was provocative. She wore her hair tied tightly in a bun, accentuating a long nose and large, almond eyes. A black strapless dress revealed her delicate collarbone wrapped in alabaster skin. She walked over to them and tilted her head back, laughing, when Andrea kissed her hand.

"You're back from Austria!" he said.

"Oh, God, I don't ever want to leave Milan again."

"Oh, my—what happened?" asked Clarina.

"Nothing like that. It's just the travel is so hard on my voice. The parties, rehearsals," she waved her hands as if tossing it all aside. "The late-night visitors," she added, rolling her eyes.

Andrea handed her a glass of wine. "Oh, the horrible life of an opera singer." He held his glass up. "I will say it certainly hasn't hurt your reputation here," Andrea smiled. "Giuseppina, I want you to meet this shy young man whom I have failed to introduce. Giuseppe Verdi, please meet Giuseppina Strepponi."

"How do you do?"

"Very well, thank you," said Giuseppe stiffly.

Clarina laughed. "I told you he's very shy. You should get to know each other because Giuseppe is an opera composer."

Giuseppe cleared his throat. "Well, I'm working on one right now at the Teatro Filodrammatici. It's why I am in Milan."

"Congratulations," Giuseppina said.

"Thank you. And of course I know who you are, Signora Strepponi. Although I am remiss to tell you that I have not yet had the pleasure to hear you perform."

"Nor will you," said Giuseppina with an exaggerated sigh. "My career is over." She held her hand to her forehead and leaned back, revealing her slender neck.

Clarina snorted. "You're so absurd."

"Vienna was tough." Giuseppina put her hand to her chin in mock consideration. "I suppose I'll recover. I'd miss all the attention."

"There you go," agreed Andrea.

"Tough break for Massini," said Clarina, turning to Giuseppe. "Who are you working with now at the Filodrammatici?"

Giuseppe squinted, distracted by Giuseppina's theatrics. "I'm sorry, what do you mean?"

"That's right, I heard something about that," said Andrea.

"What are you talking about?" asked Giuseppe, his voice uncontrollably rising.

"Massini is no longer at the Teatro Filodrammatici. He was fired."

～

Giuseppe arrived early at the Teatro Filodrammatici, his heart racing. Partly from the humidity, difficult to escape in Milan, but mostly from impatience and anger with Massini. If what Clarina Maffei said last night was true, *Oberto* was ostensibly homeless. The Teatro Filodrammatici was not as illustrious as La Scala, but the least Massini could have done was pay Giuseppe the common courtesy of telling him the bad news before he traveled all the way back to Milan.

"Giuseppe!" cried Massini, waving from the top balcony of the theatre. "Don't move. I'll be right down." He bounded down the steps, patting the sweat from his brow. "Let's go. I'm ready for a coffee."

They sat at a small wooden table in a café around the corner from the theatre. A young girl in a dress with gigot sleeves placed their coffees and a tray of sugar cubes between them. Massini dropped all four cubes of sugar into his cup, stirring vigorously like he was churning butter.

"Giuseppe, I have bad news. I won't be managing things at the theater anymore."

Giuseppe felt his forehead go hot and damp as though the coffee had been tossed in his face. "I know."

"How's that? You're the first person I've told."

"Lavigna took me to the Maffeis last night."

Massini nodded. He stirred his coffee, looking past Giuseppe. "I'm sorry I didn't say anything. I could have. But I didn't." He sipped the coffee and grimaced. "These theatre owners, they're a fickle group. They always want larger audiences. They need larger audiences. So, they make changes. Anyway, they see me as washed up."

Giuseppe bristled at the thought of being irrelevant. And with a sting of guilt in consideration of Massini's unemployment, he questioned his own prospects. Where would he go now? And what was the point of all of these trips to Milan, leaving his wife and daughter?

His mind raced. Maybe this was good timing—he and Margherita were talking about having another child. Maybe they should. Forget this business in Milan. The music director contract would be up in three years. He had been doing good work and was respected. There would be plenty of opportunities—smaller, of course, but opportunities that would actually go someplace in Busseto.

"Huh," mumbled Giuseppe, sorting his concerns.

Massini waved down the waitress. "More sugar, please."

"Why didn't you say anything?"

"Excuse me," interrupted the waitress. "You'll have to order another coffee for the sugar."

Massini's face went slack as he searched his pockets for the money he knew wasn't there. Giuseppe tossed a few coins on the table.

Massini gave a quick nod of thanks. "Because I didn't want you to give up on *Oberto* and I especially didn't want you to stop coming to Milan."

"But I'm not spending enough time with my family as it is. I could have stayed home."

"Then you should have been an accountant."

The waitress returned with the sugar and Massini immediately dropped it into his coffee.

"I can help find another impresario or theatre, but it's going to take some time. It has been difficult to keep a happy face about this."

"You seem to be doing a good job."

"I work in theatre, Giuseppe, but I'm no actor." Massini finished his coffee. "The point is I didn't want my failure to influence your decision. You're young, you can take risks."

"I have a family. And besides, I could be working on more for the orchestra in Busseto."

"The operative word being 'Busseto.'"

Giuseppe twisted the napkin in his hands, impatient. "My arrangement is guaranteed there."

"Sure, for now. But look at the effort it took Barezzi to get you there."

"What's your point?"

"The point is that nothing is guaranteed." Massini got up from the table and rolled his sleeves to his elbows. "Except that it's always too hot in Milan and I'll never pay you back for that coffee."

"Thanks."

"Just stay in Milan. Consider my advice as payback for the coffee."

Chapter Fourteen

Bartolomeo Merelli stood in the rear of the foyer at La Scala examining a mole on the back of his hand. He couldn't remember a time before the little mark punctuated itself and he wondered if its presence noted a time of rebirth, a moment when a person chooses one life for another. His success as an impresario wasn't uncommon in Milan, but for someone who preferred mulling over words rather than accounting books, it was a unique mix that he couldn't deny helped win him his long string of successes.

Merelli wouldn't go as far as to say he disliked the opera—it was just that he didn't completely trust it. There were the endless rehearsals, the constant infighting and affairs, and production budgets that could build a small country; these were all peculiarities that would make any sane man in his position weary. But it was the money—the large sums of money that somehow ended up in his pocket—that put the largest cause for doubt in his mind. How could an enterprise so unwieldy, tempestuous, and impractical make so much money? The kind of money that allowed someone to believe they didn't need it anymore, yet desperate if they didn't make more than the year before? The opera was unbridled passion in every facet, and the fact that Merelli depended on the concert season for his livelihood meant he put his complete trust in irrationality. This was a leap of logic for someone who regarded himself too sober in his approach to life.

A high-pitched shriek emanated from the murmuring crowd gathered in the lobby below.

"Oh, God," Merelli whispered under his breath, slinking into the corner as Pasetti the lawyer and his wife floated in, glad-handing and laughing, their eyes darting around the room like moths to a light.

Ignacio Pasetti had given a lot to La Scala over the years, tirelessly reinvesting in his place in society. *Maybe that's why I despise him so much*, thought Merelli as he reconsidered the absurdity of hiding in his own theatre. Both men were both cut from a similar cloth: businessmen who attached themselves to art in the only way they knew how—spending money. Considering this similarity was a bitter pill for Merelli to swallow, so he took a deep breath, sucking in so much air that it forced a smile, and walked over to where Pasetti stood with his wife.

"Excuse me, sir, but we need to ask you to leave."

Pasetti turned around, mortified, but on seeing Merelli, he broke into a smile. "Merelli, you dog." Pasetti gripped his hand and pulled him closer. "You know, you're the only person here I would do that for." He broadened his smile. "You remember my wife, Dea."

"Of course," said Merelli, stunned by her awkward, unwavering gaze.

Dea pushed herself forward, her jewels amplifying the dim light from the gas lamps hanging from the lobby walls. "How do you do?" she breathed, leaning even closer.

Finding the introduction a convenient juncture, she abruptly pulled up the hem of her long skirt and turned to her husband. "Dear, I'll be downstairs at the tables."

"Of course you will," replied Pasetti, handing her several colored chips before she disappeared.

"That may be the last we see of her this evening," he said to Merelli. He raised an eyebrow. "It's been a while since I've seen you. Keeping busy, I'm sure."

Merelli listened to Pasetti describe his latest horse trade as well as a scandalous dispute between a questionable publishing house, a well-known composer, and a lonely housewife. Stock conversation for Saturday night at La Scala. But much to his relief, the more Pasetti talked of his investments and properties, the more Merelli was relieved that they were, in fact, completely different people. The more the lawyer bragged, the more his insecurities revealed themselves and Merelli felt a sense of his younger, purer self return to his body.

Merelli loved music. But as a young man he made the decision that he was unwilling to risk a comfortable lifestyle—which, at the time, he considered daily meals and clothes—for the unlikely success of being a career musician. After four years of studying composition at a university, he immediately took a position as a theatrical agent representing any singer or composer in Milan who would trust him. Some made it and some didn't, but Merelli always believed in his clients and thought they did the same with him. That's what he was most proud of—the trust. He may not have been the next Donizetti or even a Shakespeare, but holding people's esteem in the most fickle of industries was a badge of honor.

Merelli was a competent composer and a few of his compositions were good enough for the parlor, entertaining ladies over cards. But he excelled at wordplay, and soon after he established himself in a theatrical agency, he moonlighted as a librettist, writing late into his nights. He was modest about it and often forgot that several of his librettos were made into fully produced operas. But now at forty-five he was content—proud, perhaps— to have helped others in their careers. And by any definition he was an artist, though he rarely thought of himself as such. It was this unique skill set that earned the respect of someone like Pasetti, who had little talent or aptitude.

Pasetti was explaining a lawsuit when across the foyer Merelli caught the eye of Giuseppina Strepponi, talking with Giorgio Ronconi, the actor and baritone.

"Have you met Giuseppina Strepponi?" blurted Merelli, sensing an opportunity and weary of Pasetti's drone.

"Ah, I should say I never have. You know her?"

"Of course." Merelli pulled his shirt cuffs down from under his jacket sleeves. "I can introduce you."

Giuseppina reached out eagerly as Merelli crossed the room. She kissed his cheek. "Didn't I just see you?" she exclaimed, taking his hands in hers. She wore a black satin gown embroidered with a white trim around the neck.

"You were in Austria as well?" exclaimed Ronconi.

"That's right," laughed Merelli. "We saw each other at the Theater am Kärntnertor. I completely forgot."

"We barely spoke, so it stands to reason that seeing little old me would pass through your memory."

Merelli chuckled. "That's hardly true. You were in Vienna as well, Signor Ronconi?"

"Just visiting."

"What brought you there?" interrupted Pasetti, directing the conversation back to Giuseppina. "I've never been." He smiled wildly at her.

"Oh, this and that," she said, embarrassed. Giuseppina put her hand back on Merelli's. "It would have been so nice to spend the day with you. It gets so boring there. It's all politics in Vienna."

"Is that true?" asked Pasetti with increasing fascination.

"God, no. She's just being dramatic," said Ronconi with irritation. A sudden burst of cheering erupted from the parlor and Ronconi spilled his drink in shock. "Merelli, you have to do something about those damn card games."

He shrugged. "All the other houses do it. We couldn't compete without the gambling."

"People do love their cards," appealed Giuseppina. "But it is really not in the spirit of the opera."

"It's the only reason my wife comes to the theatre," said Pasetti.

Giuseppina pursed her lips. "How charming."

Merelli coughed. "Excuse me, my manners. Signor Ronconi, Signora Strepponi, please meet one of our most illustrious subscribers at La Scala, Signor Ignacio Pasetti."

"Pleasure," said Pasetti, taking Giuseppina's hand. "Signora, you are absolutely captivating. What can we expect to see you in next?"

"It all depends on what the fine producers of Milan are looking for." She winked at Merelli.

"Well, if you ever need representation," Pasetti handed her his business card, "here is my—"

"I despise agents," said Ronconi, intercepting the card and shoving it in his pocket.

"I am a lawyer, sir."

"Even worse."

Merelli laughed. "What Signor Ronconi means is…." His face suddenly dropped as Dea charged up the stairs. "Ignacio, is something wrong with your wife?"

She bolted through the crowd, her clutch held tightly to her breast. She leaned up against her husband out of breath.

"What in the world is the matter?" asked Pasetti.

"I won, I won!"

"Ah, marvelous! That was you! We heard you from downstairs. Well done, my dear." He turned to the group. "My wife," Pasetti announced, clutching her hand as she beamed.

"Well, then, congratulations." Ronconi raised his glass. "Perhaps you can buy me a new pair of pants."

"Buy me a drink to celebrate," she said to Pasetti, oblivious, and whisked him away before he could make his appeal.

"Bye-bye," mocked Ronconi.

"That was dreadful," said Giuseppina.

"I seriously question your judgment in friends," Ronconi remarked, "which is actually making me second-guess myself now, too."

"He inherited the private box from his father. They give a lot," said Merelli diplomatically.

"Well, there you go," Giuseppina nodded.

"It looks like his wife is doing her part to help take a lot back," quipped Ronconi.

"The house always wins," Merelli assured him.

"Then surely you can afford to pay the lowly talent like Signor Ronconi and myself a little more," Giuseppina smiled.

"Touché," said Merelli, sipping his wine and laughing. "It's so good to see the both of you. Another night at the opera."

"I don't think I've had a moment to myself since I got back to Rome," Giuseppina said. "Parties, parlors, letters to so-and-so."

"If you don't go to the parties, you stop getting invited," said Ronconi. "That's my problem."

"Mmm…that sounds like a wonderful problem to have. Actually, I was at the Maffeis last night. Such a lovely couple."

"How rebellious of you," noted Ronconi.

"How's that?" Merelli asked.

"They're active in politics, I suppose," said Giuseppina.

"The Countess Maffei is a well-known supporter of the Italian unification," Ronconi stated. "Anti-Austrian."

Giuseppina rolled her eyes. "Hardly. They're…intellectuals." She hit Ronconi on the shoulder. "You make it sound so cloak-and-dagger."

"Just making interesting conversation," Ronconi replied. "Anyway, you've recused yourself from any political suspicion based on your extreme interest in a married man."

Giuseppina sighed. "Now you're just being a boor."

"A new love interest?" asked Merelli. "A lucky man."

"Actually, he might be of interest to you," said Giuseppina. "He's a composer and quite talented."

"You mean handsome," joked Ronconi. "Does he have a name?"

"I'm ignoring you now. Anyway, as I was saying, this composer, Giuseppe Verdi, has written an opera for something at the Teatro Filodrammatici with Massini—"

"Who is that?" Merelli asked.

"Pietro Massini," she answered. "He's the director, or *was* the director, at the Teatro Filodrammatici, but he's no longer there."

"So is it finished?" said Merelli.

"What do you mean, the opera?"

"What he means is, can he get it for cheap," Ronconi balked.

From inside the theatre, the orchestra began tuning and an usher rang a bell, calling people to their seats.

Merelli glanced at his pocket watch. "Can we talk about this after the show? I'd be interested in meeting this Verdi fellow."

"I suppose I could arrange it. Clarina Maffei really took a liking to him, if that means anything."

"Are you actually looking for something to produce?" asked Ronconi. "No one has heard of this man."

"I respect Signora Strepponi's opinion and maybe there's something on the back end for her." Merelli wiggled his eyebrows. "A finder's fee, perhaps."

Giuseppina laughed and made an exaggerated gasp. "Now I don't regret going out last night at all."

"God, now one of these days I'll be working for you," groaned Ronconi, shaking his head. "You're a singer, not an impresario."

"Well, I won't have this voice or my looks forever." Giuseppina took Merelli's arm. "Please join me at my seats and we can talk."

"Hey, what about me?" shouted Ronconi as Giuseppina and Merelli walked up the stairs.

"Go find the lawyer," Giuseppina called out to him. "I'm sure there's plenty of room in his box. You can tell him all about Vienna."

Chapter Fifteen

1839

Giuseppe lifted the comforter and kissed Margherita on the forehead. The evening's chill still lingered in the room and she wiggled her body deeper under the covers.

"Don't go yet," she pleaded.

"Sh, the baby."

"Mm," Margherita murmured and clutched Giuseppe's arm. "You're the baby. He's fine." She leaned on her elbow and gently rocked the bassinet next to the bed. Icilio's scrunched face twitched inscrutably. "How long will you be gone?"

"A few weeks." Giuseppe put his head on her stomach and ran his hands along the bed sheets, warming the cool patches of cotton. "We're already in rehearsals."

"I'm proud of you."

"I'm so tired."

The day following the performance at La Scala, Giuseppina and Merelli met with Giuseppe to discuss a takeover of the production of *Oberto*. Giuseppe was in rare form—loquacious and forthright. He passion for the project was unmistakable and Merelli was sold, committing himself immediately as producer. As a consequence, Giuseppe was working harder than ever before, and for months he was traveling between Busseto and Milan in preparation for the premiere of the opera in addition to performing with the Busseto Philharmonic and writing weekly choral pieces for the church. Yet despite this demanding schedule, he was relieved. Ever since Merelli ensured *Oberto*'s production at La Scala, Giuseppe felt the weight of anxiety lift itself from his body, dissipating the unknown of his life into the ether.

In July, Giuseppe and Margherita had been blessed with their son, Icilio. It was an uneventful birth and the infant had a sweet, even temperament. The midwife commented that she felt compelled to charge only half of her typical fee, having only cleaned and swaddled the baby, leaving the apartment with little more than a few words of congratulations.

Giuseppe felt a strong sense of gratitude toward the boy for saving Margherita the pain of a prolonged labor and was compelled enough to give a silent prayer of thanks to whatever god may have been responsible. Margherita's body was frail and weak during the pregnancy and Giuseppe worried nearly every day that she would collapse from exhaustion. He was gone from the house enough these past months and they both needed one less thing to worry about. The ease of the boy's birth gave them both a renewal of faith that life could be merciful from time to time.

However, the months that followed Merelli's support of *Oberto* made finding time to be together as a family increasingly difficult. Giuseppe immediately found himself spending whatever hours he could muster rewriting the music to suit the vocal ranges of the new singers employed by Merelli. The impresario felt the original libretto's dramatic pacing was unsatisfactory and hired Temistocle Solera, a known Milanese librettist, to make the necessary changes.

Solera was well meaning and easy to work with, often eating the equivalent of several meals throughout their work sessions with a joyful, determined abandon. Though Giuseppe ultimately characterized him as lazy, the librettist's casual attitude made changes to the story easy as Solera was open to any revisions as long as Giuseppe made them himself. While they worked in the back room of La Scala, Solera would often nap on the divan while Giuseppe edited the score, longing to be home in the easy comfort of his family and the predictable company of his own mind.

"I wish we could visit you," said Margherita.

"The trip is too hard on the baby."

"I know." Margherita turned on her side. "I get lonely."

The morning gray turned blue against the windows. Virginia cried out from her room and Margherita took Giuseppe's hand and covered her eyes. "Just give her a minute."

"Do you resent me?"

"No, I don't resent you. I'm just being selfish." Margherita smiled and buried her head in his shoulder. "I'm so happy."

Margherita was lucky to have several girls from town to help care for the children while Giuseppe was in Milan. And with his small pension as music director they were able to hire a maid who did the daily shopping and cooking. With the extra time to herself and the children, Margherita spent her days happily roaming the apartment hand in hand with Virginia as the girl examined every table leg, cabinet, and drawer. They were fun, blissful days. But Margherita missed Giuseppe and longed to return to the state of mind of childhood where no one else existed but herself. The immense responsibility of being an adult was harder without Giuseppe in the house.

Virginia broke into a full wail. Margherita flipped the sheets off. "I'll check on her. You should go."

"Icilio is still asleep."

"I told you, he's fine. We'll be fine."

Merelli looked down at his notes and shook his head. "I'm pushing a lot of other things around to make this work."

Giuseppe stood on the stage at La Scala, looking at what appeared to be two green hills melded together at a gray box that he supposed was the citadel. It looked nothing like the lush pastoral scene he imagined in his mind. He had already had to make more than a few concessions with Merelli on the production. They were reusing old, molting costumes and had only one set piece, which in its current form transposed the exterior of the town of Bassano with the private apartment of the princess. The suspension of disbelief was too much to ask of an audience and Verdi felt a sharp pang of despair that his music wouldn't be able to make up the difference.

"Surely the painters could render the river to look a little less like a blue line," said Giuseppe.

"I'll see what I can do," said Merelli, distracted by the tally of numbers in his ledger, "but I'm squeezing this into an opera season that has already gone well over budget." He closed his book and looked around the auditorium as if searching for his next topic of conversation. "Before I forget, do you have a few minutes to talk about the libretto?"

Giuseppe's face went slack. "Again? I thought Solera gave you his revisions."

"He did. But I was thinking about Riccardo's character. He, uh…" Merelli coughed into the sleeve of his jacket, "…he talks a lot about other women."

"He's a philanderer."

"But his character is Catholic. I don't think it looks good. The church isn't going to be happy."

"So, we won't make him a Catholic."

"It's not as easy as that. The church requires we make the leads Catholic." Merelli jotted down a note. "So he's relatable."

"But the whole premise is that he seduces one girl whom he leaves for another."

Merelli shrugged. "The way I see it, that indiscretion is forgivable. It gives us the opportunity to portray the church as…" he ran his finger along the ledger nodding to himself, "…sparing."

"So, the other affairs are too much."

"Exactly."

Giuseppe exhaled through his nose and looked at the pile of notes scattered on the table. He couldn't remember what they were keeping and what they were throwing away. "But what we have right now is no more illicit than what's in the Bible."

"That's the Bible. *You're* unknown. But that being the case," said Merelli, handing Giuseppe a heavy leather folder, "I want to change that."

Giuseppe opened the flap. Inside were several librettos neatly printed and bound. "What are all of these for?"

"I want you for three more operas here at La Scala."

Giuseppe could hardly look up from the folder. He was overwhelmed and overjoyed. "Why?"

Merelli laughed. "That isn't the reaction I typically get. Usually the composer is begging me to give them something."

"You have no idea how this opera is going to do. I can't make you any guarantees."

Merelli shook his head with a terse jerk. "Nothing is guaranteed, Giuseppe. But you're as close as I can get to a sure thing." He closed his book and tucked it under his arm. "Take a look and let me know what you think. In the meantime, I'll find you a new river backdrop. I think we can afford it."

Giuseppe returned to Lavigna's apartment late in the evening. He was exhausted from another day spent with Solera revising *Oberto* and the thought of choosing—let alone working on—another opera sent a shiver of dread through his arms and legs. He struck a match and lit the candle on his desk. Just outside the penumbra of light, he noticed a letter from his father-in-law that Lavigna had left for him on the table.

Dear Giuseppe,

I write with extreme urgency to inform you that Virginia became ill with the measles a few days after your departure for Milan. Her skin is broken out completely in a rash and her fever keeps her in bed all day. The doctor is doing his best to triage her condition, but all he can do is ensure that she eat and drink.

Margherita remains strong, but as you can imagine, she is upset beyond reproach. Thank God Icilio is not sick and the doctor has made the keen recommendation to separate him from his sister.

As you are busy with your commitments I will keep a correspondence with you as things evolve. But I urge you to come home if there is even a remote possibility of that opportunity. We think of you daily.

Regards,
Antonio

A weight emanated from the pit of Giuseppe's stomach and he became lightheaded as the mass flowed surely through his body. It felt like his blood had been replaced by sand anchoring him securely to melancholy.

He reread the letter several times looking for anything that Barezzi included about Virginia's full recovery. But each time he read the letter, it concluded that his daughter was ill and he was far away.

Giuseppe rifled through the desk hoping to find another letter determining Virginia had magically become well. But all he could recover were a few dozen pages of *Oberto* revisions littered across the table. Exhausted, he pushed them away and laid his head down. He tried to expel the enduring weight from his body with long, deep breaths. But nothing escaped, and the more he thought, the more his thoughts tumbled upon one another in a tangle of cloudy emotions, one idea clamoring for attention over another. He felt like he had abandoned his family and, in a way, he felt abandoned by the specter of happiness that family life was to provide. Being far away from Virginia was almost as tragic as the illness itself. He was like a character in an opera—his anguish the center of a bigger, dire world.

How strange that so much of our motivation to help others is really an effort to help ourselves, he thought. The trauma of thinking of Margherita and Virginia suffering alone was too much for his conscience to endure. It wasn't his daughter's illness that filled him with grief, but his own absence from the story of this experience that made it too dark to bear.

It was the consideration of his future self and the pain he would feel to not have been the husband and father he was expected to be that finally lifted him out of his chair with a clearer, more resolute state of mind. It took him only a few minutes to pack his things and he slept soundly until daybreak.

The next morning he left a short note for Merelli and boarded a coach to Busseto. Giuseppe couldn't think past his own arrival. What he would say and what he would do when he got home was beyond him. What more could he ask of himself than to enter the scene and hope that he do and say the right things? As the coach ambled along the rutted roads, Giuseppe closed his eyes and felt the sand of disquiet slowly spill from his body and blow away in the wind. For better or for worse, he would return home as was expected—and as he wanted to.

Chapter Sixteen

After Virginia's funeral, Giuseppe and Margherita resolved to move to Milan with Icilio. The decision was made less from a conversation than a shared awareness that life wasn't continuing with any joy in Busseto. Though their commitment to leave was a ray of light in dim circumstances, the guilt of Virginia's death continued to weigh heavily on Margherita. She was a ghost of her former self, floating on gusts of memories. Giuseppe found himself married to a different, more opaque being, a person with whom his words and touch could scarcely penetrate the grief. By leaving Busseto they hoped to return to a place they once were.

The funeral was modest with only Giuseppe, Margherita, and Barezzi in attendance. Virginia's body was placed in a plot next to her paternal great-grandparents, an important last-minute detail for Barezzi, who had become intensely aware of his own mortality. Little Icilio barely made a sound during the ceremony. A laugh, a whimper, or even a full-throttled tantrum would have been the antidote to the despair, but the priest's ambling prayers and the wind whipping through the open grave were all that could be heard.

In the weeks following the funeral, Icilio remained nearly silent in his own firm deference to his sister. Throughout the day Margherita would needlessly rock him both asleep and awake in fear of losing another child. Giuseppe remained able to work and continued his correspondence with La Scala and Merelli. Losing Virginia was a less an interruption of life than a test of one's humanity, he concluded. Despite her listless, fearful days, Margherita could still rest her head on Giuseppe's shoulder, searching for solace, though carefully, her emotions guarded in anxious nights. If she lost her anchor in Giuseppe, then she would be out at sea forever.

On a wakeful night before their departure for Milan, Giuseppe stuffed Virginia's soiled bedsheets into a burlap tarp and walked toward Le Roncole. At the halfway point, in a clearing of olive trees, he lit a match and tossed it on the bundle of fabric. The fire smoked and sputtered and finally roared to life as a gust of wind tore through the trees. When the flames licked the lowest branches, Giuseppe threw a thick sheath of *Oberto* revisions onto the pyre. The orb smoldered and burned with a pulse not unlike a human heart. Giuseppe considered a prayer, but for what did he need forgiveness or hope? The fire reassuringly consumed the things that were gone. When the sun rose, Giuseppe kissed the earth and walked back toward the house to pack their remaining things.

Milan offered a welcome distraction for Giuseppe and Margherita, and out of respect for the sanctity of life, the couple did their best to be happy. Margherita adjusted quickly to the city and was keen to get Giuseppe focused on his career. While she set up their new home with furniture and a small staff, Giuseppe retired to his study, musing on the books and music he took as inspiration. For the first time since he began work on *Oberto*,

Giuseppe was able to take Margherita to the salons and small parties of Milan—perks with his ties to La Scala. They spent most evenings out and would return late at night, more often than not from the Maffeis' cosmopolitan townhouse.

Margherita leaned her head to the side and removed an earring. The bedroom was warm from coals lingering in the fireplace and the shades were drawn to keep the heat in. "Aren't you going to bed?"

"I drank more than I should have." Giuseppe leaned against the bed, admiring Margherita as she removed the other earring.

"Nothing wrong with that."

"Judging from the way I feel, there certainly is not." Giuseppe removed his shoes and ran his feet through the plush rug at the foot of their bed. "Did you have a good time tonight?"

"I did."

"Anyone interesting?"

"I was with Clarina for most of the evening."

"Which means you talked with nearly everyone. Clarina Maffei holds quite a court, doesn't she?"

Margherita took off her dress and folded it over the top of the teak wardrobe. "It doesn't sound like she and Andrea are going to last much longer."

"That's impossible," said Giuseppe drily, digging his feet deeper into the rug. "They're the consummate couple. I don't think one exists without the other."

"Maybe it was just the alcohol talking," said Margherita, considering the conversation. More often than not Clarina would exaggerate and Margherita found it difficult to separate truth from fiction.

Icilio started to cry in the other room.

Margherita put on a robe. "I'll go and check on him."

Giuseppe followed her into Icilio's room. "Andrea was talking a lot about someone who's come into their circle of late. Cavour. Some revolutionary type."

"She mentioned him. You know how much Clarina despises the Austrians," said Margherita, rocking Icilio in her arms. "It makes sense."

"Andrea doesn't seem particularly impressed. Thinks he's a bad influence."

"I suppose," said Margherita vacantly. "From what she described, it sounds like this Cavour fellow loves the French as much as your father does."

"How do you mean?"

Margherita put her hand on Icilio's forehead. "He feels warm." She handed him to Giuseppe.

"I can never tell," said Giuseppe, running his hand along the baby's head. "That's the mother's realm." Giuseppe rocked Icilio against his chest and hummed. "What do you mean about the French?"

"Cavour is a big landowner, I think. Maybe it has something to do with that."

Icilio nodded off, his hand clutching Giuseppe's shirt.

"It was so kind of Merelli to toast you," said Margherita.

"I think it's only customary."

"Not like that. He was quite effusive." Margherita took the baby from Giuseppe's arms. "You need to learn to accept a compliment."

"Of course." Giuseppe watched Margherita put Icilio back into his crib. The baby yelped and then quickly turned on his stomach and fell asleep. "I think I'll stay up," Giuseppe said.

In his study, he read *Macbeth* for the dozenth time. Lady Macbeth's rage and pathological need for power had always confounded Giuseppe, but considering his recent affairs at La Scala, her disposition made sense. It was less brute force than persuasion and money that got the job done. The Scots in the eleventh century certainly had the riches, but there was much less of a compulsion to share it—best to keep it inside the family. Barezzi and Merelli would much sooner give their money away than force a man to choose his life over his livelihood. By contrast, the modern world required scheming and waiting. Always waiting. Of course, Giuseppe considered, the opportunity to become King of Scotland only came once in a lifetime.

Invigorated by the Bard's tale, Giuseppe leafed through the folder of librettos Merelli had given him to consider for the following season. They were lackluster, lesser stories from an antiquated time when audiences expected less from the singers, sets, and pomp of the production. But one of the operas, *Un giorno di regno*, though not perfect, caught Giuseppe's eye—or rather, his sense of humor. He found himself disarmingly levitated by the premise of a king in hiding and the man who impersonates him. *Un giorno di regno* was a momentary escape, much like the wine he drank that evening, and Giuseppe laughed for the first time in weeks. What more could he or an audience could really ask for?

Oberto, Conte di San Bonifacio premiered on a cool November evening to an audience of two thousand rapt in awe of this new, promising composer. When the curtain closed, the applause surged through the theatre like a wave unable to break, and Giuseppe was dazed, woken as if from a dream.

The young composer had written something that surpassed the expectations of the world's premier opera house and the patrons clapped gladly until the chandeliers shook in their moulding. Giuseppe bowed to his audience and raised his hands to the orchestra, who bowed back in celebration of his triumphant debut. The thought that a man needed a school or a title to validate oneself to the world was absurd. People didn't really know what they were looking for until you showed it to them, and Giuseppe Verdi was on full display.

Chapter Seventeen

Giuseppe looked up from his work and considered taking a walk before he lost the nerve. The morning sun heated his little room and he itched to stretch his legs. Now an independent composer, Giuseppe sought a schedule and got into the habit of going to bed just after sunset and rising early, long before the world and the news of the day polluted his mind. Now that *Oberto* had run its course, the newness of *Un giorno di regno* was a welcome change and he didn't want to lose his enthusiasm to the trivial matters of the day.

After the successful opening of *Oberto*, Merelli was quick to book another thirteen performances. He was happy with his investment and was reaffirmed of his commitment with Giuseppe when a passerby on the street would hum an aria from the opera. The premiere caught the attention of publisher Giovanni Ricordi, who published the music for a not-immodest sum from which Merelli happily took his fifty percent.

"Now you can take your lovely wife on vacation," Merelli said, handing Giuseppe the princely check.

"No time for that. I have work to do on *Un giorno*."

"Suit yourself," said Merelli, red with celebratory wine. "Lunch then. My treat."

Giuseppe watched the sky suddenly darken and he fetched his coat from the hall closet. Margherita called out for him.

"What is it?" he yelled, already halfway out the front door.

Since moving to Milan, Barezzi had been generous with the young couple, playing the role of benefactor, father, and father-in-law to his utmost capabilities. He supplemented the rent for a larger apartment, insisting they have enough bedrooms and personal space. It was a new start for the family and he wanted to give his son-in-law the environment he needed to write and space for his daughter and grandson to bond. Giuseppe's contract with Merelli was secure, but payment wouldn't come for months, not until *Un giorno di regno* premiered, and they depended on Barezzi to keep their household afloat, which he did, happily.

Giuseppe walked to Icilio's room, where the curtains were drawn. Margherita held the boy in the crook of her elbow, twisting her body back and forth, soothing his head in her hands. Icilio was silent and his shadow lay hopelessly limp against the nursery wall. The fireplace in the corner of the room wafted a small current of heat and Giuseppe lit another fire, stoking it to a steady burn

"What's the matter?"

"He's really sick." Margherita's voice was barely a whisper.

"Put him down."

Margherita placed Icilio in his crib and pulled back his nightgown. The boy was covered in red sores dotting his stomach and legs. He cried out, restless and sleepy. Margherita started to change him.

"Don't do that. You'll get infected," said Giuseppe.

Margherita hovered over the crib and wiped away a tear with the back of her hand. "What am I supposed to do then?"

"I don't know."

Giuseppe was a capable man, but faced with the reality of the world, he could do nothing more than hold a pencil in his hand and write. Being there for Margherita cleared his conscience, but it didn't seem to change the situation at hand.

"I'll fetch the doctor," he said.

Margherita remained at her vigil and Giuseppe quietly left the apartment, his walk now an imperative.

The winter sun was well over the Milanese skyline. Despite the cold, the birds darted in and out of the bare trees with surprising alacrity. The snow had fallen late in the year, but arrived just in time for Christmas. The holiday had been light and cheerful, filled with fond memories of Virginia—a relief for everyone. The crisp, clear nights were seen as a harbinger of good to come in the new year for the family.

Giuseppe knocked on the door with the large brass knocker. A girl of the house cheerfully informed him that the doctor was on call. Giuseppe left word and headed back to the apartment. He walked slower than before, taking in his surroundings and clearing his head before confronting the somber climate at home.

When he returned, Icilio was in a fit, pulling his mother, then pushing her away in spells of uncertainty. Margherita bounced him up and down as he writhed, overheated with a fever.

"He's so hot. I feel horrible for him."

Giuseppe rubbed her back and tried to give a reassuring smile to the baby. "The doctor will be here shortly. Put him down until he gets here."

Margherita shook her head and continued humming softly to her child.

The doctor arrived dressed in a black suit and tie, carrying a heavy black leather bag. He was cheerful and young and painfully formal. He immediately took Icilio from Margherita's arms and put him back in his crib.

"There's not much we can do other than feed him and make sure he's comfortable," he said, examining the sores on Icilio's stomach. "Has he been exposed to the measles before?"

"From his sister," Giuseppe answered.

"She died," said Margherita coldly.

"How long has he had the rash?"

"Just a day."

The doctor hesitated, leaning over the crib. "His fever is high. More than most children at this stage. This will either subside or the fever will go up. There's no way of telling." He placed his notebook in his case and secured the latch. "I've been advising parents to keep as little contact as possible." He gave Giuseppe a knowing look. "The only thing you can do is keep the room comfortable."

After the doctor left, Giuseppe took Margherita out of the room.

"We shouldn't have moved here," she said.

"That's not true at all. None of this would have changed."

"We did something wrong. I did something wrong."

"No, you didn't. We're just here doing the best that we can."

~

If Giuseppe had received a libretto that had two of the protagonist's children dying in six months' time, he would have sent it back for being overwrought. But reality can be stranger than fiction, and within a few days of the doctor's visit, Icilio passed. On the last night, the boy's fever nearly burned through his clothes. Giuseppe had opened the bedroom window and let the evening air cool the room. He broke the doctor's rules and held his son in the breeze, hoping to give him some respite from the discomfort. The boy's cries drifted into the winter night until he finally went to sleep, restful and trusting in his father's arms.

In the days following Icilio's death, Margherita came to Giuseppe for comfort and he was relieved to find purpose in all of this tragedy. They spent their days taking long walks and lingering over meals, finding something in their conversations to laugh and cry about. Margherita's only complaint was the headaches. Her father blamed it on unreasonable anxiety and the summer heat, and sent over several dozen bottles of wine. Giuseppe suggested calling the doctor, but Margherita refused, explaining with half seriousness that the doctor only seemed to bring death. Taking her father's prescription, she started to enjoy wine with dinner, and she gained a lightness and girlish frivolity. She insisted that the requisite headaches were simply the cost of enjoying oneself.

At first Giuseppe believed she was coming to terms with the death of her children, a manic episode of talking with ghosts. But the headaches started to bleed into the day, and at night her head swelled as if something were trying to break out. The month before she died, Margherita's fevers were so severe that she moaned incoherently through the night. The doctor instructed Giuseppe to apply cold compresses, and nearly every hour for a week, a local boy dropped off a package of ice that Giuseppe would wrap lovingly to the swelling. Giuseppe faithfully dabbed her forehead and sang the songs they practiced as children in her father's parlor.

In those last days Margherita cried for mercy and she cried for love—without it, nothing else could take the pain away. Eventually she stopped talking and stared blankly at the freshly painted walls of their bedroom. Giuseppe told her that he loved her and she smiled sweetly, her eyes slits against all of the anguish and all of the love of the world. How much could accumulate in such a small amount of time—and she died in love with it all.

Reality truly could be more tragic than fiction.

Part II

Chapter Eighteen

1840

After the premiere of *Un giorno di regno*, Giuseppe was reluctant to work, go out, or even see friends. He spent his days languishing, reading bad novels, and pacing anxiously in a small apartment he had taken on the other side of the city. It had been wearing to be so close to where he and Margherita had lived briefly with Icilio. But Milan was his new home, and if he were to stay, he had to start over once again.

The opera was an utter disappointment and Merelli mercifully cancelled the remaining performances after the first night. Margherita's death had made it difficult, if not nearly impossible, for Giuseppe to finish *Un giorno*. It premiered a mere three months after her passing, and afterward Giuseppe nearly collapsed into the shell of his former self.

"This happens," said Merelli, pouring Giuseppe a drink after the show. "But don't think you're off the hook. You'll make something great again."

But Giuseppe could no longer find the presence of mind to write. His thoughts were elsewhere and nowhere at the same time.

Finally, Clarina Maffei, desperate to help, dragged Giuseppe away from his apartment and put him in a room she set up for him in her townhouse.

"Leave your despair here; it can't come with you," she said, closing the door on his sparse apartment.

At Clarina's, Giuseppe had a sturdy desk, a sunlit room, and a friend, something he hadn't allowed himself to have for some time.

Finishing another novel, Giuseppe tossed it aside and stared out the window, listless. He eyed a libretto Merelli had recently given him. He tucked it under his arm and ambled into the main room of Clarina's townhouse, settling into an armchair. Just looking at the libretto sent a shiver of sweat down the back of his neck. It had been nearly six months since *Un giorno di regno* and the shame of its disappointment was as strong as it was the night of the premiere. But this angst was a window dressing to the despair of losing the people he loved the most. Giuseppe was tormented by the loneliness. This professional blunder only embittered him, and he was convinced that he would never find consolation in music again. Occasionally a flash of conviction to put pen to paper would come over him, quickly replaced by indifference and fear. Several weeks after the premiere, in a moment of desperation, Giuseppe had begged Merelli to release him from his contract with La Scala. Merelli had refused good-naturedly. Giuseppe could come back whenever he was ready. La Scala was his home no matter what happened.

Before the year came to a close, Merelli managed to revive both Giuseppe and *Oberto*. He diligently conducted a handful of performances scheduled to replace the hole *Un giorno* left in the calendar. The audience was appreciative, and cheered enthusiastically to show their support for Giuseppe. For a moment Giuseppe's spirits were lifted, but the longing for his family pushed the well wishes of the audience aside, making room once again for the stubborn weight of hopelessness.

"You treat me like a capricious child!" Giuseppe shouted through his apartment door when Merelli came to see him after a performance.

Merelli stood outside the door, appealing for his return. "Listen, Verdi, I can't force you to compose, but my faith in you is undiminished. Who knows? One day, you may decide to write again." He waited, listening for any movement inside the apartment. "In which case, if you give me two months' notice before the beginning of a season, I promise your opera shall be performed."

But Giuseppe couldn't shake the professional and personal tragedies. He longed for the countryside where he had grown up. The thought of a long walk, an endless walk, was the only thing that made him happy.

Late one snowy winter night when the shops were closed and the streets were vacant, Giuseppe ventured out. And as luck, fate, or ill fortune would have it, he ran into Merelli, who was on his way to La Scala.

"Giuseppe, you have to help me."

"I can't now, really. It's just good to see you."

But Merelli was in no mood to cater to his friend's despair. "It's this opera I'm working on with Nicolai."

"Otto Nicolai?"

"These damn Germans are so difficult. If he could see beyond his own ego he might be able to breathe life into this opera." Merelli pushed on the door to his office, but it held fast in the cold. "The libretto is by Solera! Just imagine. It's superb! Magnificent! Extraordinary!"

The wind picked up, blowing snow into Merelli's face as he went on, unwavering about the virtues of the opera.

"Grandiose, dramatic situations and beautiful verses. But this stubborn composer will not see reason. He calls it an *impossible* libretto."

"By Solera?"

"Yes!" Merelli's eyes twinkled, finally finding sanity. "Can you imagine!?" He pushed the door open and held it for Giuseppe. "But my problem is that I can't find a replacement libretto and the bastard is on contract for two more operas with us."

In this moment Giuseppe felt useful, purposeful. The familiar weight of self-doubt unhinged itself from his chest. He was charged by Merelli's rightful anger, giving him a sense of esprit de corps for the theatre and his friend.

"Remember when you gave me *Il proscritto*?" Giuseppe said. "I haven't written one note of it. You can have it. I put the libretto at your disposal." It was a momentary relief—the burden of work gone and his producer vindicated.

Merelli clasped his hands around Giuseppe's. "Thank you."

They walked into Merelli's office, where he poured a drink for himself and one for Giuseppe. "You don't play games like the rest of them."

"I wouldn't know how."

Merelli pulled out a thick sheath of paper and tossed it at Giuseppe.

Nabucco, read Giuseppe off the front cover.

"That's the opera that bastard Nicolai won't do."

"What on earth am I going to do with this?" Giuseppe winced. "I'm not in the mood to read anything."

"Come on, it won't bite you. Read it and bring it back to me."

Giuseppe paged through the dense pile of paper and the words blended together in one thick block of ink. He considered the work, the physical and mental turmoil it would take to give this story, whatever it was, a life of its own. He glanced up at his friend.

Merelli wore an expectant, eager look on his face. "Yes? And?"

For a moment Giuseppe forgot about his family now gone, and the failure of *Un giorno*. The mystery of the unknown of taking on something new was intriguing. Who knew what pitfalls and frustrations would befall him with this *Nabucco*?

"So, you'll do it?" Merelli prodded.

Giuseppe rolled up the thick sheath, shoved it under his arm, and walked back out into the cold.

"I'll read it."

Clarina drifted into the darkened room and scoffed. "You won't be able to read anything sitting in the dark like that," she said, opening the blinds.

Giuseppe had become closer to Clarina and Andrea, quickly endearing himself to the couple in just a few weeks. It wasn't just out of sympathy; they found him to be a forthright, albeit a humorously crass, addition to their salon. Giuseppe could be opinionated and his terse manner of speaking was refreshing. They were accustomed to the wayward intellectualizing of erudite elites who hadn't accomplished much more in their lives than attending a university and going to parties. Though Clarina was fiercely political, she found Giuseppe's complete lack of interest in the matter charming and it gave her respite from her own sense of self-importance.

Giuseppe had grown accustomed to their bohemian lifestyle, finding similarities to his stern, black-and-white view of the world. The Maffeis' salon embraced liberal ideas, and though Andrea was forceful in his arguments and Clarina persuasive with her charm and passion, Giuseppe never felt like they were out to change or persuade him. They just wanted what was good for Italians, and in his mind, they were usually right.

"That's what this candle is for," Giuseppe answered Clarina.

"Don't be silly. It's the middle of the day." She sat next to him and breathed a sigh of relief. "I've been on my feet all day." Clarina smoothed out her dress. "It's fortuitous you're here. Giuseppina will be over later this afternoon."

"I haven't seen her since the premiere of *Un giorno*. She was far too kind in her appraisal."

"Don't be ridiculous, Giuseppe." Clarina stood over him with her hands on her hips, looking over him like a nanny to her charge. "You're being morose. What if Julia brought you some brandy?"

"No, I'm fine. It's just good to be here."

Clarina put a brass bell next to Giuseppe. "Ring her if you need anything. I'll be in my study. There's always a letter to write." She stood to leave. "Have you heard about Garibaldi?"

"The politician? Isn't he somewhere in South America?"

"He's raising the anti-Austrian cause in Uruguay. Calls his army the Red Shirts."

Giuseppe nodded. "How did you come upon this?"

"I have my sources."

"Be careful writing that sort of thing. The Austrians are so strict about the theatre. Imagine if they intercepted one of your letters."

"You just worry about yourself," said Clarina, sticking out her tongue. "Let me know when you're done sulking so I can bring Giuseppina by to say hello."

Giuseppe pulled a side table up to his chair and began reading *Nabucco*. The story concerned the plight of the Jews as they were conquered and then exiled by the Babylonian king Nabucco. Inspired by stories from the Book of Jeremiah and the Book of Daniel, Solera had woven together a love plot between the supposed daughter of Nabucco, Abigaille; her "sister," Fenena; and Ismaele, the nephew of the king of Jerusalem. After conquering the Jews, Nabucco declares himself king and then god of the Babylonians. Abigaille usurps the crown, but when Nabucco regains his power, he vows to save the Jews and converts. Abigaille eventually poisons herself and the Jews are freed.

The tale of freedom was intriguing and Giuseppe quickly fell for the love affair between Fenena and Ismaele. The story of the Jews searching for their homeland resonated with him; he felt a strong connection to their wandering. It was if they both had been taken hostage by the random tragedy of life and had nowhere to go. After reading the opera, Giuseppe longed to return home to a simpler time, with his family—and especially to be back with Margherita.

Giuseppe stood at the parlor window, looking at the horse and wagons as they galloped urgently along the street below. He hummed Solera's lyrics to himself and closed his eyes, imagining the chorus of Jews longing for home:

Go, thought, on wings of gold, go settle upon the slopes and the hills, where, soft and mild, the sweet airs of our native land smell fragrant!

The melody took him to the hills of Busseto, where the fragrant wind pushed him along its windy, grass-lined roads and his clothes smelled of wet earth and petrichor. *Nabucco* was this place of freedom and salvation. When he closed his eyes, he was there in mind and body.

"Hello Maestro."

Giuseppina Strepponi stood in the middle of the room, grinning from one side of her mouth. She wore a lavender dress, the sleeves trimmed in white lace.

"Signora Strepponi," said Giuseppe, taking her hand. "So good to see you."

"It's a pleasure to see you as well. You've been missed."

"I haven't been much company to bear of late, I'm afraid."

Giuseppina smiled, baring her teeth, and laughed reassuringly. "Sit, let's catch up." She waited for Giuseppe to settle himself into the chair. "I'm sorry. I can be so haughty. I hope I'm not interrupting anything."

"Not at all. I was just—"

"You see, I told you," said Clarina, marching into the room. "I knew if we waited, we'd never see you." She plunked down a tea set laden with porcelain dishes, silver spoons, and decanters, then sat next to Giuseppina and took her hand. "I came in here earlier and he was just sitting in absolute darkness. What would men do without us?"

Giuseppina laughed. "Oh, I think they'd get a lot more done without us."

"Maybe in your case," Clarina said, then turned to Giuseppe. "Speaking of which, I am so sorry to interrupt, but I sent Giuseppina in here to see how you were doing. You don't mind, do you, Giuseppe?"

"Certainly not."

"'Certainly not,' he says. Giuseppe, we women are not afraid of conversation."

"Sometimes there can be too much," said Giuseppina diplomatically.

"Of course, but we know well enough to stay away from those types." Clarina pulled Solera's libretto toward her. "What's this?"

"It's an opera that Merelli sent me."

"Are you considering it?" asked Giuseppina.

"I wasn't." Giuseppe sipped his tea and paused, considering his thoughts. "But I don't know now."

"I envy your time off. I don't think I've had a break since I came back from Austria."

"Please don't mention them in this house," chided Clarina.

"You hypocrite!" laughed Giuseppina. "You didn't take issue with my performing there."

"I certainly didn't want you to stifle your career on account of those brutes," said Clarina in a clipped tone. "In any case, I considered it artistic warfare. The Italians are much better singers than any Austrian."

Giuseppina rolled her eyes. "Oh, Clarina. That is just patently false." She took a sip of her tea. "This is how all of this war business gets started anyway."

"Always over a girl," added Giuseppe, pulling his chair closer.

"Exactly! You think we'd learn."

"The Austrians are a stubborn bunch," said Clarina. "If the French were still here, Italy would be unified. So greedy."

"Actually," said Giuseppe, "Merelli was saying the same thing about Otto Nicolai."

"Isn't he German?" asked Giuseppina.

Clarina snorted. "What's the difference? They all come from the same inbreeding anyway."

Giuseppe stacked the loose pages of the manuscript into a pile, smoothing the sides with the palm of his hand. "It's actually about this opera. Nicolai thinks it's an impossible piece and Merelli can't convince him otherwise."

"Of all the nerve."

"Who wrote it?" asked Giuseppina.

"Temistocle Solera."

"Really!" she said, impressed. "What do you think of it?"

Giuseppe would be lying if he said he didn't like it. Until an hour ago he was considering walking away from Milan, perhaps even from Italy, and never coming back. *Nabucco* was beautiful and powerful and Giuseppe was suspicious of its sway over him. Perhaps he was too vulnerable to make a rational decision. Yet Giuseppina was so honest in her inquiry, so honest with her words.

"I think it's beautiful."

"So it's settled!" said Clarina. "You'll write this and stop moping."

"I don't think it's that easy."

"You're making it not that easy," rebutted Clarina, laughing and ringing the bell. "Regardless of what you decide, Signor Verdi—you're staying for a drink."

Giuseppina put the manuscript in her lap. "Let me know if you need anything from me."

"I will," said Giuseppe, anticipating the drink with calm relish. "Perhaps there's a part for you."

"Beautiful, eh?" said Merelli.

Giuseppe stood over his desk, holding *Nabucco* out in front of him like a specimen of rare animal. "Very beautiful."

Merelli rose from his desk and pulled a small box from the bookshelf. "Well then, set it to music!" he blustered, tossing a wad of Austrian *lire* on the table.

"I don't want anything to do with it."

"Set it to music, damn it!" Suddenly, Merelli leaped up and stuffed the libretto and the money into Giuseppe's coat pocket. "What the hell is the matter with you?"

Giuseppe put the money back on the table and rolled up the manuscript. "I'll do it," he yelled, laughing hysterically.

"What, just like that now?"

Giuseppe shrugged. "I told you, I love it."

"Off with you," said Merelli, slamming the door. "You're a crazy person!" he yelled, laughing through the window. "I don't want to see you again until it's finished."

Giuseppe hummed to himself as he traced the cobblestone streets back to his empty apartment. His mind and conscience were free again from the weight of the world.

Chapter Nineteen

1842

Merelli chuckled in disbelief as he read another review of *Nabucco* over breakfast. Giuseppe sat across the table, a pile of newspapers between them.

"This is from the *Gazzetta di Milano*," Merelli said, deepening his voice. "'Verdi has placed himself in the small but select band of composers who, ignoring the bad taste that still clouds the spirit of many, use everything in their power to overcome, even partially, the well-worn but still long-used operatic conventions.'"

Giuseppe nodded and took a bite of pastry. "That, I agree with."

"Oh, good. I'm so glad you can agree with good press." Merelli lifted a silver pitcher from its tray and refilled his coffee. "The response to this is staggering," he said, shaking his head in astonishment. "I tell you this, Giuseppe. If you can get this kind of consensus between critics, you can do anything."

"That's ridiculous."

"Oh, just take the compliment," said Merelli, fishing out another paper. "We both know how hard you worked on this."

The response to *Nabucco* was far beyond Merelli's and Giuseppe's expectations and Milan was gleefully abuzz with the name "Verdi." Giuseppe's name was printed endlessly in the papers, spoken repeatedly in the streets, and heralded in the gilded salons of high society. "Va, pensiero," the piece that first caught Giuseppe's emotions, had caught the fervent adoration of the public as well, and it was almost impossible not to hear it sung throughout the alleys and canals of Milan. Even with Giuseppina, who struggled with her voice in the opening performances as Abigaille, the consensus remained that *Nabucco* was a masterpiece.

"In any case, I can't take all the credit. Solera wrote the words."

"Ahh, but you gave them life," said Merelli. He smiled devilishly. "However, there is one voice of dissent."

"Who?"

"Otto Nicolai."

Giuseppe nearly spit out his coffee. "That's rich."

"Jealously, really. I heard he's calling it 'dreadful and degrading to Italy.'"

"That is pure nonsense. Why does everything have to turn political?"

"Giuseppe, you realize people are calling *Nabucco* the political statement of the year? Hell, the last ten years?"

"That too is nonsense."

"Of course, Donizetti is calling it beautiful. In fact, I think he said it was 'beautiful, beautiful, beautiful.'" Merelli rang the bell sitting on the table. "Goes to show we Italians need to stick together."

Julia, Clarina's maid, stood by, her hair in a tight bun.

"More of those delicious pastries, if you please," Merelli asked her.

"Of course." Julia smiled at Giuseppe. "If I may be so bold, *signor*, congratulations."

Giuseppe nodded appreciatively.

"See, you're a star," chuckled Merelli.

Julia quickly returned with a plate of sweets, placing it perilously on the pile of newspapers.

Still in her morning robe, Clarina burst into the room, trailed by a portly man in a dark suit and tie.

"Maestro Verdi!" she shouted dramatically. "An honor to have you once again grace our home."

Merelli stood. "Thank you for having us, Signora."

"Of course. I can't have Giuseppe dining alone in his shambles of an apartment."

"You do need to do something about that, Giuseppe," said Merelli.

"Giuseppe, Signor Merelli, I want to introduce you to Camillo Benso, Count of Cavour."

The count held out his hand, his fingers adorned with simple gold rings.

"Please sit," he said. His wire-frame glasses formed small opaque circles over his eyes, making his face appear disproportionately fuller than the rest of his body. "It's honor to meet you both."

"Giuseppe, the count is from the country as well," said Clarina facetiously.

Cavour laughed. "Yes, I suppose. Something like that."

A few years older than Giuseppe, Count Cavour was born in Piedmont to parents of French descent. His major land holdings, which his family had received during the French occupation, were a home base for his extensive travels throughout Europe. He was a well-read man of letters, military, and mathematics.

"How does Milan suit you then, Signor Verdi?"

"Quite well, actually," said Giuseppe. "Though of course I miss the fresh air."

"Of course." Cavour put his hands in his pockets and bowed slightly. "I am sorry to have interrupted your breakfast," he said formally, "but Clarina insisted I meet you." He smiled and threw his arms out wide. "What luck I have. I've only been in Milan a few days and all I hear is 'Verdi' this and 'Verdi' that. And here is the man of the hour."

"A fluke, really," said Giuseppe.

"The count is here from Grinzane. He is a..." Clarina wavered, reaching for the right word.

"An aspiring politician, admittedly," he said chagrined, a small smirk forming from the corner of his mouth. "I've been away from my estate for some time and the distance has given me clarity on the future of Italy."

"I don't think I've had enough coffee for this conversation," Merelli groaned, pouring another cup from the carafe.

Cavour laughed and relaxed, his arms dangling at his side. "Neither have I," he said, pushing his glasses toward his face. "I am entranced by the fervor you've created, Signor Verdi. It's really a call to arms to unify this country."

"That certainly wasn't my intent."

"It comes from an honest place, Giuseppe," said Clarina.

"That's right," added Cavour. "The people have really connected with it. You can't change how they feel."

Merelli yelped. "I'd say that's the best review yet!"

Giuseppe held up his coffee in regard. "Agreed. A bit biased, though." He winked at Clarina.

"I was just saying he can never take a compliment," said Merelli, putting the last pastry deftly into his mouth and raising the plate for more.

Merelli scheduled *Nabucco* for another fifty-seven performances at La Scala, securing Giuseppe as a household name. Organ grinders pumped "Va, pensiero" day and night, and Ricordi immediately began publishing the most talked-about opera in Europe. And despite the wear it put on her voice, Giuseppina maintained the role of Abigaille for eight performances, assuring *Nabucco* as the favorite of the opera season.

Giuseppe couldn't deny that the opera's success released him from the distress of his own tragedies—his music of freedom was, at least for now, a self-fulfilling prophecy and he felt worthy of writing once again.

Organizing his files one afternoon, Giuseppe was reminded of what his old music teacher, Baistrocci, said about being a musician: He would have to do more than just write in solitude—he had to feel a part of the world as well. And for the first time in years, he did. Whatever doubts Giuseppe had about the *Un giorno* performance now floated down the Po river and out to sea. And soon enough, Giuseppe and Solera began work on their next opera, *I Lombardi*.

Giuseppe arrived at La Scala early. The air was still cool and the buildings were dull in the morning light. He wanted to meet with Merelli before the demands of the day took both of them away from discussing the plot of *I Lombardi*.

Giuseppe was furious that the first draft of the opera was so similar to Tommaso Grossi's epic poem to which he and Solera set the opera. "We're *inspired* by—not *stealing* from—this,"

Giuseppe fumed, throwing half of the manuscript into the fire. Solera walked away in distress, tired and insulted. Giuseppe would do whatever he wanted anyway, Solera reasoned. However, Merelli was adept at this kind of editing and Giuseppe was keen to get his opinion on the matter. The sooner they started, the sooner they would be in production. Giuseppe did not want anything to slow the current of confidence he was riding.

Merelli saw Giuseppe in the hallway through the cracked door.

"Ah, Giuseppe, come in," he said. An affable-looking man sitting in front of Merelli's desk turned and smiled. "Giuseppe, this is Torresani, the chief of police," said Merelli.

"Congratulations, Maestro, on your success," said Torresani, extending his hand. He wore a dark blue uniform with brass buttons lining each side of his jacket.

Giuseppe took his hand cautiously and stood in the far corner of the office behind Merelli's desk. The three men waited in silence, only the sound from the pendulum of the clock reminding them of where they were.

Merelli smiled and cleared his throat. "Giuseppe, Signor Torresani has been kind enough to come this morning to tell us that there has been a complaint."

"A complaint," repeated Giuseppe skeptically.

Torresani straightened his back. The buttons on his uniform glimmered. "From the Archbishop of Milan. Regarding—"

"*I Lombardi*," Merelli assisted.

Giuseppe sat down and unbuttoned his jacket. "I see." He slid back in the seat and looked to Merelli. "And how would he know about it? We haven't started rehearsals."

"Come on, Giuseppe, you know we have to keep the Austrian censors informed."

"It's a complaint about the baptism scene, specifically," said Torresani.

Giuseppe sat up and leaned on Merelli's desk. "That's surprising. This is a story about Christians against infidels. The Austrian government has no problem with that?"

"Apparently not," said Merelli, wiping his glasses on the front of his shirt. "I'm as surprised as you are."

Torresani coughed. "Signor Verdi, I see my job as peacekeeper. I assure you, I do not wish to clip your wings. I am well aware that any change to this opera is a threat to public safety. There will be riots if the public finds that your work has been censored by the Austrians. Or the church, for that matter."

"What do you propose, then?"

"I leave that to you. But I do not wish to incur the displeasure of either the archbishop or the Austrian emperor."

"The emperor?" said Merelli, startled.

"Yes, the archbishop is quite serious about this," said Torresani, rising from his chair. "Whatever you decide to do, you have my support." He put on his top hat. "Good morning."

"This is absurd!" shouted Giuseppe after Torresani closed the office door. "What do you have to say about all of this?"

"Me? What is there to say? This theatre operates under the supervision of the Austrians."

"And the church, for that matter, it seems." Giuseppe looked down at the floor and laughed. "Demanding I make changes!"

"We should be grateful the chief of police is on our side."

"At least there's one of us."

"Giuseppe, there's nothing I can do. Should I not run this by the censors? Be reasonable."

Giuseppe leaned back in his chair. He focused his eyes on a point on the floor and cleared his mind, trying to find a reason to keep working on the opera. "*I am* the one who's reasonable."

Giuseppina was already at the Maffeis' parlor when Giuseppe arrived. He had left La Scala frustrated with Merelli and the inconsistency of the censors. He was certain the Austrians would criticize the political overtones of the opera and he was ready to fight it.

As much as Giuseppe hated to admit it, *I Lombardi* pandered to the anti-Austrian fervor that had caught Milan after *Nabucco*. Its story of oppression would likely feed populist demands and work as fodder for the press. At least the blowback from the Austrians was rooted in a logical place. But the church? The immunities awarded to them infuriated Giuseppe and he cursed the archbishop all the way to the Maffeis.

"You got my letter," said Giuseppe. He slumped down in the chair beside Giuseppina.

"I was just about to leave when the messenger came by." Giuseppina put a cool hand on Giuseppe's arm. "You look so tired."

Giuseppe sat up, righting his posture. "I'm fine, I'm fine." He patted her hand. "I suppose I just wanted to see you."

"How nice."

"I apologize about the informality of my note."

"Not at all. It was refreshing to receive something so effusive."

Giuseppina gazed up, admiring the room. They could hear Andrea reciting a poem upstairs, his voice muffled, as if they were listening to a performance from the lobby of the theatre. She looked to Giuseppe, her eyes glistening.

"It's kind of the Maffeis to let us come here. It's hard for us musicians to have a place to come home to."

Giuseppe leaned back, resting his head on his hand. "I forget that sometimes. Being a musician."

"You could wake up one day and everything you worked for is gone." Giuseppina's face reddened and she lowered her head. "I'm sorry, I didn't mean anything by that."

Giuseppe waved her off with a smile.

"It's true, though," she added.

Julia came in with a tray of tea and set it down between them. Both Giuseppe and Giuseppina watched her every move—pouring tea, adding sugar, placing the spoons on the saucers, and placing linens on the table.

"Will there be anything else?" Julia asked.

They shook their heads and sipped their tea, hiding behind their cups and saucers in the quiet of the room. Finally, Giuseppina broke the silence.

"I was relieved to get your letter. I've been meaning to talk to you, but couldn't find the right time." She took a sip of tea, swallowing deeply. "I'm moving to Paris."

"Oh," said Giuseppe, trying to find the right facial expression. "That's wonderful. I mean, is it?"

"Well, in a way," she said, clearing her throat. "We're both relatively young, so I think you'll understand." She flipped her hair off her shoulder. "My voice is strained and the recent touring has made it so much worse. If I feel this way now, imagine what it will be like when I'm actually old? How long could I keep this up?"

"But why Paris? You could stay in Milan. You have friends here."

"The city is different and Lombardy feels strained. I see more Austrian troops and there's all this talk of revolution." She looked at the overly familiar oil paintings, vases, and rugs of the Maffeis' parlor. "And now the church's criticism of your opera. I'm convinced that it's time to leave. Or take a break."

Giuseppina's conviction to leave Milan conjured images in Giuseppe's mind of Busseto and Le Roncole. The simplicity of life outside the city was truly a gift. Or at least a state of mind.

"I wish I could leave, too."

"No, you don't. There's so much for you right now in Milan. You would let people down."

Giuseppe shook his head. "I didn't ask for this popularity. At least not this kind of popularity. I just want to tell stories. Not politics."

"You can't separate the personal from the political. Just being an artist is a political statement."

"What's your political statement, then?" asked Giuseppe.

Giuseppina watched the tea leaves circle the cup, bobbing slowly in the opaque liquid. "Love."

Giuseppe picked at a loose thread on the arm of the chair. "Can't you find that here?"

Giuseppina smiled and took his hand. "I think so. Someday. When we both have time."

Later that evening, Giuseppe went to his apartment and packed a small bag. It had been too long since he had seen his mother and father and Barezzi, and he quickly chartered a coach to take him back to Busseto. The ride quickly brought back the painful memories of watching his family disappear one by one. Nearly every ride home since his marriage had brought tragedy. But as he watched the hills rise up and down through the window of the coach, he remembered the joyful, exuberant trips as well. The rutted road to Busseto had brought him the pleasure of sleeping with his young bride, the pride of being Busseto's music director, and the endless wonders of being a father. These were far from the political acts that had seemingly infected his life now.

He took a deep breath and let sleep wash over him. Each bump in the road brought him deeper and deeper to the center of dreams. Relief slowly coated Giuseppe's limbs as the coach approached Busseto and his soul securely nestled itself back into his body.

Giuseppe met Barezzi at his home in Busseto. The two men finally reunited after months of glum silence following Margherita's death.

"I missed her," said Barezzi as they hiked a narrow path outside of town. "I still do. And I've missed you, too."

Giuseppe stopped to take in the scenery in the valley below. The trees were tall and wispy, casting dappled shade, and the grass danced in a dozen shades of green. "Where are we?"

"This is Sant'Agata."

"It's beautiful here," said Giuseppe. "The clouds look like they were painted on the sky." He picked up a small rock and threw it as hard as he could into the bramble. "I missed you, too, but…."

Giuseppe picked up another rock and tossed it in the palm of his hand. He squinted into the sun, looking for the right words. "I've never done this before. I didn't know what to say to you." He threw the rock over the bramble. "Please forgive me."

Barezzi put his arm around his shoulder. "You needed time, Giuseppe. So did I. There's nothing to be sorry about."

Giuseppe nodded. "Margherita would have liked it here."

"She did." Barezzi crossed his arms and surveyed the landscape. "Things have changed, Giuseppe. But we're still the same people."

"I hope so." He exhaled. "I think I should live here."

Barezzi laughed. "That's the spirit. I think you should, too." He picked up a gnarled branch and tossed it over the trees. "Let's go home and have a drink. And be happy."

Chapter Twenty

1846

Giuseppe sat in a firm wooden chair, its back stiff and unyielding. His stomach churned in pain and he sank lower against the headrest, hoping to ease his aching body. Pasetti made small talk, mumbling endlessly about Vienna and Paris and bragging about his wife's ability to solicit compliments on her fashion. Giuseppe loosened his tie and patted the sweat beads flowing down the front of his neck. He was tired, miserable, and trapped in his publisher's office with a lawyer.

"You've been doing a lot of traveling lately, eh?" asked Pasetti, dressed head to toe in an impeccable cashmere suit. "My wife and I love shopping abroad."

Giuseppe mustered a nod and gazed at the books lining Ricordi's wall, where *Nabucco* sat proudly on display. It seemed like a lifetime since that auspicious premiere. Where was Ricordi? The sooner they discussed *Macbeth*, the sooner Giuseppe could get into bed and drift off to sleep for days or weeks or even years. *Attila* was scheduled to premiere in just a few months and Giuseppe's stomach flipped thinking about the trip to Venice. He still hadn't been to the theatre to prepare for rehearsals.

~

Giuseppe had been working tirelessly since *I Lombardi*. His bout with the archbishop was avoided by a sleight of pen and the premiere at La Scala went off triumphantly. Torresani, the chief of police, stood by his word and patiently waited in the wings of the theatre as the police rule against encores was broken over and over again. The audience cheered the Lombards, identifying their own struggles against the Austrians, and they carried their exuberance into the streets until sunrise shouting, "*Viva* Verdi! *Viva* Verdi!"

Before she had left for Paris, Giuseppina helped Giuseppe make the final edit to *I Lombardi*. The baptism scene was carefully, if not simply, executed. A practicing Catholic, Giuseppina suggested changing the first few lines of the opening aria from "Ave Maria" to "Salve Maria." By changing "Hail Mary" to a slightly different meaning, it wouldn't be considered a baptism. By a miracle (Giuseppina's word; Giuseppe called it "stupidity"), this appeased the archbishop and the opera went on for another twenty-seven performances.

During rehearsals, Giuseppe feared that the story depended too much on anti-Austrian sentiment. He struggled with his growing association with Italian unification and he made an effort to absolve himself of this label by dedicating the music to Duchess Marie Louise of Parma at a performance. She graciously accepted, waving to the muted audience, but the unintended irony was not lost on Count Neipperg. He sulked through the performance while the duchess hummed along, tapping her hand on his knee. Backstage, Giuseppe held his head in his hands with the realization that it would be nearly impossible to change public opinion. He would be whatever people wanted him to be.

After a short round of celebratory dinners and parties, Giuseppe dutifully began commissioned work for theatres in Naples, Venice, and Rome, and was celebrated throughout Europe as the composer of the age. But now, after three years and four operas, he was run down in body and spirit. What would it take to just be Giuseppe Verdi, simple musician, once again?

Soon after *I Lombardi*, Giuseppe and Merelli began work on *Giovanna d'Arco*, based on the story of Joan of Arc, employing Solera to write the libretto. But after months of work and pre-production, Giuseppe received an anxious letter from Ricordi. The libretto was strangely similar to German playwright Johann Schiller's play *The Maid of Orleans* and Giuseppe found himself in Ricordi's office debating the practicality of continuing with the existing libretto. There would be copyright issues and money at stake, and Ricordi didn't want to publish. Giuseppe was furious at Solera, who had a predilection for laziness and plagiarism, and he spent his days and nights anxiously editing the opera. It was one thing to be unintentionally associated with a patriotic movement, but it was another to be called a fraud.

Throughout the production, Giuseppe became increasingly frustrated with Merelli's reckless casting and frugality—La Scala was no longer living up to its reputation and Giuseppe felt sidelined to Merelli's need to fill the performance calendar. The luxurious productions of Giuseppe's operas *Ernani* and *I due Foscari* in Venice and Rome proved the slip in quality at La Scala, but Merelli seemed more concerned with appeasing the Austrian censors and saving money than with his star composer's needs and appeals.

Giuseppe's ego was hurt, but he carried on with his commitment to *Giovanna d'Arco* and the opera premiered to an audience and critics awed by its charm and simple, captivating melodies. Flowers dropped endlessly to the stage, and throughout the city, barrel organs churned arias from the opera to the boundless delight of the Milanese.

Giovanna d'Arco premiered in Rome, where it ran for three months, while *Nabucco*, *I Lombardi*, *Ernani*, and *I due Foscari* were staged in France, Germany, Austria, Algeria, Russia, and Spain. Giuseppe's reputation and fame quickly soared, and in such a position, his business arrangements became increasingly complex and he invariably committed to multiple projects and impresarios, straining his personal relationships. The contractual and social gymnastics of managing his affairs took the joy of out of work and Giuseppe's stress turned to despair. Life was becoming routine and it was harder to find his muse under the endless layers of obligations and deadlines.

While working on *Alzira* for the Teatro San Carlo in Naples, Giuseppe fell severely ill, his mind and body overworked and overwhelmed. Relieved by the doctor's prescription for rest, Giuseppe wrote the theatre's impresario, Vincenzo Flauto, that the production would have to be delayed. After an exhausting day of composing and negotiating publishing fees, Giuseppe came home to find a coarse letter from Flauto in his mailbox.

Signor Verdi,

We are very sorry to hear that you are indisposed. The illness from which you are suffering is a trifling affair and needs nothing more than a tincture of absinthe and the immediate journey to Naples. I can assure you, the air will be quite to your liking. Resolve then to come at once and abandon that troop of doctors who can only aggravate the indisposition from which you are suffering. For your cure, you can count on the air of Naples and on my advice when you get here. For I once was a doctor myself, though I have abandoned such impostures.

Through the exhausting combination of aversion and illness, Giuseppe wrote back, righteously defending his reputation as a reliable composer.

Signor Flauto,

I am terribly sorry to inform you that my illness is not as minor as you think it is and the absinthe tincture will be of no use to me. I can assure you, all I need now is calm and rest. I will not be able to meet you in Naples as you invite me to, because if I could, I would not have sent you the medical certificate from my doctor. I tell you this out of courtesy so that you can take whatever steps necessary during this period as I work to recover my health.

The tenuous correspondence with Flauto bruised Giuseppe's pride and he collapsed, unhinged, bedridden for a month.

Slouching in bed, sipping vegetable broth, he worked halfheartedly with Salvatore Cammarano, a librettist.

"We artists are never allowed to be ill," Giuseppe lamented, waiting for the stomach cramps to subside. "We should not bother to behave like gentlemen, for the impresarios please themselves whether they believe us or not."

Cammarano agreed, secretly thankful that he would never have to confront the responsibility of being Giuseppe Verdi.

After several weeks of writhing pain, Giuseppe finished *Alzira* and traveled to Naples for rehearsals. Upon his arrival, teeming crowds gathered in curiosity to see the famous composer in person. He obliged his role as musician, graciously accepting the gifts and platitudes bestowed upon him.

The opera performers surpassed themselves, presenting their effort and talent anew for the composer, acquiescing happily to Giuseppe's direction and demands. When the curtain dropped, the audience called Giuseppe to the stage for nearly an hour, showering him with flowers and applause, while afterward, thousands of Napalese escorted him to his hotel in a procession of singing and chanting. Giuseppe was affirmed by the love and adoration, but he went to sleep restless and longing for something he could call his own.

In a rare evening out, Andrea Maffei introduced Giuseppe to a playwright who had written a romantic play about Attila the Hun. After the performance Giuseppe was fascinated by the prospect of writing an opera about the feared ruler, and the Teatro La Fenice enthusiastically commissioned him to compose the work for their spring season. Despite his other commitments, his ailing health, and nonstop work since *I Lombardi*, Giuseppe was inspired. It was, he reasoned to himself at the time, to keep his sanity.

Francesco Piave had proven to be a reliable partner on *Ernani* and *I due Foscari* and Giuseppe decided shortly thereafter to employ his deft hand on *Attila*. As a young man, the librettist intended to become a priest, inspired by the prose and verse of the church. But Piave found employment sooner in the theatre and quickly began a career writing poems and librettos. Giuseppe appreciated this practical deferment from the cloth to the paper, but more importantly, he found Piave's sensitive personality made him an ideal writing partner: he conceded to Giuseppe's edits without question and was willing to bend toward his vision with little irritation.

But *Attila* proved too bloodthirsty and brash for Piave's delicate sensibilities and Giuseppe was forced to work again with the slothful Temistocle Solera. Where Piave would concede, Solera would dispute, and then, much to Giuseppe's extreme annoyance, refuse to work.

Giuseppe was horrified when he received the first draft of *Attila*. Solera took it upon himself at every opportunity to inflate the patriotic aspects of the story. Any nuance of Attila as a man, as a personality of history, was lost. After reading the libretto Giuseppe collapsed on his bed, unable to move or muster the energy to tear it to shreds. Being labeled a patriot and nationalist would surely endure for another season and Giuseppe grew weary of the responsibility.

When he found the civility to call on Solera, Giuseppe received a note informing him that the librettist had left for Madrid with his wife, leaving a big blank page for the final act of the opera. Giuseppe's lingering headaches turned to permanent throbbing, along with unyielding aches in his arms and legs. He was miserable.

Reluctantly, he wrote to Piave, and in his endless aim to please, the poet and librettist came back to help see *Attila* through. While shaping the final act, Piave suggested the Kinschi band, a popular Venetian music group.

Giuseppe felt the blood drain from his head and he collapsed on the floor, succumbing to the effects of a debilitating fever he'd had for two weeks. When he finally came to, he glared at Piave.

"That band is a piece of provincialism," Giuseppe cried through a coughing fit. He fell back into his pillows. "And unsuitable in big cities," he muttered before drifting off to sleep.

It wasn't until Piave showed Giuseppe an erroneous newspaper headline pronouncing his death that he realized his work and his ego were finally getting the best of him. Something was missing.

Alone in his apartment, with the final act of *Attila* unfinished, Giuseppe made an appeal to Margherita, whispering to the empty space in the bed. "I'm sorry, I'm not the man you married. Forgive me."

And he slept, a blank slate in his mind.

Ricordi burst into his office with a bundle of papers. He patted Giuseppe on the back.

"Verdi! May I call you that now?" he asked mockingly. "That's all I hear. Verdi! Verdi! Sometimes I forget that's you." He smirked. "But then I get the royalty checks and I remember."

"The publishing business seems to be working," said Giuseppe, lifting himself upright in the chair.

"Certainly is."

"We were just talking about Paris," said Pasetti.

Ricordi ignored the lawyer. "You don't look good, Giuseppe. Well, you requested a meeting, so here I am."

Giuseppe pushed his damp hair from his forehead. "I'm not a populist composer."

"I don't think anyone would accuse you of that."

Giuseppe shook his head. "It's a reality I can live with."

"But—"

"I need to make a clean break. I'm not working with La Scala any more."

Pasetti looked up, startled. "Signor Verdi, your contract with Ricordi publishers clearly states that—"

Giuseppe waved him off. "I need you to help ensure my rights to *Macbeth*," he said to Ricordi. "I just don't want anything to do with Merelli."

Ricordi leaned back in his chair. "We can do that," he said, crossing his arms. "That'll put your business and ours closer together."

"As long as you publish what I write and negotiate the percentage…" A sharp pang shot through Giuseppe's arm and he thought about the warm embrace of his bed. "…I'm still with you."

Ricordi nodded, smiling triumphantly like an explorer discovering a long-lost city. "So, you want to make *Macbeth* into an opera?"

"It's going to be beautiful," said Giuseppe, getting out of his chair. "I just need to get this *Attila* business out of the way. But until then, I need your blessing."

"You have it. No more La Scala."

"Will I see you at the premiere?"

"I'm too old. That trip to Venice will kill me." Ricordi laughed. "And from the look of it, I'm not sure you're going to make it, either."

"That's what I thought," said Giuseppe, making his way to the door, "but I'm suddenly feeling much better."

Chapter Twenty-One

Giuseppe stood on an arched bridge over the Naviglio della Martesana watching the water amble through the canal's muddy banks, willow branches dragging passively in the current. The morning haze lingered over Milan like dust, gently brushing the city in gray. The landscape reminded Giuseppe of a recent letter he received from Giuseppina, describing a trip to London. "If I had any thought of returning to the opera," she wrote, "it's long gone by now. The film of fog and coal coats the city like a dingy blanket and I am certain this trip has taken its toll on my health."

Downstream, an aging water wheel creaked affably, heaving water up and down in its ancient blades. *How provincial Milan would seem to a Londoner*, thought Giuseppe, admiring the portrait just the same.

Giuseppe was in control of his life again, his mind clear for *Macbeth*. After *Attila*'s premiere he spent six months in bed under strict doctor's orders to recuperate. One bright morning, after reading and having tea, he finally rose, not unlike a poppy in the revitalizing elixir of spring, rested and reborn. The months of solitude had effectively distanced him from the drudgery of the last four years. It was like another person in another life had lived the grueling schedule. After months of rest he felt enchanted, every overheard conversation or errant gesture fodder for a bit of dialogue or inspiration for a scene. Life was a stage once again.

Macbeth will capture life, its vulgar ambitions, its tragedies. Everything must say something, thought Giuseppe as he admired the pair of mermaid statues, cast in stone, flanking the ends of the bridge. *That's the important part. No allegories or comments for the climate of today. Macbeth will be its own story in its own world. Escapism.* This much Giuseppe knew. Brevity and sublimity.

The mermaids stood on their tails, demure and forceful, holding tiny water paddles like spears. They grinned knowingly, like the fate of the world was in their hands. *The witches,* thought Giuseppe. *How easily Macbeth would lend his ear to their seductive prophecies.*

"Hello over there!" shouted Andrea from the far side of the canal, his boots caked in mud. Since Giuseppe's return to the day-to-day of life, Andrea was one of the few people Giuseppe found agreeable. He was opinionated, but kept his thoughts to himself.

Andrea lit his pipe and trotted up to Giuseppe, a half-finished manuscript of poetry under his arm. "These are some lovely creatures, aren't they?" he said, running his hand over the cool statues. "I could spend the rest of my life with any one of them."

For his own constitution, Giuseppe needed to keep *Macbeth* to himself. Sharing it, even with someone as close as Andrea, would be like exposing a wound before it healed. First the divine inspiration, then the vision to make something extraordinary— and then could he offer it to others. Once he held the opera in his hands, shaping and pulling it to his taste—only *then* would Giuseppe open his palms and give it away. He would write it himself, that much he was sure, but someone like Andrea or even Piave would have to help, sanding the rough edges. Giuseppe would plane the wood and shape the door until it fit the frame he saw in his mind.

"Excellent suggestion, getting out of the house," said Andrea, puffing away. "I certainly don't do it enough of it these days. Clarina is dragging more and more people to the apartment. Questionable characters, a lot of them." He looked around and then snapped his head back in sudden realization. "How about this business with the pope?"

Clarina declared it divine intervention that Giuseppe rose from his sick bed the same day Pope Pius IX was elected to office. His unlikely appointment sent a shudder from Rome through the Italian peninsula. Pius was a liberal and vehemently opposed by the Austrians. The Catholic cardinals had exhibited their power by electing him, sympathetic to the call for Italian independence and unification.

"I've heard he's already started work on a constitution for Rome." Andrea leaned against a mermaid. "I just hope the crackpot revolutionaries don't take this too far."

"I thought you supported the movement," said Giuseppe.

"I do, but let the pope deal with the Austrians. I have more faith in the church bureaucracy than a bunch of rebels trying to overthrow a government."

"I'm surprised."

"I may be a crackpot libertine myself, Giuseppe, but I'm still a pragmatist."

"Hello, you two!" came a voice from across the bridge.

"Oh, hell," muttered Andrea. "What's she doing here?"

Clarina skipped over the bridge, her linen skirt tugging at her hips. Dressed thoroughly in black, Count Cavour trailed alongside her. He pushed his glasses back to his face, jogging to keep up.

"I hope we're not interrupting," she said.

"Not at all," said Giuseppe, relieved that he could delay the political talk with Andrea. Often forceful to a fault, Clarina was always a welcome distraction.

After his illness, Giuseppe was grateful to have Andrea and Clarina as friends. But their marriage had become contentious, their differences turning into nightly arguments over the artificial elements of life: politics, art, the social scene. This was the root of their problems and spending time with them was taxing on Giuseppe's mood. The marriage buried itself under the weight of the world and how they saw themselves in it. Perhaps Giuseppina was right. You couldn't separate yourself from your politics. It was certainly good advice to heed.

"Camillo came by the apartment and I couldn't resist showing you off, Giuseppe."

"I'm sorry," said Cavour, "you know how persuasive Clarina can be."

"To some," said Andrea.

"What?" said Clarina.

"Nothing." Andrea looked back to Cavour. "I was just agreeing with the count."

Clarina sighed, her eyes boring into Andrea's. "Be that way. We can go."

"No, no, stay," said Giuseppe. "We were just admiring the canal. So much like London. At least I've heard."

"Anyway," said Clarina, pushing Cavour forward, "we didn't come here to just see a world-famous composer."

Cavour handed Andrea a newspaper tucked inside his coat pocket. "I'm leaving Milan tomorrow and wanted you to see this before it goes to press."

"It's Camillo's new paper. Isn't it wonderful?" exclaimed Clarina.

Andrea puffed on his pipe and flipped through the pages. The text was small and dense, a dozen articles packed together on the front page. "Il Risorgimento" was printed at the top.

"We were just talking about this," said Giuseppe, looking over Andrea's shoulder and pointing to an article on the Pope's election.

"Quite extraordinary, isn't it?" said Cavour, his face suddenly animated. "With this election and the government easing up on the press, there couldn't be a better time for a liberal newspaper. Economically viable as well."

"What are you, a politician?" quipped Andrea.

"We're nationalists, to be sure," Cavour laughed. "But to answer your question, not yet."

"Be careful what you print," said Clarina. "The Austrians aren't loosening the leash anytime soon."

Cavour nodded gravely. "We're approaching this with caution." He pointed to two editorials on the election. "This is my article and this is my editor's."

"And what is your opinion?" asked Andrea, quickly examining the copy.

"Well," said Cavour, leveling out his voice, "Pope Pius is a good start. But I disagree with the premise that Italy can unite under a papal presidency. Church and state don't mix, in my mind."

"I'd rather be under Austrian rule than the church," said Giuseppe, trying to ease the strain between the two men. "At least there's logic to what they do."

"Exactly," Cavour agreed.

Andrea handed his paper back to Cavour. "So what then?"

"What do you mean?"

"Andrea always needs a solution," said Clarina.

"What do you propose we do?" Andrea asked.

"In a word: war," said Cavour.

Andrea guffawed, shaking his head in resignation.

"You don't really mean *war* war, do you?" asked Clarina.

"I do. We won't do it alone, of course. Making better friends with the French would be a good start. Make a pact. But we'll have to drive the Austrians out completely. There's only one way to do that."

"What's wrong with the pope? The church has the money to get things done," said Andrea. "Seems more realistic."

"It would take them a hundred years," said Cavour. "And don't be fooled—we're already at war. This is just a means to an end."

"Well, it's something in the right direction," said Clarina, grabbing the paper from Andrea and handing it to Giuseppe. She flipped to the last page. "Look!"

"Oh, yes," said Cavour, "I'd almost forgotten."

Giuseppe felt his pulse quicken and sweat bead down his neck as stared back at an enlarged caricature of himself, its face dour and serious. Surrounding his portrait was a review of *Nabucco*, reprinted from its premiere four years prior. An image of a unified Italy with "Risorgimento" printed boldly on top capped the article.

"What the hell is this?" Giuseppe yelled.

CHAPTER TWENTY-ONE

"Isn't it wonderful?" said Clarina.

"We thought it would inspire our readers," said Cavour. "It really brings the issue together, don't you think?"

Giuseppe was furious. The temerity to take his work and perpetuate the nationalistic myth of *Nabucco* was beyond the pale. And to regurgitate an old review, sensationalizing his involvement in politics, was an insult to his work.

"This is certainly the last thing I need," he hissed, throwing the paper back to Cavour.

"I'm sorry, I meant no offense." Cavour looked to Clarina for help.

"Giuseppe," she said, "you can't stop how people feel."

"Keep your war to yourself!" Giuseppe huffed back toward the bridge, the languid morning turned sour. "And leave me out of your little stories."

He looked out at the canal as he crossed the bridge. The clear water mutated to a brackish cloud, the bottom hidden from light. The quaint romance of the waterwheel turned ugly and old. His newfound clarity flowed down the canal, catching on the crusty, muddy banks.

Giuseppe looked back and considered apologizing to Cavour. The man meant no harm. How was he to know how trapped Giuseppe had felt? How reckless his career had become?

At the end of the bridge the mermaids lowered their paddles and their smiles tuned stern, as resolute as the stone they were carved from. "All hail Verdi!" they cried. "All hail Verdi!" Their tails flapped to the rhythm of their voices. "Not so happy, yet much happier." The mermaids raised their paddles and pointed downstream and then to the sky, beyond Milan.

"Leave. You must leave."

$\sim$

189

Giuseppe wrote to Giuseppina in Paris and waited. He read, took walks, and ate cheerfully alone—a prescription for his own good health. When the return letter finally arrived, it carried little more than a simple assertion. Yes, of course he should come to Paris. She would love to see him.

With his luggage already packed for the journey, Giuseppe left Milan for Paris, taking up an apartment along a stretch of the Seine where Parisians strolled throughout the day and night. In the evenings the gas lamps were lit and Giuseppe walked the city with Giuseppina—Macbeth, Banquo, the witches, and Lady Macbeth never far from his mind.

Giuseppe wrote *Macbeth* with the care he promised himself and sent the manuscript to Piave, his prose scrawled within neat margins.

"Here is a scenario of *Macbeth*," he wrote. "This tragedy is one of the sublime creations of mankind! If we can't make something great with it, let's try at least to make something out the ordinary."

When it was done—Piave's drafts mercilessly cut and pasted—Giuseppe dedicated the opera to Barezzi: "Here now is this Macbeth which is dearer to me than all my other operas, and which I therefore deem more worthy of being presented to you." For the first time since Margherita's death, Barezzi cried.

The opera opened in Florence in the spring and its success was immediate. The night of the premiere Giuseppe stood on the stage, deafened by applause, sustaining no less than thirty-eight curtain calls. He had taken the leap and aspired for dramatic truth, not flash or pomp or the cheap theatrics of a singer's trill. The audience understood and responded in kind. Italians were clamoring for something new and something real.

Before going back to Paris, Giuseppe returned to Busseto a local hero. Late in the evening after another celebratory dinner, Giuseppe walked to a bluff overlooking Sant'Agata. He would bring Giuseppina back one day and they would live here. They could leave the politics of Milan—of Italy—behind, and live amid their art and each other. He threw a rock as far as he could into the valley. Wherever it landed, he would, too.

Chapter Twenty-Two

1848

Giuseppe returned to Paris with a sincerity of heart that until *Macbeth* had fluttered like a flame in cool, crumbling embers. Amid the city's tranquil boulevards, ardent parks, and the serene solitude of his study, he could once again serve at beauty's behest.

Giuseppina welcomed Giuseppe to her adopted home. Paris was gray and anonymous, the ideal island to readjust to life outside of the opera. Giuseppe spent his days writing while Giuseppina conducted music lessons in her small apartment. They were relieved to be away from the routine chaos of Milanese society and soon took up residence together in Passy. Paris was forgiving in its social graces, politely ignoring their unmarried companionship as no less an offense than a sneeze.

Within a few months, Giuseppe finished *I masnadieri* for impresario Benjamin Lumley at Her Majesty's Theatre and he traveled to London before the end of the year to oversee production. Giuseppina had been right—the biting cold and the damp fog were debilitating and Giuseppe found his desire to work quickly diminished. But he was fascinated by London and English customs just the same. Where the Milanese opera houses were loud and bombastic and the Parisians distant and critical, the Londoners were silent, studying the performance from printed copies of the libretto, judging its quality against the performer's adherence to the page. In a rare moment of passion they would applaud for an encore, but never insist—a manner impossible for any Italian audience.

Giuseppina's eyes jolted open. She couldn't tell if she had been awake or was dreaming. A loud bang rang in the distance and she instinctively got up, bundling herself in a thick robe. The winter was particularly cold this year and Giuseppe insisted they keep the shutters and curtains closed to trap the apartment's lingering heat.

The bang could have been a hot coal bursting, she thought to herself as she poked the ashes in the fireplace with a brass poker. She opened the windows and checked the latches on the shutters. They were all securely fastened in their frames. Suddenly another blast and then several more, like fireworks, emanated from the distance. She opened the window to the street and looked toward the Foreign Office building, where a thin trail of smoke wiggled upward in the morning light. She pushed Giuseppe awake.

"What is it?" he mumbled.

"I think the bourgeoisie are having their day."

Giuseppe got out of bed and quickly got dressed. He tossed Giuseppina her coat and they left the apartment, taking side streets to the center of Paris, where demonstrations against the monarchy had already started days before.

Despite recent reforms, Parisians were anxious for change. A poor harvest the previous year and a lack of industrial jobs kept many of the French out of their place in the expanding middle class. The bourgeois demanded their right to work, and although King Louis Philippe I did his best to placate the proletariat, they took to the streets demanding the right to gather, vote, and own property.

A dozen people—men, women, and teenagers—milled about the murky cobblestone streets, watching alleys and doorways like sentries. A blockade of overturned omnibuses, paving bricks, and gnarled timber stacked as high as a row house lay tumbled across the Rue Martin, preventing the French guards from advancing. A top hat lay ominously in the street, a bullet hole through its top.

Giuseppe and Giuseppina passed several of these lumbering mounds on their way to the demonstrations, dodging wayward fires that dotted the city like waypoints. Several bodies, French guards, and citizens were pulled to the side of the road by soldiers and civilians alike. A boy, no older than ten, bounded up a wobbly barricade and triumphantly stuck a Tricolor on the top of the heap. The blue, white, and red flag flapped defiantly in the smoky breeze. The civility of the scene struck Giuseppe as strangely contrasting. It was like stumbling upon a lethal battle staged for one's entertainment.

"What happened here?" asked Giuseppe, examining a gaping hole in the middle of the barricade.

A young man tossed a guard's belt into the heap. His shirt was caked in blood. "They brought the cannons in early this morning."

"Where is everyone?" asked Giuseppina. "The streets are empty."

"Home," said the man. "Or...." He nodded to the bodies on the side of the street.

"Guizot resigned this morning," said another man, referring to the prime minister. He picked up the guard's discarded belt and tried it on. "And now there's fifty more dead."

"That's horrible!" Giuseppina covered her face to a foul breeze wafting over from a fire.

"What do you mean?" Giuseppe asked the man with the belt.

"A guard fired into the crowd and the rest of 'em followed." The man's face was expressionless. "I think we may have gotten a few ourselves."

"We're just here to keep this secure," said the man in the bloody shirt. He nodded to two of the guards, who were helping drag the bodies onto a makeshift gurney. "Make sure they don't do anything."

The following day, King Louis Philippe abdicated, exiled to England. That morning Giuseppe and Giuseppina took their coffee in the apartment and went back into the streets to watch the funeral processions and pay their respects. Thousands of Parisians lined the streets, their heads hung low in rueful contemplation. Outnumbered and discouraged, none of the royal guards stood watch over the somber scene. The country was ready for the Second Republic.

Life carried on for Giuseppe and Giuseppina in Paris. Moved by the February Revolution, Giuseppe vowed to stay in the city until April, when elections were scheduled for the Constituent Assembly. The French defined western civil society and Giuseppe was anxious to witness their democracy evolve firsthand. If Cavour was right and this uprising was any indication, war would be inevitable in Italy. It would take the entire peninsula, not just the kingdoms of Northern Italy, to rise to combat the Austrians. The unification was up against remarkable odds.

Giuseppina dismissed her student at the front door and returned to Giuseppe's study with a letter in her hand. He sat hunched over his desk, stuck on his composition, his head in his arms.

"This came for you yesterday," she said, handing him a tattered envelope. "It was in my coat pocket. I think it's from Piave."

Giuseppe eagerly opened the letter and read it aloud.

Dear Giuseppe,

As I have heard from others that you are safe since the recent uprisings in Paris, I write to inform of you of an extraordinary turn of events of Milan. I am assuming the news has not yet traveled to you as I write this in the midst of the fighting. The Austrians have been taking wild advantage of their tax enforcements, and since the beginning of this year, many Milanese (myself included) have boycotted tobacco. The Austrians have reacted aggressively to this, their tax coffers severely bruised, and have brought in more and more soldiers by the day. You would be alarmed by the look of it! Despite few shots being fired, we have been under siege—there is no other way to put it.

The Venetian Chancellor stepped down 13 March, and when news hit, the Milanese (our countrymen!) took to the streets and confronted the troops and the tax collectors.

Giuseppe, we fought brilliantly against the Austrians!—shooting from roofs, the streets, windows, and doors. You will be bemused to hear that our efforts have the support of the arch-bishop. And it has been a triumph—within five days General Radetzky and the Austrian troops left the city. It is chaos here but we are free. There isn't a single soldier left. The Five Days of Milan—there is hope!

I am safe, your father-in-law is safe. I urge you to come to not only see to your affairs but to see what is becoming of our home and the newfound glory of being an Italian.

Yours,
Piave

"What do you want to do?" asked Giuseppina after Giuseppe finished the letter.

"I think we should go back."

"It will be dangerous."

"No more than here. I think…we'll go to Sant'Agata. Live in the villa."

"What?"

Giuseppe considered the triumph of the French and the exuberant patriotism of Piave's letter. And *Macbeth*. How his countrymen had vindicated his ego, supporting him in his greatest effort. What use was he to anyone, himself included, in Paris?

"We'll be in the countryside. It's important that we go."

"And then what?"

"I'll write something. I'll write for Italy."

After the uprising in Milan, Italian revolutionaries held their ground in the south while Austria regained its foothold in the north. Encouraged by the success of the Five Days of Milan, Charles Albert, king of Piedmont-Sardinia, attempted to unify the country by taking Lombardy-Venetia back from Austria. With an army of Piedmontese and Tuscan troops, he went up against Austrian Joseph Radetzky with a force of 12,000 men. But after two battles King Albert's army was defeated and Milan and Lombardy-Venetia fell back to the Austrians.

Revolutionary politician Giuseppe Garibaldi returned to Italy in the summer and declared Rome a Roman Republic. Pope Pius IX left the city, creating a vacuum for a new government to establish itself. Giuseppe Mazzini arrived shortly thereafter and was appointed chief minister. In February, Albert tried again to push Austria out of Lombardy, but was swiftly defeated by Radetsky. Albert abdicated for his son Vittorio Emanuele II to rule over the Kingdom of Sardinia; for the time being, a unification led by Piedmont was abandoned.

By the middle of 1849, France would manage to dissolve the tenuous Roman Republic and Pope Pius was placed back in Rome, forcing Garibaldi and Mazzini into exile, paving the way for the Austrians to reinstate themselves in central Italy.

Chapter Twenty-Three

1849–1851

Sant'Agata proved to be the perfect refuge for Giuseppe and Giuseppina. A day's journey from Milan and far enough away from Busseto, they were able to work and live in relative obscurity. Though the old farmhouse left something to be desired, its walls warped and chipped and the bedrooms drafty, it rooted itself as a home they could grow into. "Like any relationship," said Giuseppina cheerfully, shivering under a second overcoat.

Inspired by Piave's account of the uprising, Giuseppe fervently began work on *La battaglia di Legnano*. With Austrian control of Venetia weakened, and shortly after the Five Days of Milan, Piedmont, in alliance with the Papal States and the Two Sicilies, declared war on Austria. But mistrust among the kingdoms and fear of one rising against the other caused a rift in the accord, and without help from France, Northern Italy fell once again to Austria.

Far from discouraged by these events, however, Giuseppe wrote with Cammarano, with whom he collaborated on *Alzira*. Cammarano suggested the story, which, he assured Giuseppe, "stir every man with an Italian soul in his breast."

La battaglia di Legnano premiered in Rome to an audience primed for a story that spoke to the movement. The opera was patriotic, the antagonists stand-ins for the Austrians. Giuseppe and Cammarano feared reprisals from the censors for its nationalistic message, but the authorities were overwhelmed with a tense political situation in Rome. In a turn of position, Pope Pius IX refused to send military assistance to Lombardy, fearful of the backlash from Habsburg, Austria, a Catholic stronghold. Local republicans retaliated and murdered his chief administrator, and within days of the opera's premiere, Pope Pius escaped to the seaside town of Gaeta.

The republicans called for an election and won by an overwhelming majority. With the newly elected assembly scheduled to meet the following month, the theatre was packed with sympathetic, restless Italians, excited for Giuseppe Verdi's latest opera.

The chorus defiantly sang its opening lines, "Long live Italy! A sacred pact binds all her sons!" and hysterical cries of "*Viva* Verdi!" "*Viva Italia!*" sprung from the balcony. During the third act, a soldier overcome with emotion flung his coat, sword, and epaulettes onto the stage, and then every chair in his box. The crowd cheered and the performers carried on, inspired by the bravery of Verdi's opera.

But the city of Rome was an exception, the political climate perfect timing for such a performance. Fearful of reprisals, the opera houses in Naples and Venice refused to produce *La battaglia di Legnano*. Yet it continued in Rome, a powerful testament to what the rest of the country could become.

Giuseppe was vindicated after the run of *La battaglia di Legnano*. It avoided censorship on its own terms. It was rebellious without breaking any rules. Satisfied, he wrote to Piave to find a new opera.

Stiffelio premiered the following year and found its critics again in the church. The opera, portraying the marital difficulties of a clergyman and his unfaithful wife, struck the ire of a reverend in Trieste. After the Royal Directorate of Police issued their approval, the reverend demanded they eliminate any depiction of a married priest. Disgusted, Giuseppe and Piave were forced to revise the scenes until the opera was a shell of its former self. It opened to a warm reception, though the critics poked fun at Piave's mutilated libretto.

Verdi laughed after he read the initial reviews. "You're a martyr for artists everywhere!"

Piave grumbled, comforted that Giuseppe was, at the very least, bemused.

Their next triumph, *Rigoletto*, did not come without its battles against the Austrian censors. Like the French who banned the story twenty years before, the Austrians took issue with the depiction of the king as a womanizer and immoralist. After arguments between the Austrian censors, the Teatro La Fenice, and a severely rattled Piave, they eventually came to compromise: The setting of the opera would be moved from the royal court of France to a minor duchy in France or Italy, and the duke would rule over a house long extinct. Any sexual encounters would be changed from intentional to provoked. It was a bitter pill for Giuseppe to swallow, his work stifled, but he moved ahead with rehearsals, keeping the music and details closely guarded from the press and the public.

On opening night, the baritone in the title role, Felice Varesi, refused to go on stage.

"Signor Verdi," he cried just minutes before the curtain was to open. "I look so foolish in this costume. I'll be a laughing-stock, please." He tugged at his ragged, over-the-top costume. "I'm a buffoon."

Giuseppe pulled him toward the edge of the stage. "You are a buffoon, but not because of this costume." He hit the baritone on the shoulder with the script. "Why now, Varesi?"

Varesi shrugged.

"Off with you," muttered Giuseppe, pushing the singer onto the stage, where he staggered and stumbled.

The theatre erupted in laughter, anxious for what would be a captivating performance. At the end, Giuseppe stood for a full twenty-minute ovation, bowing appreciatively for as long as it would take.

The next morning, the papers gushed over the overwhelming originality of the opera in the music, costumes, and style. Giuseppe was praised as an innovator.

The secrecy behind the production was well founded. The day following the premiere, nearly every Venetian could be heard humming "La donna è mobile," and barrel organs cranked day and night with the airy sound of the opera's signature song. *Rigoletto* carried a dramatic passion that was unprecedented in the opera.

"I don't think we could have done better," said Piave after the opening performance.

And though Giuseppe didn't agree, it was hard for him to imagine how they would.

Clarina opened the door and quickly latched it shut.

"Come in, come in." She pushed Giuseppe and Giuseppina into the foyer. "Sorry to be so suspicious," she whispered, kissing both their cheeks, then hit Giuseppe on the shoulder. "You're partially to blame."

"If it's not the police, it's the people," said Giuseppina. "I feel like we're being watched all the time."

"Don't be absurd," said Giuseppe modestly. He took off his coat. "There's no one watching us. Where's Andrea?"

"Right here." Dressed in a silk robe, Andrea took Giuseppe's coat and swung it over his shoulder.

"Where are you going?" asked Clarina.

"We're out of wine," Andrea replied.

"Julia can do that."

"And miss an opportunity to leave the apartment?" Andrea jiggled the front door, trying to unlatch the lock. He turned to Giuseppe and Giuseppina. "Excuse my wife. She thinks we're under attack." Andrea opened the door and raised his eyebrows conspiratorially. "See you in a bit."

Clarina locked the door behind him. "I should tell you before rumors spread. We're getting a divorce."

Giuseppina put Clarina's hand in hers and pulled her into a hug. "I am so sorry to hear that."

"Don't be," said Clarina, forcing a smile. "We're not saying anything to anybody until it's finished. You know how it goes."

"You should move to Paris," said Giuseppe. "They're all in bad marriages."

Giuseppina slapped him playfully with her glove.

"But I am sorry, Clarina," he added.

Clarina stepped closer and lowered her voice to a near whisper. "I'm surprised you both are living together at Sant'Agata."

"It hasn't been easy," said Giuseppina, taking Giuseppe's arm. "Even in Milan, people don't approve of an unmarried couple."

"Of course, he doesn't care." Clarina squeezed Giuseppe's cheek. "So you know," she said, jerking her head back toward the dining room, "this crowd isn't as liberal as you might think."

"*We* should have stayed in Paris, then," said Giuseppe, putting his arm around Giuseppina.

"Why would you do that?" Count Cavour came out of the dining room, a half-drunk glass of wine in his hand.

Giuseppina stepped back from Giuseppe, nearly toppling a Chinese vase from a side table.

"Count Cavour, it is good to see you again." Giuseppe hesitated. Their last conversation had been less than ideal. "Clarina didn't tell me you would be here."

"It was short notice." Cavour leaned in, taking on a conspiratorial look, not unlike Andrea. "Giuseppe Mazzini was here."

"The politician?" asked Giuseppina. "I thought he was out of the country."

"He's a wanted man!" said Giuseppe.

"Of course he is," said Clarina. "And Andrea thinks I'm being paranoid."

"He was here? In the apartment!?" exclaimed Giuseppina.

Cavour took a swig of wine. "He was in Switzerland and is now on his way to London. I'm trying to discourage him from coming back. For the time being."

"Garibaldi," said Giuseppe. "He's in exile, too."

"In New York right now," said Cavour. "He came here after the uprising. Both of those men are extreme, to be sure."

Clarina smiled furtively. "He stayed here as well. Andrea had no idea."

"Good lord," said Giuseppe. "Half of Europe has been after him."

"Both are good for the movement, but we need to keep things peaceful for as long as possible," said Cavour. "I'll admit I'm more of a politician. Anyway…." He looked at his empty glass. "We were supposed to be having fun until I ruined everything with my talk." He took Clarina's hand. "Where's that husband of yours?"

"Getting more wine."

"Good man. I just wanted to gloat."

Julia, the maid, whispered in Clarina's ear.

Clarina nodded. "It's almost time to eat. Go and talk," she said to Giuseppe, and pulled Giuseppina away to the recesses of the apartment.

Giuseppe wandered out to the balcony, where Cavour was lighting his cigar.

"Funny about the pope, isn't it?" said Cavour. "I knew he wouldn't go up against the Austrians."

"Mm," agreed Giuseppe, hoping to avoid politics.

"But," conceded Cavour, "Andrea does have a point. Italy will need help." He tapped his cigar on the railing and the ash floated into the trees. "Anyway, how have you been?"

"Fine. Fine, really."

"'Fine,' says the world-famous composer!" Cavour shrugged, laughing. "Fine." He took a drag on his cigar and exhaled. The smoke flowed over his beard like a thick mist. "You don't smoke these?"

Giuseppe shook his head. "Headaches."

"Hm," said Cavour, examining Giuseppe. He leaned over the railing, examining the street below. "I want to publish a letter asking for French support against Austria. I was hoping to get your signature."

"Wouldn't they have offered it already?"

"We don't have a prime minister they can come to." Cavour took another drag on his cigar. "Can I get your help?"

"What are you proposing?"

"Piedmont and France join a pact against Austria. If France helps us, we give them Lombardy."

"I'm not sure." Giuseppe sat down on a wooden bench near the railing, lightheaded. "Something serious must be emerging within Austria. Some insurrection. If we could seize that moment to fight," he said, rubbing his temples, "Italy could be free."

Cavour howled. "Well, there's an option. It's the hopeful, let's-do-nothing-and-see-what-happens strategy."

"I think an appeal to France is silly."

"Why is that?"

"They look down on us. We write operas for them. Nothing else."

Cavour shook his head, disappointed. "You sell yourself and your profession short, Giuseppe. And I think your opinion is misinformed. We can't just wait for the rest of the world to take notice of us."

Giuseppe remembered Barezzi groveling for an appointment with the duchess in Parma so he could go the conservatory. It was humiliating.

"France doesn't want us united. We'd just become another enemy, right at their front door," Giuseppe said.

"And watch Austria get bigger instead? Don't be naive."

"Even if France did help us and we won, the Austrians would sack everything in Lombardy. France would be left with a smoldering backwater."

"Even with all your success, you are a pessimist." Cavour tossed his cigar butt over the railing.

"Hey, up there!" called a voice from below.

Giuseppe and Cavour peered down into the street. Andrea was below, waving up to them.

"Toss me one of those," he said, motioning with his hand.

Cavour dug into his pocket and pulled out a cigar.

Giuseppe grabbed his arm and leaned over the railing. "Not in my coat!" he yelled, waving Cavour's cigar above his head. "You were supposed to bring wine!"

"Damn it," mumbled Andrea. "I just wanted a lousy cigar." They could see his grin under the gas lamp. "Nothing's open right now!"

"You have a decent reputation! Ask a neighbor!"

"There you go," said Cavour, impressed. "A negotiation where everyone wins." He put his arm around Giuseppe. "Think about signing the letter. Your name means a lot."

Chapter Twenty-Four

1852–1853

A thundering crash shook the house and Giuseppe woke with a start, the couch still wobbling beneath him. The low trill of hammers and saws came to a sudden stop. A dozen men bounded into the house, looking for the cause of the sound. A midday nap had become a welcome part of Giuseppe's routine, but it was impossible to get anything else done.

Giuseppina screamed from the bedroom and Giuseppe bolted upstairs. She stood in the bedroom doorway, her mouth agape. Above their heads a patch of blue sky hung directly over their bed. Half the ceiling lay scattered in a hundred pieces across the floor and a single plaster slab sat squarely in the middle of the rug. A small bird swooped into the room and perched itself on the edge of the hole, whistling an aria. Giuseppe begrudgingly began to clean, pulling the pieces of plaster out one at time with the other workmen. Remodeling Sant'Agata was proving to be as stressful as producing any opera.

They had spent so much of their time at their well-appointed apartment in Paris that they found it hard to come home to their modest estate, where every floorboard bowed and every window creaked in the slightest wind. After years of humbly describing the villa as "charming," it was time to make the house a home, and Giuseppe committed to remodeling the farmhouse from floor to ceiling in case he lost the nerve. After writing Ricordi that his contractors were threatening a lawsuit if he didn't pay his invoices, his publisher finally sent his overdue royalty payments. The check arrived several weeks later by post with an overly apologetic note: *"Please forgive our oversight."* It was getting harder and harder to manage these things.

It was also time to stop visiting Busseto, the town that had fostered Giuseppe into opera. Giuseppina was increasingly distraught over her treatment in their unwed relationship. The ideology of the church held sway over the provincial town and she fared the worst of the community's derision of her and Giuseppe. They grew weary of uncomfortable gatherings with their friends, conversations tinged with vague insults, and they longed for the more liberal salons of Paris and Milan. The din of daily construction was preferable over the false pleasantries of civil society, and Sant'Agata proved to be the ideal refuge.

The sun was setting by the time the workmen cleared the bedroom. The ceiling was covered with a tarp, and from his study downstairs, Giuseppe could hear it gently banging, pushing air in and out like a lung. Giuseppe's pen hovered over his latest opera, *Il trovatore*, and, indecisive, he closed the leather ledger of the score. He was exhausted—again.

Cammarano the librettist had fallen ill the previous month, leaving Giuseppe with as much of the lyrics to write as the score. They had found their rhythm, trading their work by mail. But with nearly everything, there were complications. And as soon as *Il trovatore* was finished, Giuseppe would have to leave for Venice to fulfill another commission. He slogged through the score and the libretto, writing through his evenings, making sure it would be finished in time for the premiere in Rome.

Giuseppina put a plate of sliced apples on the table.

"Did you see this?" she asked, handing Giuseppe the newspaper. She brushed the plaster from his hair.

"He's done it, hasn't he?" said Giuseppe bemused, reading the headline.

Count Cavour was now Prime Minister of Piedmont. With his close ties to the French and keen sense of diplomacy, Cavour was now in a key position to bolster Vittorio Emanuele and Piedmont-Sardinia against the Austrians.

"He wants to improve the railroads," said Giuseppina, reading the article over Giuseppe's shoulder. "That would be nice. I could visit you in Milan." She tapped Giuseppe on the arm. "What do you think?"

Giuseppe considered the extraordinary turn of events that put Cavour in the position of prime minister. The man had a vision. He knew what he wanted and had influenced those around him to fit that mold.

Giuseppe felt the throbbing in his head. He had embraced his role as Italy's composer, but it had left him ragged and defeated. He begrudged every new opportunity given to him as if it were a curse. Again, he was tired of life's expectations. All he wanted was peace and quiet. Now Cavour and the rest of the revolutionaries could carry the torch of independence.

A chunk of plaster fell from the ceiling, tumbling into Giuseppe's lap.

"I think it's time for bed."

≈

Il trovatore premiered in Rome in January to huge anticipation and it left the city reeling, with chants of "Long live Verdi!" echoing throughout the night. The tragic story of a mother accidentally killing her own child was unexpected and the reviews saw it as the end of the high romance of opera. But Giuseppe was indifferent.

The next morning, deftly avoiding fans in the street, he was able to meet Giuseppina for coffee.

"They say it's too sad, too many deaths," he said.

"Well, is it necessary for the story?"

"It doesn't matter, Giuseppina. Life is death. What else can be said?"

"People want glamour. This opera isn't."

"Which is exactly why I am getting the praise." Giuseppe laughed. "Now on to the next one."

Chapter Twenty-Five

1859

Giuseppe pulled the end of the trowel into the soft, crumbly dirt and tossed a handful of seeds into the trench. His legs were sore with the pleasant ache of manual labor.

The summer had been warm and dry, the birds only venturing out of their trees for water, hiding back under the branches until nightfall. Giuseppe and Giuseppina spent their evenings that summer pacing languidly around the house, conspiring for a breeze to blow through the windows. But the air remained still and trapped the heat in the rooms like an oven. By August the rain finally came and the earth eagerly soaked it up, making a fresh bed of soil to cradle the vegetables for winter.

As he dug another trench, Giuseppe made plans to walk into town. Giuseppina loved brined cheese. It would pair well with the small harvest of kale that he pulled that morning.

He might also mail the letter back to Cavour in Turin. He just wasn't sure how to decline his offer. Giuseppe was just a farmer now and an infrequent composer, much less a member of Parliament in a free and independent Italy.

~

A few months earlier, Giuseppe announced his retirement from opera. They were gathered at his apartment in Milan for a dinner party—writers, librettists, and journalists enjoying the pleasure of each other's wit and words. After several bottles of wine, impresario Vincenzo Jacovacci of the Teatro Apollo in Rome stood and toasted Giuseppe's legacy. Milan was still reeling in delight from the recent premiere of *Un ballo in maschera*, and the impresario offered, with full sincerity, as many blank contracts as Giuseppe wished. Italy loved him, and Jacovacci found it his duty to continue the composer's legacy. The table applauded graciously for Jacovacci, Giuseppe, the opera, and Italy, and they raised their glasses in celebration, beaming at their host.

Giuseppe joined the toast and put his arm around Giuseppina. "The scheme is splendid and does you honor, but I no longer compose," he said.

The table laughed, thinking it a wry joke from a man for whom leaving the opera would be a distortion of reality. But with humor Giuseppe stood his ground and dispelled the tepid admonishments of his friends. For now he was content to just *be*.

Since *Macbeth*, Giuseppe had worked hard to pursue truth in his art. But the opera and its machinations had demanded more of him and less from the music. The needs of Italy and, increasingly, the dictates of the censors projected themselves onto the music and Giuseppe was no longer in service to his art—he was in service to an idea of what it should be. The public had fallen in love with his creations, but what he had created was dishonest. What the public didn't know, and his friends failed to appreciate that evening, was that his art was a product of concession and defeat. He was guiding it faithlessly down a river it didn't want to travel. Giuseppe needed the world to trust and love the music he wrote. Instead, they loved the idea of the man behind the arias, the marches, and the trills.

Dazed by the informality of the announcement, Jacovacci and the other dinner guests conceded and the evening went on its merry way without a word of contradiction. Giuseppe later confessed to Giuseppina that he knew his announcement would shock. He was, in many ways, looking to add a touch of thrill to the evening. But whether he held his word or not, the sentiment remained. He was tired, and without a muse, he needed to recede back into the comforts of the country.

Un ballo in maschera had premiered a few months before, in February, at the Teatro Apollo, to much acclaim. In the weeks leading up the opening, Rome was mad for Verdi. During rehearsals his actors informed Giuseppe that barbers were selling locks of his hair and street merchants had set up booths selling pirated librettos, fake sheet music, and what they claimed was his discarded refuse—all for sale. People continued to scrawl "*Viva* Verdi" on public walls and the exclamation had taken on even greater meaning with the growing popularity of Piedmont's King Vittorio Emanuele. A clever acronym of his name solidified Giuseppe in his role as patriot and confirmed the country's need for unification: "Vittorio Emanuele, Re D'Italia"—VERDI.

The opera had faced a difficult journey to its premiere. A year earlier, while Giuseppe and his librettist Antonio Somma were working on *Gustave III*—which, after many changes, would become *Un ballo in maschera*—a member of the Carbonari had thrown a bomb at Napoleon III while the emperor was on his way to the opera in Paris. The event sparked sympathy for the Italian unification and Napoleon III saw the assassination attempt as a message that France could do more to lessen the hold Austria had on the Italian states.

Giuseppe was dismayed to find that the San Carlo theatre in Naples was sensitive to *Gustave III*, which depicted the assassination of the Swedish king. After heartbreaking revisions and a tiresome lawsuit, he brought the opera to the Teatro Apollo, where the Vatican took inexplicable offense to the operatic version of this well-known story. Giuseppe was at his wits' end, and Somma even more so. Giuseppe made an appeal to his librettist, but Somma bowed out, writing:

> *In your letter, you ask me if I can write other verses with these changes in mind, but in a manner that will not offend the Roman censor. How can I do this? As long as a change has some element of reason, some compromise could be found. But instead of a reasonable change, there is only ignorance.*

Upon reading the letter, Giuseppe nearly capitulated. He could not have agreed more. What tortured Giuseppe was censorship of his work and the curse of the terrorist attack on Napoleon in Paris that only served the outcry for unification. Milan was celebrating a rebel when all Giuseppe felt like was a conformist. Here he was, the supposed face and sound of Italian independence, cut short by the overlords of church and state. But with the heavy burden of obligation to the theatre, he lost his ability to fight against censorship and the opera opened at Teatro Apollo. From its ashes, the opera was enthusiastically received and Giuseppe was no less a hero to the cause than before. But unbeknownst to his audience, the fight for what was right was lost, and after it was said and done, so was Giuseppe.

And by summer, finally able to rest, Giuseppe fell into the swing of country life. The remodeling at Sant'Agata plodded along, and he took to his land, overseeing its landscaping and enjoying the simple, backbreaking pleasure of farming. But amidst the tranquility, the battles that he longed to leave behind came back to the solitude of his estate. In June, hundreds of thousands of men from Piedmont, France, and Austria fought the key battles for Italy's crusade for independence, miles from the peaceful endeavors of Giuseppe's home. In the evenings while he and Giuseppina tried to stay cool, the violent blasts of canons and rifles and the ghostly screams of thousands of men dying could be heard in every room and corner of the house. The guilt inside Giuseppe's heart was thick as mud.

The following month, the smoke finally cleared from the battlefields and the letter from Cavour arrived in the mail.

It was a chess move that wasn't his own and one Giuseppe never could have predicted. His heart fluttered in indecision, trying to break free from the sticky morass. What more could he give Italy than he already had?

The political events of the past year and a half had been turbulent for Cavour.

He had graciously accepted an invitation from the French diplomatic envoy. They wanted to discuss his proposed treaty with France. His efforts of late had fallen on deaf ears and it was a relief to finally get an audience. The French had been unwilling to go to war with Austria for the sake of a land grab, much less help with the unification of Italy. Cavour had offered Savoy and Nice, but France wasn't willing to fight for those territories and he feared that in his position as prime minister he was doing a disservice to King Vittorio Emanuele and the patriots of Piedmont.

But the assassination attempt on Napoleon III had created an interesting opportunity in Cavour's scheme.

The explosion had been tremendous, the bomb falling directly underneath the emperor's carriage, killing eight and injuring dozens. Napoleon left the scene unharmed and attended the opera, assuring France they were safe from harm. At first blush, the assassination attempt appeared to be a dagger to the heart of the unification's cause. But Napoleon saw it as an opportunity to stabilize and bring peace to the region—who knew when and where this would happen again? And as a side, though it was Cavour's main meal, Northern Italy could unite with France against Austria and seal Italian independence for the rest of the world to see.

In a secret meeting, Cavour and Napoleon discussed the terms of their agreement, circling the town of Plombières in a horse-drawn carriage until the terms were met. France would protect Piedmont from any act of aggression from Austria. It was up to Cavour to design that opportunity.

About nine months later, in April, Cavour bulked up his troops and stood defiantly against the Austrians, rejecting an ultimatum to stand down. Provoked, Austrian troops crossed the Ticino River, invading Piedmont. Adhering to the agreement, French forces quickly traveled by rail in time for the first battle and through July nearly half a million men from all sides fought for peace, independence, and pride. By the end, France and Piedmont pushed Austria out of Northern Italy and the road was paved for Italian unification.

But the agreement was tenuous. Fearful of German support of Austria, Napoleon signed a secret treaty with Austria creating a federation of Italian states under the leadership of the pope.

France would still get Lombardy with the understanding that they would cede it to Piedmont. Cavour was deceived.

He was devastated, and to the Italians, it was a betrayal of the highest order. He stood disheartened beside King Vittorio Emanuele as he signed the treaty.

But the defeat was short-lived. Exhausted and depleted from war, Austria lost its hold on the Italian territories and shrank back, ceding Piedmont back to King Vittorio Emanuele.

Italy was now free.

Cavour retired to his study and schemed his next move. Unification would still take years, but the slate was clear for a new country, a constitution, and a democracy. Italy would now need forceful, trusting leaders to take its citizens to the global stage.

He pulled out a sheet of paper and wrote a letter. He needed Giuseppe Verdi for the parliament of a united Italy.

Chapter Twenty-Six

1861

The snowcapped Alps rose proudly against the horizon as Giuseppe's coach rumbled into Turin. The crisp, clear air revealed the mountain's sharp peaks and shallow valleys, so distinct they looked unreal, like an elaborate painted backdrop embellished for dramatic effect. It was a fitting scene for Italy's new capital.

It was a three-day journey to Turin from Busseto, the roads still pitted with ruts and mud. But the Austrian troops had long since left their posts along the highways and Giuseppe kept his passport safely tucked away in his bags, his journey uninterrupted by toll collectors. He was no longer a foreigner in his own country.

The trip gave him time to practice what he would tell Cavour: that he was unfit for anything other than music—and these days he was even unsure of that—and good luck with building a new country. Mostly he would express admiration for the man who had brought Italy together and he hoped his compliments would avoid any further discussion about joining the Parliament. Giuseppe was a scribbler, not a statesman. If the country needed another opera, Cavour knew where to find him.

Cavour stood over a gaping hole, cold wind gently puffing from the Po River, winding its way through the city. The two men stood in silence, looking into the chasm.

"This is going to be a synagogue," Cavour explained.

"It's massive," said Giuseppe, bundling his collar around his neck.

"What I like about it," said Cavour, pulling an envelope out of his hand, "is that life moves on. The world doesn't stop just for you. We keep going." He handed the envelope to Giuseppe. "You've already read this letter."

"So why are you giving it to me again?"

"In case you didn't show up. I was going to mail it to Sant'Agata."

"To make me feel guilty."

Cavour smiled, validated. "So you know it's the right thing to do."

Giuseppe shook his head, boring his gaze into the pit. "I'm a musician."

"You're a man. A person, like everyone else," said Cavour, taking the letter back from Giuseppe's hand. "What if I tossed this in?" He waved the envelope over the hole. "It would either be buried forever or someone would read it and discover that Giuseppe Verdi, world-famous composer, turned down his place in history."

"Or I could jump in and pull it out."

"That wouldn't change anything." Cavour crumpled the letter into a ball. "What do you want?"

"I'm a farmer now."

"Ha!" Cavour grabbed Giuseppe's soft hands. "With these? Come on, Giuseppe."

"It took me a long time to get where I am. I'm not going to leave it all behind."

"I'm not asking you to stop being who you are. If you want to farm, farm. If you want to write, write. I'm just asking you to consider what's brought you here. What's brought you to Turin standing next to me."

"I don't really know anymore."

"This isn't about you, Giuseppe," Cavour sighed. "You've given your life to music and this is where it's gone. If you're looking for the next step, if you're looking to be who you are and respect what you've created, I'm giving it to you."

"I'm not a politician. I'm a musician."

"You're also an Italian now. Does your life's work mean nothing to you? Because it means a lot to the rest of us." Cavour threw the crumpled letter into the pit. "Are you going to take it back and leave everything behind?"

Giuseppe looked out to the mountains. They stood stoic, unmoved for centuries, for tens of thousands of years. Defiant, but yielding, they were a part of their environment whether they asked for it or not.

"You realize I'm only going to vote for what you vote for."

Cavour smiled. "If that's what it takes."

"I trust you on this."

"Good. The feeling is mutual."

Church bells rang in the distance, reminding the city that the hour had passed and a new one approached. The peal floated over the river and Giuseppe followed its ambling path, humming to himself, an orchestra already thrumming in his mind.

Chapter Twenty-Seven

The heat in Turin's Palazzo Madama was stifling, a tiresome weight pressing on every curve and corner of the body. The sun streamed through the former palace's outlying windows, warming the assembly chamber like an oven. The red curtains and swirling crimson wallpaper climbing toward the ceiling only added to the sense that the heat would endure. Giuseppe undid the top button of his shirt and the sweat trickled down his neck in several tense beads.

The patter of the deputies bounced off the palazzo's columns in short bursts, indecipherable and coded. The mumbling old men, their snaps of laughter over coughing and sneezing, coalesced into a disagreeable din. Giuseppe took a deep breath, mollified that he was doing the right thing, and waited for the gavel. Cavour stood and took his position on the raised platform at the front of the chamber. Parliament was in session.

"Gentlemen, please take your seats," Cavour announced from the pulpit, his eyes meeting every other pair in the room. "Signor Verdi has prepared a briefing on our policy toward the arts." Murmurs of uncertainty rose from scattered pockets in the room.

Giuseppe reviewed the few notes he had written to himself. The words blurred into a ball of twisted lines and he shuffled his papers in an attempt to buy time. He didn't have a policy or a financial plan or even a list of well-funded impresarios. Giuseppe's strategy was to simply stand before his fellow deputies with a story and an appeal—it was the argument of an artist, not a statesman. He tried to meet the gaze of his colleagues, but their faces only revealed an eagerness to challenge whatever sound came from his mouth. The room went silent and Giuseppe cleared his throat, making a final appeal to himself that he was not a fraud.

He longed to be back in the familiar arms of the estate at Sant'Agata. It would be hot there, to be sure, but outside among the pungent fruit trees and rolling gardens he could breathe in air laced with the dank aroma of fresh soil and flower blooms. He could stroll the grounds absentmindedly, bathe at his leisure, and fill his time with the idle pleasantries of a successful artist. And Shakespeare. There would be ample time to linger in the Bard's wordplay and pithy observations. Sant'Agata, his own mind, was where he needed to be.

If the opera attracted the misfits of the world, then politics attracted a group cut from a similar cloth. Within hours of their first meeting, the infighting and self-interest of the Parliament emerged with little warning. Conversations polarized themselves as naturally as oil and water and tenuous bedfellows made plans to collaborate while patting the shoulder of another. Amidst disagreement on what to do about Rome and the pope, Italy's diplomatic relations with France, and questions about each state's benefits, there seemed little chance that unification was possible. It was no wonder that Austria (or any country, for that matter) had been able to keep such a firm grip on the states for so long—there was a clear understanding of who was in charge.

As prime minister of Piedmont, the leading state of the Parliament, Cavour was the obvious target of the other deputies' ire and grievances. Giuseppe felt bad for Cavour. He was a friend, and it pained him to see the man who had given so much to the country get smothered by his peers.

Cavour's health visibly waned as the initial days of Parliament dragged into weeks, and though his voice still demanded the attention of the deputies, it belied the fact that he was exhausted. The road to unification created more distance than cohesion, like dancers on their own time, each unsure of who would lead.

Giuseppe cleared his throat. "I am sure most of you have heard of me. If not for my music, then for some offense I may have inadvertently caused you or someone you know," he said drily. The room sat as indifferent as an icebox. "Whether this qualifies me to speak for all artists, I can't be sure. But I am here with only my experience to share."

"*Viva* Verdi!" someone shouted from the upper balcony. Laughter erupted throughout the chamber.

Cavour knocked his gavel on the table. "Order, please!" he shouted. The room went still.

Parliament reminded Giuseppe of his school days and its cloud of estrangement. Group work eluded him, and as he presented his case in front of grown men—as a world-famous musician, no less—his ideas still held little purchase. Reason would suggest that it wasn't personal, it was politics, yet it was hard to avoid the reality that persuasion and respect were difficult rings to grasp when egos were on the line. Instead of disinterest in Giuseppe, as was the case in school, there was an overt interest in his presence: "The world-famous opera composer, a deputy of Parliament—how quaint!" It was antipathy part and parcel.

The other deputies saw Giuseppe as nothing more than a superficial symbol. He was a distraction and they were not going to let him forget it. It was a bizarre reversal of identity, as if Giuseppe had spun full circle, wholly transformed from his childhood, but still the same to everyone else. He had lamented this fact to Giuseppina in a letter he wrote upon arrival in Turin. "You do not need to be any more or any less than what you are," she replied with other smatterings of encouragement. Giuseppe picked up the faint scent of Sant'Agata's earthy rosemary entangled in the stationery fibers and grew wistful for home. Giuseppina's words helped, but only as a salve, sinking no deeper than the iris of the eye that read them.

"So, on the question of funding the arts," Giuseppe continued, pushing his misgivings down as far as they could go, "my story is simple. I was born with little means, but I was given the gift of support from a family friend. This is something that only luck and circumstance can provide. And despite some initial fumbles, which I blame on politics, something our nascent country can address, I won the support and trust of the Austrians, who—"

"Boo!" hissed several voices.

Cavour rocked his gavel, but to little avail.

Flustered, Giuseppe's prepared speech seemingly burned up in the heat of the room and the deputies quickly lost patience with their celebrity statesman.

Giuseppe raised his voice. "We must admit it's the one thing the Austrians did right. By all means the Kingdom of Italy should—"

More admonishment came from the gallery. The gavel rocked and Giuseppe took a step back from his table, defeated.

Cavour addressed the room, still banging the gavel. "Gentlemen, consider this an export that we must protect."

A rigid voice emerged from the middle of the gallery and a diminutive man stood and waved to the other deputies for their attention.

Ruggero Settimo had fought, written, and politicked for Italian independence for most of his life. Fighting alongside the British Navy in the Mediterranean, he battled the French during the French Revolutionary Wars and governed Sicily after its revolt against King Ferdinand II. Like Cavour, he helped build the wave of nationalism that made Italy's unification possible. Elected president of the Parliament, he enjoyed a comfortable position of leverage. His eighty-one-year-old frame stood upright and stiff, aided only by a lacquered cane.

"With all due respect to the Maestro, art and music are important issues, to be sure," Settimo proclaimed with a whiff of sentiment, his voice soft. "But are we not perhaps putting the cart before the horse? Wouldn't our time, our resources, be better spent implementing laws of governance and laws of education?" Shouts came from the floor and several men stood and clapped, echoing their support. "This is not the time for artistic welfare."

Certainly not someone to defend charity for charity's sake, Giuseppe's stomach turned. His speech, such as it was, was being elegantly twisted by a skilled orator and politician. Giuseppe knew that none of the deputies failed to see the importance of arts funding. Yet the support of Settimo's belief made it clear that what was at heart wasn't the issue, but the person taking it to the table. Or the one trying to take it off, as it were.

This group was so conflicted in their views of governance that commonsense ideas were tacked up on any dartboard the Parliament could find. Improvement of an aging sewer system was pitted against the urgency of new roads, and Cavour's insistence on the railway caused continual controversy. Every idea was better or worse than the other, depending on whose hand had drafted the bill. The committees and the mutual decision-making aggravated Giuseppe. He preferred the genteel dictatorship he held over his librettists. At least one half of that endeavor ended up happy whether they liked it or not.

Cavour looked around the chamber as the murmur of the men turned to agitation. The morning heat was taking its toll and the group had barely found its bearings, its compass, or even the ocean on which it wanted to set its course.

"Gentlemen," Cavour called in appeal, trying to level the rising impatience, "may I suggest that we hold on this particular agenda item until Signor Verdi has created a more thorough report of its viability?" Though Cavour was visibly agitated, sweat dripping from his pale jowls, he held sway and the men diligently began to leave the chamber.

Giuseppe busied himself at his table, avoiding eye contact with his colleagues as they clapped each other on the back and scheduled evening plans.

"Time for lunch," Cavour pronounced gregariously, knocking his fist on Giuseppe's table.

"How can you eat in this heat?" asked Giuseppe, finally slumping back in his chair in exhaustion.

"Typically I drink first, and then..." Cavour closed Giuseppe's attaché and pushed it gently into his chest, "...I'm ready to eat."

Giuseppe pulled his glass back as the waiter approached with a carafe of wine. "None for me, thank you."

"More for me," said Cavour, handing his menu back to the waiter. "We'll have the usual, Tommaso."

"Very good, *signor*." The waiter set the carafe on a side table. "I'll be back with your first course shortly."

"I can't eat in this heat."

"It might help you relax." Cavour handed Giuseppe his glass. "I'm no doctor, but this should help."

Giuseppe grasped the crystal stem with the tips of his fingers and swirled it. "Parliament is more contentious than I anticipated. I thought we knew what we were doing."

"There's an order to all of it. We're just making our plays," said Cavour, grinning. "I'm used to the long fight."

Giuseppe took a sip of wine and pushed the glass back to Cavour. "I don't know how the Romans did it."

"It was a different time. Our politics have evolved since then."

"What, to get nothing done?"

Cavour laughed. "That's one way to look at it." He took large gulp and pushed the glass aside, eying the red liquid. "We're like a group of orphans trying to start our own family. That we're even in the same room is a miracle."

Giuseppe nodded and reached absently for Cavour's glass.

"I think we should order you your own," said Cavour.

"How about we share? *Esprit de corps*."

"Capital idea." Cavour stretched his arm toward the side table when his body suddenly slipped from the chair, sending him crashing to the floor. His head slammed on the hard tile with a flat bang.

Giuseppe leapt from his seat and thrust his arms under Cavour's. He strained, lifting his dense frame against the wall. "Are you all right?"

"Fine, fine," exhaled Cavour, catching his breath. "This heat is making me a bit punchy." He closed his eyes and got to one knee and slid into his chair. He rolled up his sleeves. Black and blue gashes lined the inside of his forearm.

Giuseppe winced, trying to hide his disgust. "Have you been going to a barber?"

Cavour rubbed the back of his head and took a deep pull of wine. "Under the advisement of my doctor," he said, running a chubby finger along the edge of a small abscess. "This one got infected recently. They use leeches to clean it. Too early to tell if it's working, though."

"That's archaic."

"Well, I don't have a lot of time for much else. Being bled out will have to do for now."

The waiter returned, placing a plate of *lepre al civet*—rabbit stew—between them.

Cavour's face brightened. "I don't want to talk about it, frankly," he said, dipping a silver spoon into the steaming broth. "Giuseppe, take the time to rewrite the arts proposal."

Giuseppe drummed his fingers on the table, caught off guard by the change of topic. "I don't know what else to say. The benefits of state funds are obvious. Where would the opera be if it weren't for the Austrians, honestly?"

"Says the famous musician." Cavour tore into a piece of bread. "Not everyone is in your position or talent," he said between bites. "You'll have to make your case some other way. Think of your presentation like a music score. Every word and phrase has its meaning."

"This is nothing like music, believe me. I'm stating the obvious."

"Take advantage of this time off. Let your mind clear." Cavour filled Giuseppe's bowl with stew. "You have my support. You know that, right?"

"I know." Giuseppe took a mouthful of soup and a sip of wine. His eyes widened. "Bravo."

"I told you," said Cavour. "It would have been uncivilized to not have any lunch."

Giuseppe smiled appreciatively. "Are you sure you're all right?" he asked, waving a finger at Cavour's swollen arms.

"Besides this heat, I've never felt better."

Giuseppe swallowed and tried to think of something to talk about other than politics or health. He watched his friend take another cumbersome bite of food and refill his glass to the brim.

Giuseppina crossed her arms and leaned against the doorframe, watching Giuseppe write. Once every minute Giuseppe would steal a gaze out the open window, where a lush bloom of white azaleas crowded into view, their perfumed scent wafting into the study on warm puffs of air.

His attention to work never ceased to amaze Giuseppina, and although she considered herself a careerist of sorts, she cherished these days spent reading and napping or giving the infrequent voice lesson to a student from the village. She enjoyed writing the occasional poem, but those days of inspired reflection were few and far between. It was reassuring to have Giuseppe at Sant'Agata and for now that was enough. He was a reminder that her life had not stopped.

"It's so hot in my room," she said, pinning her hair up in a bun. She kissed his cheek. "I think you have more shade in your room than mine."

"That's true. I planted the trees myself."

Giuseppina slapped him on the head with a playful tap. "You would."

"Sunlight makes my little flower happy," said Giuseppe, returning the kiss to Giuseppina. "I only had you in mind."

Giuseppina lifted the hem of her skirt and settled herself in Giuseppe's lap. "And as thanks, you now have the pleasure of my company." She eyed the scattered paper, mostly blank, on Giuseppe's desk. "This doesn't look like the work of a man who has been in his study all morning," she said jokingly. "Are you not doing your assignments, Signor Verdi?"

Giuseppe pushed the paper aside. "You're nosy."

"Well, if you are going to be home so briefly, I'd prefer you wasted your time with me and not on yourself."

Giuseppe sighed and stood, pushing Giuseppina off his lap.

"Too heavy?" she pouted.

Giuseppe leaned over and touched his toes. He took a deep breath and sighed.

"What is it?" she asked.

"Cavour barely made it through dinner the other night."

"What do you mean?"

"He's exhausted." Giuseppe nodded toward the papers littering his desk. "I was starting a memorial, some sort of speech for him."

"That's morbid, even for you."

Giuseppe shrugged. "I'd rather do that than work on this arts policy."

"Did he say anything to you?"

"We talked about Parliament and what I need to do."

"No, how he's feeling."

"Other than defending going to a barber, nothing." Giuseppe ambled toward the window. "For someone so perceptive, he hardly seems to know himself." He leaned over the windowsill and took in the azaleas. "Anyway," he said, picking a flower and placing it gently behind Giuseppina's ear, "I thought you came here to see me, not spy on me."

Giuseppina took Giuseppe by the hand and raised it toward her ear, squeezing his hand gently. Counting softly, she extended a foot and led him in a waltz. They paced the room to a silent tune, their bodies turning in threes. "It's so good to have you home."

"It's all I've been thinking about." Giuseppe took the lead, guiding them into the hall. "Come back with me to Turin."

"Mm," Giuseppina pondered. "There would be so much to take care of before I left."

"Well, that's where I'll be."

"It's hot in Turin, too." Giuseppina laid her head on Giuseppe's shoulder. "What about France?"

"I have Parliament."

"When you're done, silly. Who do you take me for?"

"It will be fall by the time we're ready to leave."

Giuseppina ran her hands through Giuseppe's hair and tugged as though testing its strength. "We can spend Christmas there."

Their waltz took them into the kitchen. Giuseppina pushed Giuseppe back and bowed. "Sit down," she said abruptly, pulling out a chair. "I'll make lunch."

"How did I get so lucky?"

Giuseppina brought a pitcher of water and poured Giuseppe a glass. "Luck has nothing to do with it."

Giuseppe took a long drink of water and drummed his fingers on the table. "Marry me."

"What?"

"If you want to."

Giuseppina sat next to Giuseppe, taking his hands in hers. "Do we want to?"

"Yes."

"Why now?"

"I don't want to lose you."

"You're silly."

Giuseppe refilled his glass. "I know."

"When should we do it?" asked Giuseppina, pulling the pin out of her bun. Her hair cascaded around her face.

"When I get back from Turin."

She smiled, the edges of her lips meeting the crinkle of her eyes. "And what should I do in the meantime?"

Giuseppe ran his fingers through her hair. "Just be here when I get back."

It took several days for Giuseppe's coach to rumble over the ancient Roman roads on the journey from Sant'Agata to Turin. On the final stretch into the city, Giuseppe finally began to work on his speech for the arts proposal. Sant'Agata was the respite he needed from his duties in Parliament. So much so that the distance from his responsibilities gave him little imperative to do any work. It was a challenge to build enthusiasm for a policy he knew was on the back of everyone's mind.

As he turned into the city gates, a messenger riding a horse galloped alongside the coach and handed Giuseppe an urgent letter from Cavour. Sealed with red wax, the note was terse and shaky, written in Cavour's hand: *"Please see me before anything else."* Giuseppe instructed his coachman to take him to Cavour's apartment on Via Po.

Giuseppe trudged up the apartment steps, the marble solid under his feet. The stairwell was one of the few cool places in Turin and Giuseppe wished he could sit on the stairs until Parliament figured everything out in his absence.

The maid led Giuseppe into a sparsely furnished parlor that looked out on the western portion of the city. Cavour sat slumped in a tufted armchair, his body spilling over like an overgrown plant. Giuseppe sat across from his friend on a leather loveseat and extended his legs, still stiff from the long journey. The immense fire Cavour carried within was nowhere distinguished in his eyes.

"I didn't consider it when I first moved in, but this apartment has a tremendous view of the Torino Porta Nuova."

Giuseppe looked out the window, where Turin's train station sat half built.

"We'll catch up with the rest of Europe sure enough. Mark my words." Cavour coughed into a handkerchief and groaned. "Most of the deputies already know, Giuseppe. I sent letters to everyone who stayed in Turin over the break."

"Already know what?" Giuseppe asked, knowing the answer.

"That I'm sick."

The maid reappeared with a tray of brandy. Cavour leaned in to pour a drink, revealing a face that was gaunt and pale, given over to dehydration and exhaustion. "I've really taken a turn for the worse over the last few days."

Giuseppe put his hand on his friend's back, helping him pour his drink. He thought about telling him he knew—that he knew how sick he was and that he regretted not saying more when he had the opportunity.

Instead, Giuseppe just nodded and smiled reassuringly. "What are we going to do without you?"

"I know I'm supposed to say that you'll be fine. But that's not true. It won't be easy." He winked. "But you knew that already."

"I'm never going to pass this bill without you."

"Maybe that will give me something to live for," Cavour joked. The blanket covering his legs fell from his lap revealing a smattering of swollen lesions. Cavour shooed Giuseppe away as he tried to lay the blanket back across his legs. "You're not thinking about quitting, are you?"

Giuseppe looked out the window at the train station and the Mole Antonelliana, diligently creeping up into the sky. "You've done all this," he mused, looking out on Turin's skyline.

Cavour laughed. "If my colleagues gave me half the credit I deserve, then they wouldn't have named the street it sits on Vittorio Emanuele Boulevard."

"Eh," said Giuseppe, pouring himself a drink, "the meaning will get lost in time."

"I don't want you to quit. It's not in you, Giuseppe."

"I suppose it's just another three and a half years," said Giuseppe sarcastically.

"I didn't put you in this position to pass laws. That would be unrealistic. I also didn't put you in to fail. Just having the title is enough. It's so the country understands what we stand for."

The room began to go dark as the sun set over Turin. Giuseppe struck a match and lit a candle on the table between them. "How am I going to vote without you there?"

Cavour stared at his feet and vainly tried to lift them. "Think about what you would want, Giuseppe. And don't look back." He wheezed and sat himself upright in the chair. "Now, tell me about your next opera."

"I have nothing planned."

"Well, you'd better," Cavour chuckled maniacally, "because they are going to eat you alive in Parliament."

Giuseppe laughed out loud. He felt a hint of cool air from some corner of the room and he relaxed, admiring the view.

On the day Giuseppe was to present his proposal to Parliament, he received a letter from Giuseppina: "Our next trip shall not be to France, but rather to Russia. Think of it as a honeymoon."

Enclosed with her letter was a note from the tenor Enrico Tamberlick. Writing on behalf of the director of the Russian Imperial Theatre, he offered generous terms for any opera of Giuseppe's choosing. The details were brief but explicit, and between the creative license and the pay, Giuseppe felt like himself once again, back in a world where he could pull the strings.

It was a welcome letter, one that Giuseppe luckily happened to pick up on his way to Parliament. If all went awry in session, he now had an out, a definitive plan to move forward. Like Macbeth, fate was working in his favor—at least for now. It was refreshing that Giuseppina would be amenable to such an arduous trip and one so cold. A creature of habit, she could be painfully predictable, so her enthusiasm could not have been better timed.

The return to Parliament proved expectedly to be a sad day. The deputies took a moment of silence for Cavour, paying their respects with short tributes and remembrances. But business was to be attended to and Giuseppe was given the floor, as promised.

Giuseppe's presentation was no different from the first, his appeal heartfelt but without a plan. Isn't that what everyone else was for? To write the details? Worse than being followed by argument or jeers, his speech concluded with a quick knock of the gavel and the next item on the agenda. Giuseppe's bill went silently to pasture.

Without Cavour by his side, Giuseppe found himself outcast and pleasantly alone in Parliament. He took his seat and quietly absorbed the chance to fall back into his former life. He would not be missed and it was a familiar, pleasurable feeling.

That evening he boarded a coach back to the estate at Sant'Agata, where he and Giuseppina, after twelve years together, married upon his return.

"What are you doing?" Giuseppe chided, lifting a heap of winter pants and skirts from the floor. He examined them like a bin of questionable vegetables.

"St. Petersburg gets to twenty-two degrees below zero," said Giuseppina with a look of horror and wonder. She tossed a thick stack of furs at the end of the bed. "You should get your pants lined as well."

Sant'Agata continued to be in the throes of a deep summer heat and staring at the wool and fur made Giuseppe nauseous. Considering the oppressive summer, freezing to death didn't seem half bad.

"Are you sure you need this many?" he asked.

A tailor dressed in a dark suit appeared at the bedroom door, a sheen of sweat upon his forehead.

"It's better safe than sorry," said Giuseppina, handing the man a bundle of skirts.

Giuseppe shook his head and paced the room. "I can't think about that right now. I have an opera to write."

Giuseppina rolled her eyes. "Suit yourself," she said, collapsing on the bed.

A chorus of men's voices singing "La donna é mobile" drifted through the bedroom window. Giuseppe peered down into the courtyard and waved.

"What are they doing down there?" Giuseppina asked.

"I've got my own preparations to make." Giuseppe closed the curtains. "I've started the crush early so we have enough wine for our trip."

"I thought you had an opera to write," said Giuseppina, closing her eyes, drifting into an afternoon nap.

"You'll thank me later," said Giuseppe, singing to himself.

In early September, Giuseppe and Giuseppina boarded a coach in Sant'Agata and traveled to Berlin, where they caught a train to St. Petersburg. Lumbering north, the temperature in the train dropped at an alarming rate, the chill steadily coercing itself through every panel and window of their private compartment.

Giuseppina knitted a wool cap, the needles pinging in time with the clack of the train.

"How are you able to do that in this cold?" asked Giuseppe, rubbing his hands vigorously against his thighs.

Giuseppina lifted the hem of her skirt, revealing the thick pelt lining its underside. "Maybe next time you'll listen to me."

Giuseppe grunted begrudgingly and with both hands stiff from the cold, poured a glass of wine. An icy mixture edged itself out of the end of the bottle, falling into the glass with a plop.

Suddenly, the train hit a curve, the car lifting on one side like a boat in choppy waters. Giuseppe bounced off the compartment wall and landed with a crash. He quickly scrambled to his feet, deftly collecting a dozen errant wine bottles rolling precariously on the floor.

Giuseppina stifled a laugh. The wine had frozen through and Giuseppe had spent the morning sitting on a rotating batch of bottles in an attempt to thaw them back to form.

Giuseppe carefully placed the wine on his seat and covered them with a towel. "It's not funny," he admonished. "They could have all broken." Like a frenzied hen on her eggs, Giuseppe settled back into his nest, exhausted.

He cautiously handed Giuseppina her glass. She looked out the train window on a vista of vast, perpetual white. "It's hard to believe we exist in all of this," she said, taking a protracted sip. "But this helps." She smiled and put her hand on Giuseppe's knee. "You're helping."

Despite the frigid conditions on the train, Giuseppe was able to put the finishing touches on *La forza del destino*, the opera he had chosen for the Russian Imperial Theatre. Adapted from a Spanish drama, the opera told the story of a young nobleman and his lover, torn apart by her father and brother. He had initially read the story with disinterest, but found himself moved to tears by the end, the sister stabbed in the heart by her brother, revenge for the grief her affair caused their father. It would be a devastating performance for his Russian premiere. A dramatic crowd pleaser, to be sure.

Satisfied, Giuseppe looked out at the bleak landscape, confident he had found a tragedy suitable for his new audience. He wiped his nose on the back of his hand and brought his jacket tight around his neck.

"I knew you would catch cold," said Giuseppina, placing the knitted cap on his head. "You should have listened to me."

"I'll be back to myself in no time."

"I have no doubt," said Giuseppina, bemused.

The reception that the Verdis received in St. Petersburg warmed them from any chill that survived the train journey from Berlin. Barely a bag in hand, they were immediately but carefully whisked from the station to a whirlwind tour of the intellectual parlors and salons scattered throughout the city. Russian statesmen, countesses, writers, and military generals showered Giuseppe with praise that was as flattering as it was distressing.

Their appreciation, though well meaning, made Giuseppe wane with every handshake and compliment. By the third salon Giuseppe felt a definite illness take hold. He grasped the banister of the staircase to catch his breath, the murmuring of admirers in the parlor causing flashes of hot and cold.

"I don't think I can make it to the premiere tonight," he confided to Giuseppina.

She rubbed his back. "You can always blame it on me."

Giuseppe smiled over the exhaustion. "I might. No one would ever fault my beautiful wife."

Yet despite feeling unwell, Giuseppe couldn't see himself letting down these well-meaning people. He saw no difference in them from his fellow Italians, whom he would never deny an audience. This was the price to be paid for celebrity.

That evening, the premiere of *La forza del destino* caught the longing passions of the Russian audience and they cheered not only for the opera itself, but also for the man who wrote it and the hope and love he had stoked in their souls. It was by any measure a rousing success.

After the performance, the tsar and empress invited Giuseppe and Giuseppina into their private box at the Imperial Theatre. Giuseppina wiped Giuseppe's brow with a damp handkerchief in an attempt to conceal the impending illness. They opened the heavy curtains from the box's antechamber.

"Giuseppe Verdi!" Tsar Alexander II cried with unexpected familiarity. Lit by nearly two hundred candles, the private balcony was gilded in thick gold molding and crimson panels made of silk. Seats for two dozen guests looked out on a privileged view of the stately theatre and its stage.

The tsar was popular among the Russian people, and having recently emancipated the Russian serfs he was viewed as a reformer, bringing Russia closer to the rising social values of Europe.

Dressed in formal military wear, a blue sash the color of a robin's egg crossing his broad chest, he extended a rough hand, easing the formality of the circumstances.

"What an honor it is to have you here," he said, clasping Giuseppe's back and kissing Giuseppina's hand. The tsar beamed and took a deep breath, savoring the moment. He gently hooked the empress in the crook of his arm. "My lovely wife, Empress Alexandrovna," he said with sincerity.

A German by blood, Empress Maria Alexandrovna had moved to Russia when she was just sixteen years old. She had spent her life cultivating an air of gentility and worldliness that she hoped would bridge the cultural divide between her adopted country and the rest of the world. "I echo my husband's sentiment. This is truly an honor."

Giuseppe and Giuseppina blushed at the praise.

"You both speak French so well," said Giuseppina with deliberate pronunciation.

"I have my wife to thank for that," the tsar smiled.

"My mother was quite serious about my education," said the empress, taking a seat in an ornate velvet wing chair and adjusting the cuff of her mauve gloves. "Not only does it allow me an audience with you, but it keeps me interesting to my husband as well."

Giuseppina laughed. "I'll have to take notes."

"Please sit," implored the tsar as a servant presented a tray of caviar and crackers.

"I understand you are an opera singer," the tsar said to Giuseppina, reaching for the tray and placing it between them.

"I was," said Giuseppina. "But now," she scooped a dollop of caviar on her plate, "well now, I teach. Sometimes."

Giuseppe managed to sit up straight, adeptly feigning interest in the conversation. "She sang in Paris and Vienna while still a teenager. Quite remarkable, really."

"It's just so hard on the body." Giuseppina covered her mouth, talking between bites. "I know that sounds ridiculous. There are so many talented singers. I had my run." She took Giuseppe's hand. "Now we travel and work on our home."

"Please, Monsieur Verdi, try the caviar," said the empress, preparing a plate.

Giuseppe's stomach turned at the sight of the black orbs.

"It's from the Caspian Sea," said the tsar. "Much better than the stuff from the Baltic. Unfortunately for us."

"I'll be leaving for Crimea shortly," said the empress. "These Russian winters are simply too harsh for me. I should come to Italy."

"Oh, you must!" said Giuseppina.

"Did you know that the Po River produces some of the world's finest caviar?" asked the tsar, heaping more of the fish eggs in front of Giuseppe.

"Really? How interesting." Giuseppe tilted his head back, trying to keep the briny scent from getting too close.

"Oh, yes. There was a war over it. Caviar should be the pride of Italy as far as I'm concerned."

"I'll keep that in mind," said Giuseppe, ebbing.

"I hope you do come to Italy," said Giuseppina, trying to divert the tsar's attention from Giuseppe. "It would give you a chance to practice your French as well." She pulled the plate of caviar out of Giuseppe's olfactory range.

"I am sure that is changing, no?" asked the tsar, turning back to Giuseppe, undeterred. "With the unification."

Giuseppe managed a genteel smile, relieved that the caviar was away from sight. "We have been talking about standardizing the language, it's true."

"It's an issue we share as well in Russia," said the empress. "It's one of the greatest challenges for our stability."

"The world is quickly coming together, isn't it?" suggested Giuseppina.

"Your music must have had quite an impact with the unification efforts, I am sure," said the empress.

"I suppose," Giuseppe replied quickly, hoping to avoid any further conversation on the matter.

"My husband is being modest," said Giuseppina. "It's earned him a seat in Parliament."

"Really?" the empress said, impressed. "You're a man of many talents, Monsieur Verdi."

The tsar shook his head. "A government like that would not work here in Russia. Too many different people."

"Oh, it's no different in Italy," said Giuseppe, compelled to express an opinion despite the bubbling in his stomach.

The empress smiled. "You must be quite the diplomat, then. Your colleagues should be in awe."

Giuseppina managed a cautionary glance toward her husband.

"On occasion," said Giuseppe, taking Giuseppina's cue.

"You have not tried the caviar," observed the tsar, visibly disappointed.

"Oh yes, of course," said Giuseppe, cautiously reaching for the plate. Anticipating the inevitable sickness that would come, he casually reached into the inner pocket of his overcoat. "Before I forget, I want to present you with this," he said, pulling out a bottle of wine. "From my vineyard to you."

The tsar was overjoyed. "Italian wine from Monsieur Verdi!"

"How lovely," replied the empress.

"My pleasure," said Giuseppe, placing his plate aside, relieved by the distraction.

"Now, if you would indulge us," said the empress, "I would love to hear about the writing process of the opera you graced us with tonight."

A wave of exhaustion poured over Giuseppe, the sweat pouring down his back as he built up the courage to have a conversation about opera. Quietly, an assistant quickly padded into the room and whispered into the tsar's ear.

"I am terribly sorry," said the tsar, "but we must excuse ourselves."

The empress looked to her husband for explanation, smiling apologetically. "Oh, how tragic. I'm so sorry we couldn't talk longer."

"Not at all," said Giuseppina, rising from her seat.

Giuseppe bowed and the tsar and empress left the box, leaving them completely alone for the first time since arriving in Russia.

"Let's get you back to the hotel," said Giuseppina. "I think you've done your duty here. Fate was on your side."

Giuseppe took a deep breath and grabbed Giuseppina's arm to steady himself. "I think you were right about going to France, originally."

"Why is that?"

"They're much too nice here in Russia. In France they wouldn't have been bothered if I ever made an appearance."

"Oh, they would. You would just read about it in the papers."

"My wife, the realist," said Giuseppe, taking her arm and stumbling gratefully to the exit.

Giuseppe and Giuseppina were in Paris by Christmas, stopping at Sant'Agata to tend to the gardens and vineyard. Although Giuseppe had been eager to return to France, he already missed the tranquility of the estate. It was rest and it was life away from the opera.

"It will give you something to look forward to in the spring," said Giuseppina.

Giuseppe longed to be at rest. As a creature of habit, like most after a certain age, he wanted to be in the calm of home. The unbridled enthusiasm he had received in St. Petersburg reminded Giuseppe of the passion he instilled in his fellow Italians. Had he forgotten that? Or was it just harder to see, like missing the forest for the trees?

"I've been skipping on my duties in Parliament," said Giuseppe, suddenly remorseful, while he and Giuseppina took an evening stroll along the Seine.

"Let them think what they're going to think," said Giuseppina. "You said yourself, your vote is lost without Cavour."

"You don't understand."

"Giuseppe, we were unmarried for years. Do you think that was easy for me?"

"What does that have to do with anything?"

"People's judgment didn't keep me from doing what I wanted. And I wanted to be with you." Giuseppina nestled her head into Giuseppe's shoulder and looked out on the river, the light from the streetlamps reflecting off the water. "I'm glad you finally listened to me," she said, running her fingers along the side of his pants.

"It's too warm here for fur-lined anything."

"Well, I'm happy you took my advice."

They continued their walk, laughing about the whirlwind trip to Russia and their plans for Christmas dinner.

It wasn't until he went to bed that Giuseppe realized he hadn't been thinking about Parliament or his next opera—nor did he want to. He was happier, for now, without it.

Chapter Twenty-Eight

1870

Giuseppe walked up the narrow staircase to the steamer's top deck and leaned against the polished guardrail, catching his breath from the shaky climb. In the reflection off the brass fixtures securing the wood beam, he could see the ship's twin smokestacks spewing boiler steam upward, the clouds of black soot and vapor streaming the sky like food coloring in water. A salty breeze floated across the deck, gently tossing the errant strands of a woman's hair or flipping the pages of an open book, abandoned on a table.

"Would you like a recliner, Signor Verdi?" invited a steward, quickly wiping the striped red-and-white canvas of a chaise lounge with a brush.

"I'd never get out of that thing," said Giuseppe, poking at it with his cane. He pointed to a lone wicker chaise by a cache of life preservers. "How about that one?"

"Very good, sir." The steward handed Giuseppe a soft woolen blanket tucked implausibly inside his double-breasted blazer and motioned him toward the chaise, positioning it toward the sea.

"And one for my wife," said Giuseppe, sitting carefully on the creaky lounge chair.

He took appraisal of his corner of the deck and leaned back, placing the wool blanket behind his head. He undid his coat button and finally took a breath, inhaling the warm air of the Ligurian Sea. The morning fog lingered to the east, mercifully keeping the Mediterranean sun at bay. Giuseppina napped downstairs, catching up on her sleep. She had spent a restless week preparing for their trip: hemming shirts and pants, arranging food, and packing small plants from the estate gardens to give as gifts. There were five trunks between the two of them, Giuseppe having unceremoniously discarded the contents of three others the night before. "We're not going to war," he said as the footmen quickly loaded their coach in the driveway at Sant'Agata. They were on their way to Paris, where the set pieces for Giuseppe's latest opera, *Aida*, were being held at customs.

It was a cool September day, the preludes to fall mixing judiciously with the remnants of summer, and the ocean beat calmly against the hull of the boat with the rhythm of a drum. Giuseppe looked out at the coastline dotted with cliffside homes, jagged, as if cut from the rock itself. The ocean felt like the edge of the world, a place where one could jump safely off the earth into their own. Giuseppe considered a life along the coast, a place where he could have one foot in and one foot out—a primer for escape. A melody entered his head and he tapped his knee, hopeful that Giuseppina would emerge rested, no longer angry for leaving their luggage at the front door.

In March, Giuseppe had been to Paris at the behest of Camille du Locle, co-director for the Paris Opéra-Comique, who sought Giuseppe for a new production. Though he liked du Locle, Giuseppe had grown tired of the French theatre's laissez-faire attitude toward his operas, their eye for detail in the productions increasingly lacking. And he detested a culture that invited the opinion of everyone from the actors to the stage manager. He had told du Locle as much, and though he had thick skin for the critiques of the Parisian audience and critics, Giuseppe was tired of having his music misrepresented. There were always too many cooks in the kitchen.

A few months after his explicit note, Giuseppe was surprised to receive a return letter from du Locle offering a large sum for an original work at the newly opened Cairo Opera House in Egypt. It was almost too considerate—artistically and monetarily—to pass up. Giuseppe could hire the librettist, arrange his own conductor, and have the publishing rights for every performance outside of Cairo—all for the princely sum of 150,000 francs.

After *La forza del destino* in Russia, Giuseppe had committed himself to his estate and his marriage—everything he loved outside of the opera. But after nearly ten years, the request for *Aida* had come at the right time. Being sufficiently recharged and inspired, Giuseppe took the offer with his sights on emboldening his nest egg and retiring.

But now, this journey to Paris was his penance and Giuseppe was paying for whatever artistic and monetary freedom *Aida* could afford him.

In July, France had declared war on Prussia, hoping to break the consolidation of the German states. By August, Napoleon III was captured by the Germans. And just days before Giuseppe and Giuseppina left for France, the French government established the Third Republic, resetting their fight against the Kingdom of Prussia. News reports wrote in terrified awe of Germany's superior military technology, an unstoppable machine instilling fear and intimidation throughout France.

With its resources severely restricted, Paris, where *Aida*'s set pieces were built, was far too embroiled in the hurdles of war to release the artwork to Cairo. Yet the city was still open and, undeterred, Giuseppe was determined to get the art to the theatre in time for the premiere. *Aida* was the start of his retirement and he was loath to let it go.

"Good morning, sleepyhead."

Expecting Giuseppina's fingers gently upon his arm, Giuseppe awoke to the pounding of furry paws and a wet tongue on his nose.

"Violet!" yelled Giuseppina through stifled laughter, pulling a small brown terrier off of Giuseppe. She whipped the dog up into her arms and nuzzled her face. "You mean, cute little thing."

The steward returned with another wicker lounge. "Signora Verdi," he said, extending his arm toward the chair.

Giuseppina raised her eyebrows and settled next to Giuseppe, setting the dog in his lap.

"Who is this?" asked Giuseppe, scratching behind the dog's ears.

"I ran into a few of Clarina Maffei's friends." Giuseppina nodded toward a group of men gathered at the far end of the deck. "This cute little ball of fur is the duke's," she said, waving her hand absently. "I guess he couldn't resist making a beautiful woman happy." She took the dog back from Giuseppe. "They're going to Marseille to see the Palais Longchamp."

"Dilettantes," muttered Giuseppe. "Don't they know there's a war?"

Giuseppina hit him on the arm. "You should talk." She settled in with the dog, stroking its head with the full of her hand. "You may have met the duke, actually."

"There are too many dukes and governors and all of that other foolishness running around," said Giuseppe, covering his eyes with his arm.

Giuseppina leaned toward Giuseppe. "They're saying that the Papal States have fallen," she whispered.

Giuseppe whipped his hand from his face and the dog leapt back, nearly clobbered by his arm. "What?"

"The Italian army took Rome a few days ago. The pope has secured himself in the Vatican."

Protected by France, the Papal States were the last holdout for a truly unified Italy. With Prussia forcing France to fight at home, the French had no choice but to extract their troops, leaving Rome and the pope vulnerable to attack by the Italian army. Seizing the opportunity, the Italians took Rome, nearly unopposed.

Giuseppe sighed. "Italy is completely united and I'm on a boat to France."

Giuseppina shook her head. "And where else should you be?"

"Home. In Italy. I am a member of Parliament, Giuseppina."

"They won't miss you," she replied, teasing. "You're the great Italian opera composer, Giuseppe Verdi. You are where you're supposed to be."

Giuseppe started to protest, but thought the better of it, seeing Giuseppina in such a good humor. Battles are won as much as they are lost.

When they arrived in Marseille, the port was abuzz with confusion. Du Locle met them at the bottom of the ramp, taking them to a nearby café where they waited for their trunks to be unloaded from the ship.

Settled at the table, Giuseppe took a grateful drink of water and looked around the crowds. "What's happening here?"

"The Prussians have made their approach on Paris."

Giuseppina grabbed du Locle's arm. "Good lord, already?"

"The ramparts are holding them off for now," said du Locle unconvincingly, sipping his coffee, his eyes cast downward.

"Have you heard about the pope?" asked Giuseppe.

Du Locle nodded, pouring Giuseppe the last of the coffee from the silver carafe. "Europe is going to look a lot different very soon."

The next morning, a hot air balloon precariously floated into Marseille like a dandelion flower righting itself in the wind. A French army officer wearily climbed out of the basket, his skin blotchy and red from the sun. Several young men escorted him under the shade of an oak tree, where he was given water and wine. An old woman carefully cleaned his face of soot and grime with a warm towel.

After a quarter of an hour, the officer recovered from his air journey and assumed an official stance addressing the crowd that had gathered around him. Paris had been captured by the Kingdom of Prussia. The city was now closed indefinitely.

Audible gasps came from the crowd and shouts of "*Vive* la France!" came from the young men who stood next to the officer. From the edge of the crowd, Giuseppe turned and walked back toward the café.

"Where are you going?" shouted Giuseppina. She looked to du Locle, who shrugged and chased after him.

Giuseppe returned a few minutes later, du Locle in tow, with two return tickets to Italy in hand. "There's nothing left for us to do here."

"Please, you came all this way. They may come to an armistice sooner than we think," said du Locle, in an attempt to convince Giuseppe to stay.

But Giuseppe was anxious to get home, impatient with the whims and conspiracies of the world. *Aida* and retirement now had to wait.

"I have a life to lead," he said, ordering another coffee from the café and thinking of the cool grounds of Sant'Agata.

After four months of fighting, peace finally came to Paris. In the wake of the punishing Prussian siege, the Parisians emerged from the blockade starving and homeless, their lives shattered. Like Italy, the Kingdom of Prussia was now consolidated under a single flag. The German Empire was now one of the greatest powers in Europe.

Giuseppe and Giuseppina had enjoyed a mild winter at Sant'Agata after returning from Marseille. The orange trees blossomed and gave fruit, and the roses persevered through chill, their bare stems protected with sheets Giuseppe had lovingly laid over their branches to prevent the ravages of frost. But more than anything else, Giuseppe took the time to enjoy life with Giuseppina, away from the demands of writing and the frustrations of politics.

Though a few years younger than Giuseppe, Giuseppina was visibly aged, her shoulders stooped and her gait slow. She complained of her sore hips, which Giuseppe stretched and massaged to help relieve the pain. They took frequent trips to the spas at Montecatini Terme, relaxing in the natural spring water and enjoying their time with the other guests.

While Sant'Agata's plants slumbered, the next harvest delayed until spring, Giuseppe and Giuseppina lingered in their unadulterated time together. With Italy fully united and Rome officially installed as the capital, Giuseppe was finally able to breathe a sigh of relief that his time as a legislator could extend no further. Italy was on its way, and his work, his music, would sustain his legacy.

In February, Giuseppe received a letter from du Locle: *Aida*'s set pieces had survived the invasion and would be sent immediately from Paris to Cairo. Giuseppe had more than six months to prepare for the premiere at the end of the year.

In the spring, word came from Ricordi, his publisher, that Alessandro Manzoni, the activist and novelist, had died. Recalling the writer's profound influence and the lively conversations his work had spurned in Andrea Maffei, Giuseppe was compelled to make the trip to Milan for the memorial. It would give him a chance to pay his respects as well as start a conversation with La Scala regarding the Italian premiere of *Aida*. It had been over twenty-five years since Giuseppe had allowed one of his works to be performed at the opera house and he was in the spirit to let bygones be bygones.

In the days leading up to the memorial, Giuseppe and Giuseppina stayed with Andrea in his apartment in Milan. Over a late dinner, Andrea showed Giuseppe a set of half-finished translations he had been working on with Manzoni. The fervor and passion in the writing reminded Giuseppe of the longing he felt in reading *The Betrothed* for the first time. The novel's jab at the Austrians and its meditations on suffering influenced Giuseppe to write again and he pained to bring those sentiments to life.

"I'm sorry," said Giuseppe later that night, helping Giuseppina into bed. "I'd be remiss if I didn't honor Manzoni in some way."

"I would never expect you to stop writing."

"I want to do something lasting."

CHAPTER TWENTY-EIGHT

"You've loved me," said Giuseppina, running her hand along his cheek.

Giuseppe blew out the candle by her bedside table. "Then I can rest well," he said, curling up by her side.

Giuseppe soon found himself back to the grindstone, preparing for the Cairo premiere of *Aida* and writing the *Messa da Requiem* in honor of Manzoni—a relief from the rote detail of a fully produced opera. He worked late into the evenings, his mind clear from obligations with Parliament and focused solely on the music.

Finally, on Christmas Eve, *Aida* premiered at the Cairo Opera House to a packed and enthusiastic theatre. It was an opulent affair, the ornate sets and lush costumes gleaming against the brand-new stage. But it was a premiere that Giuseppe did not attend. The trip too far and too cumbersome, he could not imagine taking another journey west. And with Giuseppina unable to travel such a distance, he used his celebrity power to remain at the estate with little consequence.

Aida told the story of Radames, a captain in the Egyptian army, and his love for Aida, the daughter of the king of Ethiopia and a slave to the pharaoh's daughter. Radames was chosen to lead the army against the Ethiopians, and during his absence, the pharaoh's daughter discovers that Aida has fallen in love with Radames. She becomes enraged with jealousy, punishing Aida. Radames returns victorious, with Aida's father, the king of Ethiopia, in tow. However, the king tricks Radames into revealing the position of his troops, sabotaging the war. As punishment, Radames is thrown into a tomb to die. Aida lies in the grave, hoping to spend eternity together with her true love.

The audience, mostly dignitaries, royalty, and politicians, did not restrain their ardor for the story and the love between

Aida and Radames—two lovers held back like Romeo and Juliet—cheering again and again, despite the absence of the opera's composer.

When word came back that the Cairo premiere was attended only by the Egyptian elite, Giuseppe was despondent and he doubled his efforts to produce a version of *Aida* worthy of the Italian people—no matter their social standing.

When the opera finally premiered at La Scala, the sensation for Verdi struck the country once again—the prodigal son returned. Among his peers, the Italian people, and perhaps now even to himself, Giuseppe was second to none. With another creative endeavor behind him, he found comfort that he could truly give something everlasting to the opera and Italy.

Chapter Twenty-Nine

1885

"You're walking too fast," said Giuseppina, shuffling behind Giuseppe, her right hand lifting the hem of her skirt out of the mud.

"So sorry, my love," said Giuseppe, reaching back with his cane.

Giuseppina grabbed the brass tip and pulled herself toward Giuseppe's hand, lifting her feet onto the curb. "This is exciting, I know," she said, catching her breath and smoothing out her skirt.

They crossed the traffic circle at Via Tiziano hand in hand. Camillo Boito waited for them at the edge of an empty lot, a roll of blueprints in hand.

"Signor and Signora Verdi!" he cried out, removing his hat and bowing his head. "If I had known you were going to walk, I would have called my coach for you." He took Giuseppina's arm and walked the couple into the lot.

Giuseppina elbowed Giuseppe playfully. "We'll make sure to do that next time."

"I like to walk."

"As if he doesn't do enough of that at home already," she remarked to Boito.

"Ah, I've heard your gardens are quite lovely, Signor Verdi. You're an accomplished gardener? You've done the work yourself?" Boito asked.

"Certainly," said Giuseppe, uncharacteristically boastful in his role as groundskeeper. "And I want to make this project better than my estate." He tapped the plans in Camillo's hands.

They walked to the end of the gravel drive, where a pile of felled alder trees sat in a neat stack.

"This is it," said Boito with a grand sweep of his arm. "The future home of Casa di Riposo per Musicisti."

"Casa Verdi," said Giuseppina proudly, causing Giuseppe to blush. She took his arm and rested her head on his shoulder. "Well, we'll keep it between us for now," she reassured him.

Aida's success was confirmation to Giuseppe that he could move on from music, his ego intact. The acclaim, as it had always been, was fleeting and Giuseppe sought recourse in something to leave a lasting legacy. After a brief trip to Milan the previous summer, he decided to build a retirement home exclusively for aging musicians and opera singers. It would be his way to give back to the community that had given him so much. This would be Casa Verdi.

In addition to meeting Boito, the architect for Casa Verdi, Giuseppe and Giuseppina were in Milan to assuage Ricordi's insistent demands that they visit and discuss Giuseppe's next opera. Giuseppe knew it would be a burden to continue with anything as large and as grand as *Aida*. Where could he go from there? Giuseppe was tired, as he had been for some time. He only wanted happiness in his waking moments, not anguish or despair over deadlines, rehearsals, and productions.

He discovered renewed passion for music in the *Requiem*, the performances less demanding yet as rich and profound as opera. Despite his continued success, how could he predict how his legacy would be received in fifty or a hundred years? No doubt he was a great composer, but the pragmatist in Giuseppe sought something deeper, more relevant to the realities of life.

Casa Verdi would be his mark. Childless and with few relatives, Giuseppe had nowhere to send his work's royalties—a sum that would perpetuate for generations—after he and Giuseppina passed. He did not wish to dismiss the help he had provided Cavour or the millions of Italians he had touched with his music. But the opportunity to provide a home for his musical brethren would be the greatest reward for his success. If there was any meaning to his existence and his life's work, then this home was the physical embodiment of it.

"Let me show you how I've designed the main building," said Boito, unrolling the blueprints. "Foremost, I think this selection of land is excellent. It's close to the city center, not too far on the outskirts of town."

"It's very peaceful," observed Giuseppina, taking a careful seat on the wood pile.

"Precisely," said Boito, shuffling the plans nervously. "Signor Verdi, what are your thoughts?"

Giuseppe leaned forward, both hands on his cane. He took in the property with the full of his body and sighed with relief.

"It's perfect."

Boito grinned. "Well, the land is yours, so I am at your disposal to begin the building's foundation any time. I have some thoughts if you'd like…."

"Not right now," said Giuseppe, noticing Giuseppina's fatigue. "Perhaps sometime soon."

"Of course," said Boito, rolling up the blueprints. "Are you in Milan to discuss a new opera, Signor Verdi?"

"Hardly," said Giuseppe, helping Giuseppina up. "I'm here to discuss business with my publisher. I want to ensure that this retirement home will be well endowed long after my death."

"Tito Ricordi?"

"Pardon?"

"Tito Ricordi is your publisher?"

"Yes, you know him?"

"I know him well. My brother Arrigo is a librettist and a friend of his."

"Opera is a small world," said Giuseppe. "One that I hope to leave soon."

Giuseppina yawned. "Excuse me, Signor Boito," she said, leaning against Giuseppe.

"Not at all, Signora." Camillo took her arm. "Please allow me to give you a ride back to your hotel."

"How generous," said Giuseppe, helping Giuseppina into the coach.

"And you, Signor Verdi? Won't you join us?"

"I'll take this opportunity to walk the property. Get a sense of what I'll leave behind," said Giuseppe, raising his hat. "I am far too happy to sit right now."

Giuseppe returned to the hotel just before sunset.

"I thought you might have gotten lost," chided Giuseppina.

Giuseppe sniggered.

"I hope he's taken the time to review the contracts," Giuseppina said, dabbing perfume behind her ears. "At least you know what you're getting yourself into."

Giuseppe swung his dinner jacket across his shoulder and adjusted his tie. "Not at this age, I don't."

"Come on now," said Giuseppina, standing up from the vanity mirror. "I think you know what you're doing."

Indeed, Giuseppe did. Since writing the *Requiem*, he had amassed dozens, if not hundreds, of performances, each date recorded in his journal. With this in hand and some previous disagreements on his opera royalties coming to accord, Giuseppe could anticipate his legacy at Casa Verdi to be funded through perpetuity—as long as Ricordi and the publishing house kept their books straight.

"How are you feeling, my love?"

"Wonderful," said Giuseppina. She gave Giuseppe a kiss and put on her shawl.

He took her arm and they walked carefully down the main stairwell into the lobby of the Grand Hotel.

Tito Ricordi sat at a corner table at the rear of the restaurant, waiting for Giuseppe to arrive.

"Verdi! Verdi!" he exclaimed, as Giuseppe and Giuseppina arrived arm in arm. He pulled seats out for the both of them and kissed Giuseppina on the cheek.

"Good to see you again, Tito," said Giuseppina.

"It's so good to see you both," he replied, beaming. "What are you drinking?" he asked, settling himself into his seat.

Giuseppe pulled a wine bottle from his coat. "I've brought this for our special reunion. It's straight from the estate."

Ricordi took the bottle from Giuseppe's hands and examined the liquid in the light from the wall sconce. "The fruits of your labor—splendid!" He motioned to the waiter to pour them each a glass. "And a fourth, please."

"Who else will be joining us?"

"Sorry, I'm not late, am I?" came a voice from behind Giuseppe.

Arrigo Boito stood nearly six feet tall and maintained a full mustache that hung from his nose like a brush. He smiled nervously, waiting for an introduction. When none came, he nodded and sat down. He placed a bouquet of flowers in front of Giuseppina.

"For the *signora*," Boito said nervously.

"How nice," said Giuseppina, placing the flowers between herself and Giuseppe.

"Giuseppe, I want you to meet Arrigo Boito, librettist," said Ricordi.

Giuseppe took a sip of wine, ignoring Boito. "Now Tito, I thought we were here tonight to discuss finances."

"There's nothing to discuss, Giuseppe. I've already made arrangements to settle any disagreements we've had. I didn't come here to quarrel. Every *lira* will be accounted for. Today, tomorrow, and all of the ones after that."

"Good. Long live Casa Ricordi," said Giuseppe. "Then can we talk of something other than opera? I've retired, Tito."

Ricordi smiled. "Arrigo has a very promising career ahead of him."

"And I wish him well." Giuseppe raised his glass, nodding at Boito. "I wish you well, *signor*."

"Thank you."

Giuseppe's eyes narrowed. "Aren't you Camillo Boito's brother?"

"I am."

Giuseppe sighed. "Never a moment's peace," he lamented, casting a glance at Giuseppina, hoping for some sympathy.

"Now, now, Giuseppe," said Ricordi. "Don't get upset. Camillo didn't orchestrate this meeting. It's mere coincidence. Fate, actually."

"Pray tell."

Ricordi nodded toward Boito.

Boito cleared his throat. "Signor Verdi, it's no mystery that you are a fan of Shakespeare. And I am as well, understandably. Signor Ricordi thought it would be prudent that I should send you my latest project."

"Well, spit it out," said Giuseppe impatiently.

"It's a complete libretto for *Otello*."

Giuseppe raised his eyebrows, considering. He took a long sip from his glass. "I'm not interested."

"It's excellent," said Ricordi.

Suddenly, a group of waiters descended on the table, laying platters of roasted vegetables, fowl, and fish. Two more bottles of wine appeared.

"Oh my," said Giuseppina, taking a bite from a small dish of black orbs. "Is this caviar?"

"From the Po River," said Ricordi assuredly. "Apparently it's one of the best in the world. Who knew?"

"Oh, we know all about it," said Giuseppe drily. He cracked a smile. "I feel like we've been ambushed."

"I'm sorry," said Ricordi. "You're loved, Giuseppe." He poured more wine around the table. "But life isn't over yet and I know you have more in you."

"What you don't understand is that I'm happy without the work."

"But this isn't work, Giuseppe. It's *Shakespeare*. You can write it at your leisure. Signor Boito has finished the libretto. It's on your time."

"If I may," said Boito, clearing his throat. "It goes without saying that I am open to any of your suggestions and edits on the libretto, Signor Verdi."

"You see, it's settled," said Ricordi with a smile.

"It's certainly *not* settled," huffed Giuseppe. He took Giuseppina's hand and kissed it. "She is the most important thing to me right now. But when I'm working on anything worth doing, I'm not with her."

"Of course," said Ricordi, laughing. "I understand, Giuseppe, I do."

Giuseppe took a deep breath and eyed his publisher. He considered the work to be done on Casa Verdi and Sant'Agata. And he considered himself. He was tired, to be sure. But he still loved life. And he still loved music. And he especially loved Shakespeare.

"No deadlines?"

"No deadlines," assured Ricordi.

Giuseppe stood, his hand outstretched. "Good to meet you, Signor Boito. It seems as though you and your brother have several of my interests in mind."

The two men shook hands.

"To Shakespeare and Italy," said Giuseppina, raising her glass.

"What else is there?" said Giuseppe, taking a drink and pouring the rest of the table a glass.

"Love, of course," said Boito.

Giuseppe took Giuseppina's hand. "Of course there is."

Chapter Thirty

1897

Giuseppina shuffled into the study, where Giuseppe was working. He paused to look up at her.

"What are you doing up?"

"I saw the light was still on," she said, sitting next to Giuseppe's desk.

"Can't you sleep?"

She coughed and rested her head against the headrest. "I don't want to. I just want to spend time with you."

Giuseppe got up to rub her back. She pushed him gently back to his seat.

"You're sweet. What are you working on?"

"I'm just replying to a few letters," said Giuseppe, retaking a seat at his desk. "Santa Cecilia gave a performance of *Requiem Mass*."

"I'm sure it was lovely," said Giuseppina, clutching her chest and catching her breath. "Before I forget…I've started making a list of things for us to take to Genoa. Can you take a look at it tomorrow and let me know if there's anything else we need?"

"Are you still up for the trip?"

"I feel good." Giuseppina closed her eyes. "But if not now, we'll go eventually."

Giuseppe searched for something more to say, but was at a loss. Giuseppina was getting more and more tired each day.

Otello had premiered just a few years after Giuseppe and Arrigo Boito met at dinner with Tito Ricordi. After its rousing success they collaborated on another Shakespeare story and character, *Falstaff*—Giuseppe's first comedy since the tepid production of *Un giorno di regno* over half a century before. Nervous that his old age would cause him to miss the comedic marks, Giuseppe wrote *Falstaff* with the enthusiastic collaboration of Boito. He had confided in the librettist that he wrote *Un giorno di regno* shortly after the death of his first wife.

"You must have had a happy marriage," Boito reasoned. "If you had been unhappy, the opera would have been much better."

"Why is that?" asked Giuseppe.

"The relief of a bad marriage finally let go."

Like *Otello*, *Falstaff* opened to enormous success. After the premiere's thirty-minute standing ovation, Giuseppe told Boito, "I was missing this the first time around—the ability to laugh at myself. Falstaff is conceited, like me. Who better to write it?"

"Then I daresay you'll end your career on self-parody."

"Beautiful, isn't?"

After *Falstaff*, Giuseppe and Giuseppina lived their days among friends. Winters in Genoa and trips to Paris and the spas around Sant'Agata. For the first time in his career, Giuseppe rejected requests for commissions, premieres, and parties without regret, confident in his retirement and that he had served Italy as well as he could. Not wanting to condemn the public to his prose, he declined a request for his memoirs. Even well-deserved conceit could not bring him back to the desk. Only the drama of real life would get him out of bed. And having come full circle in his career with the success of the humorous *Falstaff*, his account was settled.

Giuseppe woke suddenly. He looked over to the empty chair where Giuseppina was sitting the night before. He remembered he took her to bed and returned to his study to finish his letters. Resting on his chest was the list of things they were to take to Genoa for the winter holiday. He must have dozed off, barely through the list.

He stumbled into the hall where the blinds had been left up and a cold draft came through the leaky windows. Several trunk cases sat at the base of the stairs, ready to depart.

Giuseppe called up the stairwell. "Love, I'm preparing coffee!" He waited for an answer, but it was silent upstairs.

A cold wind blew through the kitchen and Giuseppe closed the windows that had been left open overnight. He lit the stove and boiled a pot of water and prepared the beans. Making coffee, a longtime ritual for Giuseppe, had never grown tiresome. He could start and finish preparing a cup in a few minutes and enjoy the result. Everything else in life that was halfway worthwhile seemed to take a lifetime to finish.

Giuseppe took the tray of coffee upstairs to the bedroom and opened the door. Giuseppina lay in a motionless heap under the comforter. Her eyes were open when Giuseppe approached the bed. He put the coffee on the dresser and knelt by the bed, pushing her hair aside.

"I made coffee."

Giuseppina didn't look up or down or away; her eyes just lingered on Giuseppe's face, his long nose and narrow eyes. Though the rest of her body didn't move, her eyes still had life. They glistened and a tear ran down her cheek.

Giuseppe wiped her face. "Are you in pain?"

She shook her head, mouthing the word "No."

The coffee grew cold through the morning as Giuseppe sat by the bed, running his hands over Giuseppina's back and arms, talking about Paris and the opera, her voice, their gardens, and how much he loved her. She managed to lift her head and squeeze his hands. And she could still smile. In the end she smiled, and Giuseppe smiled back.

Giuseppe was despondent after Giuseppina's death and unable to leave Sant'Agata after the burial in Milan. By Christmas, Giuseppe finally allowed Boito see him, and the librettist convinced him to go to Milan to spend time with friends. Giuseppe took long carriage rides, played cards, and even took to having lunch alone at the railway station, taking in the daily crush of travelers. It was anonymity in its most perfect form.

1901

"I'm sorry I can't see you at the door," yelled Giuseppe from the hall. "Just let yourself in."

Boito walked into the house at Sant'Agata and removed his coat. "How are you this afternoon?"

Giuseppe tossed down the newspaper. "My old age has nothing on the injustices others are trying to impose on me."

"What in the world are you talking about?" asked Boito, pouring Giuseppe a sherry.

"Are they trying to kill me?" Giuseppe picked up the paper and shoved it in Boito's face. "The Milan Conservancy of Music is announcing its intentions to rename the school after me."

Unaware of Giuseppe's history with the school, Boito nodded appreciatively. "What a nice gesture."

"They rejected me! Well, I'll certainly reciprocate the favor."

Boito handed Giuseppe the drink, happy to see some spirit back in his friend. "Cheers to what could have been."

"These eighty-seven years are weighing me down." Giuseppe got up from his seat and started down the hall. "But there is still work for us to do. Are you ready?"

"Begrudgingly, yes."

For the next few days, Giuseppe and Boito collected Giuseppe's student manuscripts, old compositions, and false starts and brought them into the yard in dusty, forgotten stacks to be burned.

"Are you sure you want to do this?" asked Boito.

Giuseppe pulled a matchbook out of his pocket and struck a match. It fizzled in his bent hand. Boito took the book and struck another match. The flame took and he handed it to Giuseppe and turned his back. Unceremoniously, Giuseppe threw the match onto the pile and it lit instantly, burning everything to embers with little more than a hiss.

"The only thing that will be left is public opinion."

"I think you've done more than that," said Boito.

Giuseppe shook his head. "The music is no longer mine. It never was."

"That's a sobering thought."

"I don't know why I wrote, but I did. And if you're willing to listen, then it's as much yours as it is mine. Does that make sense?"

Boito shrugged. "Not so much. But I'm not you. No one is." He kicked dirt over the smoldering fire. "Do you still want to go to Milan?"

"Let's leave in the morning. I want to eat together."

The next morning, Boito and Giuseppe left for Milan by coach, arriving at the Grand Hotel a few days later. On New Year's Day, a letter sent on behalf of the archbishop of Milan arrived on Giuseppe's desk.

"What's this?" he asked Boito, opening the letter.

"Ah, it was left for you earlier this morning."

Giuseppe read the letter and put it down, his face slack. "This is a horrible thing."

"Why, what's wrong?" asked Boito.

"The archbishop is wishing me a happy new year."

Boito laughed. "Oh, how horrible."

"It's a sign."

"That hardly sounds like you, Giuseppe."

"I'm old, Boito. I am certainly not myself anymore." He laughed. "So please excuse me."

"No need," said Boito. "There's nothing to apologize for."

"No, I suppose there isn't. We are all just trying to do the right thing." Giuseppe walked to the window and put his hands on the cold glass. "I love Milan in the winter. I could sleep for a thousand years here."

Boito went to Giuseppe's side. "What do you remember most about the city, Giuseppe?"

Giuseppe sighed and looked out on the snow now falling on the streets. "The love. Everywhere I went here, there was love. I don't know if it was deserved, but I want to give every drop of it back."

"Have you?"

Giuseppe turned and walked to the bed. "Some of it. Time will tell. I wish I could tell everyone how much I love them, truly."

"They know, Giuseppe."

"Do they?"

Boito considered for a moment. "Somewhere, someone is singing 'La donna è mobile.'"

"Well, that is something, isn't it?" Giuseppe crawled into bed. "Close the blinds, Boito."

The next morning Boito called the doctor when Giuseppe was unable to get out of bed. He had suffered a stroke.

Six days later Giuseppe passed at the Grand Hotel, surrounded by friends. The hotel staff wore black in mourning and two hundred thousand Italians lined the streets to say goodbye and give tribute to their hero. "Va, pensiero," sung by a choir of eight hundred, emanated throughout Milan and wreaths from around the world encircled Casa Verdi.

Giuseppe was buried with Giuseppina among his musical brethren at Casa Verdi, his lasting gesture of love to his people and the country of Italy.

The world-famous composer's legacy would endure.

About the Author

Collin Mitchell is graduate of UC Santa Barbara with a degree in Comparative Literature and Film Studies. Originally from the Bay Area, he now resides in Los Angeles. This is his first novel.

Leonardo's Secret
A Novel Based on the Life of Leonardo da Vinci
by Peter David Myers

Marconi and His Muses
A Novel Based on the Life of Guglielmo Marconi
by Pamela Winfrey

Saving the Republic
A Novel Based on the Life of Marcus Cicero
by Eric D. Martin

Soldier, Diplomat, Archaeologist
A Novel Based on the Bold Life of Louis Palma di Cesnola
by Peg A. Lamphier

COMING IN 2018 FROM THE MENTORIS PROJECT

A Novel Based on the Life of Alessandro Volta
A Novel Based on the Life of Angelo Dundee
A Novel Based on the Life of Henry Mancini
A Novel Based on the Life of Maria Montessori
A Novel Based on the Life of Publius Cornelius Scipio
Fulfilling the Promise of California

FUTURE TITLES FROM THE MENTORIS PROJECT

A Novel Based on the Life of Amerigo Vespucci
A Novel Based on the Life of Andrea Palladio
A Novel Based on the Life of Antonin Scalia
A Novel Based on the Life of Antonio Meucci
A Novel Based on the Life of Buzzie Bavasi
A Novel Based on the Life of Cesare Becaria
A Novel Based on the Life of Federico Fellini
A Novel Based on the Life of Frank Capra
A Novel Based on the Life of Galileo Galilei
A Novel Based on the Life of Giovanni Andrea Doria
A Novel Based on the Life of Giovanni di Bicci de' Medici
A Novel Based on the Life of Giuseppe Garibaldi
A Novel Based on the Life of Guido Monaco
A Novel Based on the Life of Harry Warren
A Novel Based on the Life of John Cabot
A Novel Based on the Life of Judge John Sirica
A Novel Based on the Life of Leonard Covello
A Novel Based on the Life of Luca Pacioli
A Novel Based on the Life of Mario Andretti
A Novel Based on the Life of Mario Cuomo
A Novel Based on the Life of Niccolo Machiavelli
A Novel Based on the Life of Peter Rodino
A Novel Based on the Life of Pietro Belluschi
A Novel Based on the Life of Robert Barbera
A Novel Based on the Life of Saint Augustine of Hippo
A Novel Based on the Life of Saint Francis of Assisi
A Novel Based on the Life of Vince Lombardi

For more information on these titles and
The Mentoris Project, please visit
www.mentorisproject.org.